Helen Phifer is the bestselling writer of twenty-seven books, including the hugely popular Annie Graham, Lucy Harwin, Beth Adams, Maria Miller and Detective Constable Morgan Brooks series.

She lives in the busy town of Barrow-in-Furness surrounded by miles of coastline and a short drive from the glorious English Lake District.

Helen loves reading books that scare the heck out of her and is eternally grateful to Stephen King, Dean Koontz, James Herbert and Graham Masterton for scaring her senseless in her teenage years. Unable to find enough scary stories she decided to write her own and her debut novel *The Ghost House* released in October 2013 became a #1 Global Bestseller.

You can find her over on Instagram @helenphifer, or on her website at www.helenphifer.com

Also by Helen Phifer

The Annie Graham series
The Ghost House
Secrets of the Shadows
The Forgotten Cottage
The Lake House
The Girls in the Woods
The Face Behind the Mask

Detective Lucy Harwin
Dark House
Dying Breath
Last Light

Beth Adams
The Girl in the Grave
The Girls in the Lake

Detective Morgan Brookes
One Left Alive
The Killer's Girl
The Hiding Place
First Girl to Die
Find the Girl
Sleeping Dolls
Silent Angel
Their Burning Graves
Hold Your Breath
Stolen Darlings
Save Her Twice
Poison Memories

Detective Maria Miller
The Haunting on West 10th Street
Her Lost Soul
The Girls on Floor 13

Standalone novels
The Good Sisters
The House on West 10th Street
Lakeview House

The Girls in the Woods

HELEN PHIFER

ONE PLACE. MANY STORIES

HQ
An imprint of HarperCollins*Publishers* Ltd
1 London Bridge Street
London SE1 9GF

www.harpercollins.co.uk

HarperCollins*Publishers*
Macken House, 39/40 Mayor Street Upper,
Dublin 1 D01 C9W8
This edition 2025

1
First published in Great Britain by Carina,
an imprint of HarperCollins*Publishers* Ltd 2016

Copyright © Helen Phifer 2016

Helen Phifer asserts the moral right to be identified as the author of this work.
A catalogue record for this book is available from the British Library.

ISBN: 9780008737184

This novel is entirely a work of fiction. The names, characters and incidents portrayed in it are the work of the author's imagination. Any resemblance to actual persons, living or dead, events or localities is entirely coincidental.

All rights reserved. No part of this publication may be reproduced, stored in a retrieval system, or transmitted, in any form or by any means, electronic, mechanical, photocopying, recording or otherwise, without the prior permission of the publishers.

Without limiting the author's and publisher's exclusive rights, any unauthorized use of this publication to train generative artificial intelligence (AI) technologies is expressly prohibited. HarperCollins also exercise their rights under Article 4(3) of the Digital Single Market Directive 2019/790 and expressly reserve this publication from the text and data mining exception.

Printed and bound in the UK using 100% Renewable
Electricity by CPI Group (UK) Ltd

This book contains FSC™ certified paper and other controlled sources to ensure responsible forest management.

For more information visit: www.harpercollins.co.uk/green

For Gail O'Neil, Wendy Smith, Amanda Rawlinson, Diane Sullivan, Adele Dean, Gill Tyson & all of the other fabulous ladies in the Lookin GOOD and Feelin GREAT Charity Group.

Prologue

Summer 1895

The smell was always the big giveaway – no matter how many fresh flowers were placed around a room, the stench of decomposition would always seep through the cracks. Maybe not at first because the sweet scent from the roses or sweet peas, dependent upon the season, would infiltrate your nostrils with their heady fragrance, but after a few minutes you would realise that the underlying, more cloying scent wasn't such a fragrant one after all. In fact you would more than likely wonder which flower it was that was giving off the almost too sweet, sickly smell. The black cloth covering the large ornamental mirror above the fireplace confirmed what you already knew. That this was a house of death. Upon further investigation, as you looked around the room at the waiting subjects, one would always stand out just that little bit more than the others; it was always the hands that would give them away. Those petite hands that had once been ivory coloured were now mottled purple and black. The rest of the body, underneath the layers of petticoats, pinafore dresses and thick tights, was probably turning the same colours – but the face you could disguise, if you worked your magic with the thick, heavy cosmetic face powder.

The three girls were all dressed in identical long white nightgowns; the only flesh showing was their hands, necks and faces. He smiled at the two who were hovering to the side of their dead sister looking uncomfortable; he wouldn't want to have to stand next to a dead person and pose for the camera even if it was his brother. The dead girl was on her own, lying on a chaise in the middle of the room. He tilted his head to ensure that the pillow supporting her decaying body looked clean and that her nightgown had been arranged properly. The girl had died with her eyes partially open, so it looked as if she was still watching everyone. A life-sized, human doll that would probably be the cause of many years of nightmares for her siblings. Her mother was in the opposite corner being comforted by a much older woman. Both of them dressed all in black. He cleared his throat.

'Should we begin?'

The girls stared at each other, both of them holding hands. It was the older woman who nodded her head. He set his tripod up and placed the heavy camera onto it; a couple of photographs and he would be done. There was a certain beauty about death that he found very attractive but he had never told anyone this; it wouldn't be the right thing to do or say. His wife would be mortified at the thought of him enjoying photographing corpses; she hated that he did it for a living anyway, but if she knew he enjoyed it she would make him stop.

'Mabel, Flora, go and stand either side of your sister.'

He felt a little sorry for the girls, who both looked as if they were about to burst into tears. They were staring at each other and still holding hands.

'Now, please. The longer you continue to fuss about it the longer it will take. What on earth is wrong with you both?'

Mabel looked the oldest out of the three of them; she implored Flora with her eyes. He folded his arms across his chest and watched them. Mabel stepped forward pulling the younger girl, who let out a sob.

'Please don't make me touch her; she's cold and she smells. I'm scared – I don't want to stand next to her. Why do we have to do this?'

Her mother looked up from her crumpled handkerchief, surprised by her daughter's outburst of insolence. She didn't need to speak because the girl's grandmother walked across and slapped Flora across the face.

'Stop that at once, child – that is your sister, not some stranger from the street. It is the very last chance your parents have to get a photograph of you all together. Now you will stand next to your sister and smile for the camera before she is taken away and buried.'

The girl stopped speaking but her hand came up and rubbed at the red finger marks that had appeared on her pale, perfect skin. She let Mabel take hold of her shoulders and position her next to the dead girl, then Mabel took her position on the other side. Neither of them looked at their sister. He put his head underneath the cover to take the picture but it was no good. Those red marks on her cheek would stand out on the still when it was developed and it wasn't as if he could arrange to come back and do this all over again; he only had this one chance to get it right. He lifted his head up and walked across the room, taking hold of Flora's shoulders.

'I'm sorry but the mark on your face is too prominent. I need you to turn and face your sister. I promise I'll be quick and you won't have to stay there for very long.'

He didn't think he'd ever forget the look the young girl gave him then; obviously this was a huge ordeal for her. This must be her first brush with death and an experience that would no doubt stay with her for the rest of her life – but her parents had made it quite clear when they asked him to call around yesterday. They could only afford to pay for two stills so he couldn't make any mistakes; these two pictures needed to be perfect. He gently turned her to face the dead girl and could feel her entire body shaking; he then went to Mabel and turned her in a similar position so they were both staring at their sister with what he hoped would be assumed was loving attention and not abject horror. He then went back to his camera and buried his head back underneath the cloth. Holding up the flash he snapped first one, then another still.

'That's it. Thank you for your patience, girls. You can leave now.'

Flora scurried away from the girl that she had no doubt shared a bedroom with for the last twelve years; they had possibly even shared the same bed. How sad that two such close sisters should now be so torn apart by death. Still it wasn't his place to say anything; his job was done here. He would pack his equipment away and go back to his house so he could develop the films. He would of course keep a copy for his own records; he was getting quite a collection in his brown leather book. People were dying of all sorts of diseases, and more and more families wanted their loved ones photographed before they were buried. When he'd taken up photography as a hobby he'd never envisaged that memento mori photography would prove to be such a lucrative business move.

He packed up his things and carried them out to the waiting horse and carriage; he lived too far away to carry his equipment around town. The grandmother walked him out to the front door, leaving her sobbing daughter alone with her dead granddaughter. The other two girls had run from the room as fast as they could once they had been dismissed; it was indeed sad to watch such grief day in day out, but it was also providing his family with a way of life they could only ever have dreamed of.

'How long will it be before you can bring the pictures?'

'As soon as they are ready, I will personally hand-deliver them. It should only take two days but it depends how busy I am tomorrow.'

'Thank you for your time, Mr Tyson. It is very much appreciated.'

He nodded his head then turned and ran down the last few steps and climbed into the waiting carriage. As it pulled away from the side he looked up to see the two girls watching him from the upstairs window. Flora's face was damp, no doubt with the tears she had finally been able to shed, but Mabel looked as if she was weighing him up. Seeming embarrassed they had been caught staring, Mabel stepped back, pulling her sister with her, and he gazed straight ahead, pretending he hadn't noticed either of them.

1995

'Beautiful, really beautiful – that's it, hold that position.' The camera flashed several times. 'Gorgeous, you look stunning. So demure yet so damn sexy. I love it.' Heath Tyson walked towards her and pushed her head to the left, just a touch. 'That's it, don't move; we're almost done. You're going to love these pictures; I swear you've never looked so good.' He snapped a few more shots then let his camera drop around his neck and clapped his hands.

'Bravo, bravo. You have been the best model I've ever had. Thank you so much for your patience.'

He walked away towards his darkroom, eager to develop his films and add these very special photographs to his secret album. Left lying on the chaise longue, she didn't move to get up and change out of the long, cool, linen nightgown he'd dressed her in. She would stay there until he came and lifted her onto the makeshift trolley he used to push her to and from the freezer in his garage. When he was happy with his photographs he would undress her and put her back inside the cold blackness of the large freezer he'd bought when the village butcher had been closing down. Slamming the metal door, he would lock her in until he had no further use for her or until her body started to decompose too much, whichever came first. Probably the decomposition because he didn't think he would ever get tired of staring at her. There was something so beautiful about death that was never present in the living. Her hands had already begun to turn black despite the freezing temperatures. He wondered why it was they did that. In his collection of Victorian mourning photographs you could always tell the deceased family member by the discoloration of their hands.

It had fascinated him the first time he'd seen a photograph of three sisters, all no older than fifteen – he had been eight years old when he found that photograph album. Heath had been sent to bed but he could hear his father whispering on the phone; he knew he shouldn't be listening in because he shouldn't be out of bed, but he couldn't sleep. He loved his granddad but that day's visit had been playing heavily on his mind; his normally fun-filled granddad had been lying in a bed in the front room of his terraced house in the busy town-centre street. The smell had been pretty bad. He didn't know what it was but as soon as he'd walked in he'd had to screw his nose up and try not to breathe through it.

His mother, who refused to come into the house because she was 'not going to be there when he croaked', was back at home and for once he wished his father had left him at home with her. His older brother didn't care; he had gone straight into the converted front room that was now a bedroom and stood by the frail old man who was asleep. Heath watched the shallow rise and fall of his chest underneath the covers; the rattling sound of the breaths he was struggling to take would stay with him forever. They could hear their father in the kitchen banging around. He turned away for a split second and when he turned back his brother, who had just celebrated his eleventh birthday, was stroking the old man's hair. Heath shuddered; this wasn't the happy, funny man he remembered and he wanted it all to stop. Their dad came in, his tear-stained face a mask of grief.

'Right, you two, go in the kitchen and get yourselves something to eat. I need to sort your granddad out.'

His brother leant down and kissed the man's forehead and Heath tried to force himself to move towards him to do the same but he couldn't. His legs wouldn't move. As his brother walked past he whispered in his ear '*Scaredy cat*'. His dad came over and placed his hands on his shoulders, then pushed Heath out of the room and shut the door behind him. Finally finding his feet, he went into the kitchen where his brother was sitting eating a packet of crisps.

'He's going to pop his clogs any minute.'

'How do you know that?'

'I just do. You wait and see.'

Sometimes he hated how his brother was such a know-it-all. It made him feel stupid and like a big baby. He got himself a packet of crisps out of the cupboard and they both sat on the high stools near the breakfast bar waiting for their dad to come back in. After what seemed like forever he finally did. His eyes were red and he'd been crying. Heath had never seen his dad cry. He walked over and hugged them close to him.

'Your granddad's gone to heaven now; you can both go in and say goodbye.'

This time it was Heath who wanted to go in first – he desperately wanted to see what you looked like when you were dead – and it was his brother who lingered behind. Heath jumped off his stool and went to the room where the door was ajar. The first thing he noticed was how peaceful it was now that horrible sound his granddad had been making had stopped. He stepped inside. The sheets were no longer moving and he walked closer to look at the man on the bed. The second thing he noticed was how different he looked; his skin appeared yellow but it was no longer scrunched up and wrinkled in pain. It was smooth, his mouth was open and his false teeth had slipped down. He'd expected his eyes to be closed but they were open slightly, staring straight ahead.

Heath marvelled at how wonderful his granddad looked now he was dead – how much younger. It was amazing. Did everyone who died look like this? His foot kicked something soft and he glanced down to see one of the pillows from the bed there. It puzzled him how it had got there; it wasn't there before when they'd been in the room and his granddad hadn't moved at all. His dad must have taken it from under the old man's head but he didn't understand why. He picked it up and felt a warm patch in the middle. Placing it on the chair next to the bed he thought nothing of it.

It wasn't until some years later when he replayed that last scene in his head that he realised that the pillow was warm in the middle because that was where his granddad's last breaths had gone. He had known all along that the grief his dad had shown had been filled with guilt – but he hadn't known why until his dad's own dying confession had confirmed the sneaking suspicion he'd always held. His dad had been the one to end his granddad's life that morning all those years ago; he could have gone to prison but he'd decided it was worth the risk. The only regret that Heath had was that he'd had no means to photograph how wonderful his granddad looked, more wonderful than he ever did when he was alive. It was as if his true inner beauty had been revealed and it was something Heath never forgot; in fact he thought about it an awful lot. When most kids his age had been playing with action men or cap guns, he had spent all his time locked in his bedroom wondering how he could see more dead people.

There was a certain beauty in death that could not be achieved at any cost in life, even with the number of plastic surgeons and all the cosmetic surgery available. When he was ten years old he knew that he wanted to be a photographer but he did have a backup plan. He would probably one day become a funeral director if his photography didn't take off but his one passion in life was photography. What he really wanted to do was photograph the dead. He didn't really want to have to deal with the grieving families; he just wanted to photograph their loved ones like his great-great-grandfather had back in the Victorian days. It had been quite normal back then, but if you told anyone now that you liked photographing the dead they'd lock you up and throw away the key. There were some things you didn't admit to and getting your rocks off over corpses was almost certainly one.

He spent hours locked in his room studying the photos in the album they'd found when clearing their granddad's house out. Luckily for him, he'd been on his own in the bedroom when he found the dusty album at the back of the wardrobe, wrapped in faded yellow newspapers. His brother had gone to the tip with his dad and a car boot full of their granddad's belongings. At first he hadn't realised just what it was he was looking at, but he knew there was something strange about the pictures in the album. It had *Memento Mori* in gold letters engraved into the soft brown leather cover. He'd had no idea what that meant, but he would try and find out.

There was no one in the pictures that he knew and they looked as if they were very old. Not wanting his dad to throw it out on his next visit to the local tip, Heath ran downstairs and stuffed it into his backpack. It was his secret, and he wouldn't tell anyone about it – not even his brother. Well, not unless he was going to help him somehow find dead people to take pictures of. That photograph album had started this obsession with death, be it in male or female form – although he much preferred females; they were so much more elegant and prettier than men. His warped obsession with death had now resulted in the dead girl in front of him.

She was his first and quite possibly his last; it was too risky. He'd briefly considered the implications before it all happened but he hadn't realised just how seriously a missing teenager would be taken. He thought they'd assume she'd run away and that would be that – the reality had been far different. The police had been crawling all over the village, surrounding fields and woods looking for the missing girl who had been on her way to visit her friend who lived at the opposite side of the village. It had scared him, seeing the crowds of villagers that had gathered with their dogs and the many police officers who'd been drafted in to search for her. He'd known her since he had moved back to the village he'd lived in as a child and set up his business, taking her first photographs when she had been seven. Then every year since until she was seventeen.

Sharon Sale had come to him alone this time, asking him to take some photos she could send off to a modelling agency, only he wasn't to tell her parents because they would freak. She had told him she would pay him but he had shaken his head, telling her that he would do it for her if she would do a big favour for him and she'd agreed. Perhaps if she'd known what it was he'd wanted she would have run away as fast as she could and never come back. He knew her by her name, just like he knew all the local children that the parents brought to him to have their portraits taken.

It had been two weeks now and he deemed it safe enough to take her to the woods behind the cottage and bury her. He had already dug a deep grave in the early hours this morning; it had taken him hours but it had been worth it because the woods had been searched three times now, by police, the villagers (including himself) and then searched again with sniffer dogs. Yesterday they had publicly declared that they thought the girl had left the area. He wished he could keep her forever but if they did come looking, how would he explain to them that he had a dead girl in the freezer in his garage? It was far too risky. He was a patient man and was happy enough to wait until the fuss died down, even if took a couple of years, before he tried it again.

At least now he had started his own collection of photographs of the dead, and it was a work in progress – the best works of art weren't achieved in a day. He would wait until the opportunity arose and it was the right time to do it all over again. He had no doubt that soon enough another girl with big ambitions of becoming a model would turn up at his doorstep and, when they did, he would be ready.

Chapter 1

2015

Annie Ashworth let out a sigh and turned on her side. The heat from the late afternoon sun was warming her skin and even though she'd tried her best to keep out of the direct sunlight she still had a warm, golden glow. Her husband, Will, had a deep, bronze tan. His normally clean-shaven chin was covered in dark stubble and his dark blond hair had lightened considerably with the sun. He looked the picture of complete health and happiness but she knew differently. He was lying on his side with his back to her and her eyes fell on the angry red scar that ran across his right kidney. It would take a long time for it to fade into oblivion and when it did she hoped the memories would go with it. She was so lucky he was still alive, that they both were.

She shivered at the thought of that man, Henry Smith, and his accomplice, Megan. What she would have given to have watched their bodies being brought up from the cellar of Beckett House in black body bags and wheeled out to the waiting private ambulances. But she'd had to go with Will; he had been so badly injured and she had needed to be by his side. Jake, her best friend and colleague, had stayed along with Cathy and Kav, their inspector and sergeant when they were both stationed back in Barrow, to watch on their behalf.

They had brought Megan up first because her body had been the most straightforward to bag up. She'd fallen down the cellar steps from top to bottom at Beckett House and instantly broken her neck. Henry, though, had got what he deserved. That strange man/monster thing had sliced his throat open with its long sharp claws, but not before Annie had watched the terror on Henry's face as he had stuck his knife into its strange, grey body. Jake had told her when he came to see her in the hospital that even Matt the pathologist had been horrified to see the mess of blood and limbs. No one had ever seen anything like the strange creature that lived in the drains below Beckett House, and it had been badly injured by Henry because there had been a trail of blood that led to the huge drain in the corner of the cellar – but then it had disappeared.

Search teams had been brought in with special infrared and thermal-imaging cameras and, apart from a trail of blood that stopped suddenly in the sewers, there had been no trace of it. Annie suspected that it had gone deep underground to another lair and either died or gone into hibernation. She hoped for Martha Beckett's sake that it had curled up and died. The last time she had spoken with the elderly woman she had arranged to have the drain filled in with concrete and the cellar door permanently sealed shut. She had told Annie about the long letter she had written detailing the history of the house and everything that had happened there. She had given it to her solicitor with strict instructions that when the day came that someone was eager enough to buy Beckett House they would be given a copy of the letter so they were fully aware of the circumstances.

It had made Martha feel much better but Annie knew that the house would be snapped up by some property developer who wouldn't be remotely interested in the letter or the history of Beckett House. They would turn it into luxury apartments and move on to the next project. Annie just hoped that history wouldn't repeat itself and no one with small children moved in there. All of this had been kept hush-hush and out of the media for the sake of Martha who had kept the terrible secret of the thing hidden for years. One day they could make a film about what happened at Beckett House; it was that horrific no one would ever believe it was all true.

She picked up her Kindle. It was amazing how Will could lie there for hours and not get bored. Turning to face her, he smiled as his hand reached out for hers and she held it tight. His fingers trailed across the baby bump and he let them rest there.

'I thought you were asleep again.'

'What do you mean, again?' He opened one eye and winked at her, 'I'm just making the most of the last day before we have to go back to reality. I've been thinking about it, and you know I'll have to go back to work soon, don't you?'

She nodded, wishing they could stay here – cocooned on this island forever, away from the madness that seemed to take over their lives on a regular basis.

'I know you do, but are you ready to go back? I mean they couldn't exactly say no if you had a bit longer off, could they? You almost . . .'

She couldn't say the words because it set her heart racing every time she thought about what had happened at the Lake House where she'd almost lost him.

'I think I'm ready, Annie. As much as I love spending time with you I'm getting a bit fidgety, restless. I need to be doing something a bit more challenging with my life than pottering around pretending everything is OK.'

She knew how he felt – she was on restricted duties because she was six months pregnant and she was bored, bored, bored. Although she was glad to be away from the prying eyes of the public and every weirdo who seemed to be attracted to her, she still liked to do her job.

'If you're ready that's fine; I'm just being completely selfish, but I love having you around. Although I suppose you're bound to start getting on my nerves sooner or later.'

She grinned at him and he shoved her arm. Jumping up he bent down and kissed her lips then he moved further down and kissed her swollen stomach.

'I thought I was already getting on your nerves; you were a right grump before we came on holiday.'

'Well, maybe just a little; you know I like my own space and I was getting fed up of doing nothing myself. But I've forgiven you because you brought me here.'

'So it was a good choice coming here?'

'Yes, probably the best idea you've ever had apart from marrying me. I'd never even thought about a holiday in Hawaii until you showed it to me on the internet. It's so perfect – just how I imagined paradise to be. Could you imagine living here? It must be so wonderful.'

He smiled and she knew that he loved to please her and she also knew she was very lucky that both of them were still alive to be here enjoying this perfect holiday.

'Come on, how about we take a dip then go and get ready for tea?'

She held her hand out for him to pull her up, tucking her Kindle under her towel.

'I'm starving.'

Will laughed. 'Funnily enough I thought you might say that; after all it's been, what, two hours since you last ate?'

'You know I'm feeding for two; it's the only time I'll ever have an excuse to eat what I want without worrying.'

'You could eat for three for all I care; as long as you're happy, then so am I.'

They walked hand in hand towards the crystal blue ocean, which was gently lapping at the sand. She didn't hear her phone, which was at the bottom of her beach bag ringing; she'd switched it to silent – in fact she hadn't bothered to look at it for days. She wasn't bothered about telling the whole world on Facebook what she was doing every single second of the day, unlike most of her friends. They walked into the water, which made her yelp at the coldness. Will splashed around and she sank into the water and began swimming, relishing the sudden change in temperature that cooled her warm skin. Further down she could see the beach was full of people but their hotel had its own private beach, which was never busy. Even their ground-floor room had sliding patio doors that looked out onto a lush green lawn, with palm trees towering above to provide shade from the constant heat. It also had the shortest walk to the Pacific Ocean she could imagine.

When Will had booked this holiday he had thought about everything, knowing that if it was hot she wouldn't feel like walking far. Her phone kept on ringing in the bottom of her bag but oblivious to it she swam towards the floating sundeck not far from the shore, to work up an appetite before they went back to get ready to go out and make the most of their last evening together in paradise.

Chapter 2

Matilda Graham had finally plucked up the courage after dithering for days and told her mum, Lisa, she was going with a friend for a job interview at a hotel in Bowness. She had known she'd object to it because she always did.

'How ridiculous – you can't drive, Tilly. How on earth do you expect to get up to Bowness day in day out and home again? It's at least a thirty-minute drive there and back on a good day, without traffic or bad weather.'

'It's not ridiculous, Mum. They might let me live in – and if not I'm pretty sure Aunty Annie would let me stay with her. She has plenty of room in that big house and I wouldn't get in her way. She wouldn't mind at all.'

'No, she might not mind but I certainly would; you never know who's going to turn up knocking on her door. It wouldn't surprise me if the Yorkshire bloody Ripper decided to pay her a visit.'

And so it had continued for the next ten minutes until Tilly had stormed out of the kitchen and up to her bedroom, slamming the door for good measure. They hadn't spoken for the rest of the afternoon and when Ben arrived home Lisa was drinking her second glass of wine. He walked in, looked at the half-empty bottle of Chardonnay on the table and nodded.

'Rough day?'

'You could say that. Your daughter has got it into her head she can go for a job interview at some hotel in Bowness and live and work up there – for Christ's sake, she can't even keep her bedroom tidy.'

'It's not the worst idea I've ever heard, Lisa. At least she's looking for a job.'

'Are you having a laugh, Ben? She said if the hotel won't let her live in then she'll go and stop with your Annie. Which is never a good idea. I love your sister to bits but she has more nutters and serial killers chasing her than the bloody detectives on the television. No, it's not a good idea at all – and you should go upstairs and tell her that.'

'Yes, you're right about Annie but she's pregnant now and that man who was stalking her is dead. For all we know it's not as if Tilly will even get the job; the least you can do is let her go there and have an interview. It will be good experience for her and if she does get it then we'll discuss what's going to happen then. How does that sound?'

'Fucking ridiculous, Ben. The day you actually stand by me and my opinions I'll probably drop dead with shock. Do what you want, but I'm not being a part of it. You can tell her and if anything bad happens then on your head be it.'

She rolled her eyes towards the ceiling. Ben walked across and kissed his wife's forehead, then he sighed. All he seemed to do lately was try to keep the peace between them but it was getting more difficult each day. Then he went upstairs to talk to his daughter, who had music blasting from her room so loud the floor was vibrating underneath his feet. No doubt it had been to drown out the noise of him and Lisa arguing. Tilly hated it when they argued, which seemed to be an awful lot lately. What she didn't realise was that she was the cause of most of the arguments. He'd never imagined teenage girls could be such hard work.

He knocked on her door and waited for her to open it. She

did and he followed her inside and sat on the end of her bed.

'God, she told you to say no, didn't she?'

Ben nodded. 'Tilly, I can understand where your mum is coming from. She's only worried about you.'

'No, she isn't. She doesn't want me to have a life – she wants me to be stuck in this crap town for ever and pregnant before I'm twenty-one. For God's sake it's only an interview. I probably won't even get the job.'

'When is it?'

'Tomorrow.'

'How are you going to get there? Me and your mum are both at work – you know that.'

'I'm not an idiot, Dad. I can get the bus or a train – and besides, Gemma is coming with me and her mum who isn't a total psycho might be taking us yet.'

Ben stifled a laugh. 'All right, you can go, but if you get stranded make sure you phone one of us, OK?'

'Thank you, Dad, I promise I will. You do both realise I'm almost eighteen, don't you?'

'Yes, but you have to realise that whether you're eighteen or fifty-eight you're still our little girl and we'll always worry about you.'

She rolled her eyes and lifted two fingers to her head, pretending to shoot herself.

'Very funny. Now make sure you look smart and don't be cheeky when they ask you straightforward questions. Look them in the eye and do your best to answer them.'

'Argh, Dad, get out. Now you're just being insulting.'

He stood up and grinned. 'Just checking. Oh, and I wouldn't mention that you're allergic to the hoover or washing machine either.'

He walked out and as she shut the door behind him, she felt her stomach churn. She didn't care about lying to her mum but she hated lying to her dad. But hopefully he'd never find out. She only had to meet the photographer, have her photoshoot and then come home again. Tilly had found his details through Facebook. Some of her friends had liked his page so she'd clicked on it and had been impressed with some of the photographs. There were lots of prom photographs and a few before and after makeovers; one of the women had looked like an old dog before so he must be good to have taken the after photo where she looked quite nice.

There was a voucher on there for a free photoshoot, no obligation to buy the photos if you didn't like them. He sounded perfect and he didn't look like some sort of major pervert. He wasn't based in Barrow, he was in Hawkshead – which was a bit far away and trickier to get to – but she could do it. There was a bus route and if she got stuck she could go and see Annie for a lift home. She would tell them she didn't like the manager at the hotel and didn't want to work there anyway, so that would put an end to this argument. Then hopefully she would be able to send off her portfolio to the modelling agencies in Manchester and London.

Her mum would have a complete shit fit when she found out that she wanted to move away to a city, but she wouldn't be able to stop her once she was eighteen. She would be able to do whatever she wanted and get out of this dead-end town. The last three years she had done nothing but dream about becoming a model and living a far more glamorous life than the one she did now. If she didn't try she'd never know, and would spend the rest of her life regretting it.

Chapter 3

Joanne Tyson opened her eyes and wondered why she was lying on a damp, hard, concrete floor. For a moment she didn't have a clue as she blinked and her vision semi-cleared, then she remembered exactly where she was. One eye was swollen shut and she opened her good eye. He had gone; she couldn't hear him stomping around. Which was good. She tried to sit up but felt queasy and light-headed. He'd managed to really do some damage this time. Joanne wondered what it was she'd said to make him fly off the handle; she thought back but couldn't remember anything that had warranted him giving her a black eye and knocking her unconscious.

He was getting much worse – for a while everything had seemed OK and he seemed to have forgotten about using her as a punching bag, but lately . . . She shuddered. Well, lately it was getting more painful to be around him. The floor was freezing and she remembered where she was. She had come into the garage to ask him if he wanted some dinner, and he'd flipped. Now here she was. She heard his heavy footsteps as he came back through the door and walked towards her. She sat up, tucking her knees under her chin and wrapping her arms around them. She felt the air cool as his dark shadow loomed over her and she flinched once more; he bent down and stroked her head.

'I'm so sorry, Jo. I didn't mean it. You caught me off guard – you know I don't like you coming in here when I'm working. It puts me off my stride. If you put me off I lose my momentum, then I can't get it back – and the bills won't pay themselves, will they?'

She whispered, 'I'm sorry, I forgot. I just wanted to see you. I get so bored on my own all day.'

He reached down and stroked her hair like she was some kind of pet dog. 'I'm nearly done for now. How about you go and clean yourself up and I'll come inside, make us both a sandwich?'

He reached down, putting his hands under her arms, then pulled her to her feet. He brushed her down and she had to stop herself from flinching at his touch. Keeping her one good eye on the floor, she didn't look across at the bank of steel fridges that were now lined against the back wall. She remembered now that she had stared at them when she'd come in and that had been why he'd hit her. She'd never seen them before and wondered why he wanted those monstrosities, which looked like something out of a television morgue. He must have seen the shock on her face and that was when he'd hit her.

She pushed the thought to the back of her mind. They weren't morgue fridges. What would her husband want with second-hand fridges that had been used to store dead bodies in? It wasn't right and he had no use for them – he was a photographer, not a pathologist. Maybe they were for keeping his equipment in, or something to do with developing his films. She pushed all thoughts of them to the back of her mind and stored them in the little black box where she kept the flashbacks of the kicks and punches he had hurt her with previously. She would lock them away and forget about them. She had no right prying into his business. If she kept out of here and did as she was told, then he would be happy with her. She cursed herself under her breath. What on earth had she been thinking, coming in here?

She walked out of the garage, through his workshop and out

through the studio, keeping her head down. He had been so busy lately and she had been so restless it had seemed like a good idea to come and see him. He hadn't hit her for at least six weeks; what a fool she was, thinking that once again he had realised how cruel he was being to her and was a changed man – the same old stupid dream that had kept her going year after year. It was never going to come true. Now they were back at square one. She wouldn't be able to go out of the house until the swelling had gone down and it was the height of summer; the weather was glorious. She supposed she could potter around the garden and there was nothing stopping her walking through the woods at the back of the house, although she didn't really like them.

On the rare occasions she'd gone walking out there she had always felt as if someone was hiding in the trees watching her and it freaked her out, even though she knew it was just her imagination running wild. She didn't need to go into the village really; it was easy to do an online shop now that every supermarket did home delivery, and the swelling would go down before she knew it. She went straight to the downstairs cloakroom to look at her reflection in the mirror. Her swollen eye was already turning blue. She'd never learn. Running the cold water tap she put the flannel underneath it, wrung it out, then sat down on the toilet and pressed it against her eyelid. 'Ouch.' She stayed that way until she heard the loud footsteps coming down the hallway towards the toilet. They paused outside the door and she felt a cold shiver run down the entire length of her spine, making her drop the flannel into the sink. She picked up a towel and patted the water from her cheek.

'I'm coming, sorry; I won't be a minute.'

Then she flushed the toilet, blew her nose and opened the door. There wasn't anybody outside. She could have sworn she'd heard him walking towards the bathroom door. She looked around, not daring to call his name in case it made him angry again. Maybe she'd knocked her head when she hit the floor and was hearing things. After wringing out the flannel and folding it up, she put it back so it didn't look untidy. She glanced into the mirror one last time, and screamed. There was a much younger woman watching her from inside the glass. Her face was pale, with huge dark circles under her eyes. Her long dark hair hung around her face and the left side of her head was covered in thick, almost black, dried blood. Part of her skull was showing where the flesh had been eaten away.

Jo gasped and stepped away from the mirror. Terrified the woman was behind her, she turned to look . . . but there was no one there. She looked back at the mirror, hoping she had gone – but the woman was still watching her. The fear that filled Jo's heart was different to anything she'd ever felt. It was a cold, creeping feeling, like her entire body was freezing itself from the inside out. The woman in the mirror watched Jo for a little while longer, then lifted her hands, which were bruised purple and black, and slammed them against the glass of the cabinet. The glass bent with the force of the blow and Jo turned and ran, expecting it to shatter everywhere. After slamming the door behind her she ran into the kitchen to see him coming through the door that led from his studio.

'What's the matter with you? You've gone white.'

Instead of telling him like she wanted to, like she should have been able to, she shook her head and tried her very best to make her voice not shake.

'Nothing, sorry, I just gave myself a bit of a fright.'

He looked her up and down. 'Well, that's hardly a surprise. I mean you've had better days. Have you looked in the mirror lately?'

She bit her lip. Yes, she bloody well had and the mirror had looked back at her. Who was that girl and how did she get in there? It wasn't possible – that mirror was hung on a plasterboard wall, and on the opposite side of that wall was the garage, so there was no way someone could have been standing there watching. Her heart was racing. All she wanted to do was go outside and get some fresh air, get away from this house, from him. But thanks to him and his twitchy fists she couldn't even do that. Willing herself to calm down before he got angry again she opened the cupboard and took a loaf of bread out. He walked across and took the bread from her.

'Sit down. I told you I'd make lunch. I have no idea what is going on with you, but you need to sort yourself out.'

She sat down, crossing her hands so he wouldn't notice how much they were trembling. Then she recited a prayer in her mind over and over again. She didn't know if she had really seen that woman or whether she was hallucinating because of the knock to her head, but she prayed to God to make it all go away. Her gran had been a very spiritual woman and when Jo had been little she would watch her through the crack in the curtains that separated Gran's front room from the living room. Her gran would have people come around for readings, or to speak to their dearly departed. They'd sit around the small round table in the front room and dim the lights, the glow from the candle making them all seem very eerie.

Jo's mum didn't believe in any of it and once, when her gran had told Jo she had the gift and one day she would be able to do what she did, Jo had gone home crying and her mum had gone mad. She'd stormed round to her gran's house – which was a few doors up the street from them – and told her not to scare Jo and to keep her rubbish to herself. Jo's mum never believed any of it and Jo definitely never believed in anything remotely paranormal. She hated horror films, much preferring to watch a nice feel-good film where the girl always got the guy and he would turn out to be the kind of man every woman fantasised about. No, her own life was a big enough horror story – so she didn't want to add any further distress to it than she had to.

He slid a sandwich across the table to her and she thanked him, not wanting to eat because she felt sick, but not daring to turn it down because he would go mad at her for wasting his time and food – so she picked it up and nibbled on it. He chattered away; when he did occasionally talk to her there was no stopping him, but today she couldn't be bothered. Her eye was throbbing and her head hurt, not to mention that her heart was having palpitations because she couldn't get the image of the woman from the mirror out of her mind. Jo wanted to scream at him to shut up; she wanted to pick up one of the pans from the hanging rack and smack him across the head with it to see how he liked it, give him a taste of his own medicine. Instead she listened to him going on about what a fabulous photographer he was and how he had this idea for a great project, something that no modern-day photographer had ever done. She nodded and agreed with him whenever she thought it was necessary, anything to keep the peace and stop the pain.

When she looked up from her plate to face him, she felt her blood freeze. The rack of pans that hung down from the ceiling behind him was moving. The pans were swaying from side to side; they were heavy-based copper pans that she struggled to lift most of the time so how they were moving like that was beyond her. She glanced across at the window to see if it was open and letting in a breeze, but it was shut tight, as were all the doors. Even if she did leave the windows and doors open she had never seen them all move like this all at the same time, ever. He looked at her.

'What the hell is the matter with you today? What are you looking at?'

Jo shook her head. 'Nothing. I don't feel well. I must have banged my head when I fell over in the garage.'

She emphasised the 'I', careful not to accuse or throw any blame his way – even though it was completely his fault. The pans were still moving behind him. Why weren't they making a noise? They should have been clanging together but they weren't. She coughed, choking on a bite of her sandwich, and the breath that came out of her mouth was surrounded by a plume of white smoke as if it were a crisp, frosty December day – not the end of August. He looked at her as if she was mad, shoved the last of his sandwich in his mouth, then stood up to go back to his studio.

'I have clients in this afternoon, Jo. I do not want you to come in or disturb me – do you understand?'

She nodded her head. She was going to go upstairs and lie down.

'Good, I'm glad we cleared that up – because if you disturb me again when you've been told not to, I'll fucking kill you.'

And with that he walked out of the door, turning the key in the lock from his side. She looked up at the pans, which were now still, then towards the door that he'd just locked. She stood up and put the plate on the side, and then she forced her hand to reach up and touch one of the pans; her fingers brushed against the cold metal and she pulled back. It felt as if it had been in the freezer for an hour. She turned and stumbled her way upstairs to her bedroom . . . She needed to lie down. She wasn't well at all.

Chapter 4

Will loaded the cases into the back of his car then took the trolley back. It was drizzling in Manchester and the airport behind them looked grey and gloomy. Annie was sitting in the front passenger seat, not quite believing that they were back in England after such a perfect holiday. She pulled her phone out of her handbag and rooted around in the glove compartment for the charger. As it vibrated back to life she saw that she had twelve missed calls from her sister-in-law. She also had a message box full of texts saying 'ring me' but not what it was about. If it had been urgent then she would have said there was something wrong. Annie liked the woman but she was a bit too tightly wound up for her – she made a huge fuss over everything and insisted on sharing every trial and tribulation over her social media accounts, which drove Annie mad to the point where she had unfollowed her. Annie didn't want to know about every argument that Lisa had with her brother and her niece and neither should anyone else.

She pressed the green button to ring her back, hoping this wasn't going to be a thirty-minute phone call about Ben being late for dinner three times this year. Will got in the car and she mouthed the word 'Lisa' to him, and he smiled and turned the key. By the time they got back to Hawkshead the conversation might have finished.

'Well, I'm sorry, Lisa, but I agree with both Ben and Tilly this time. You don't know if she'll even get the job.'

Annie held the phone away from her ear and Will laughed a little too loud, making Annie slam it back against her ear.

'What no, it was the radio. You know she's welcome to stop with me and Will if she does get it. I don't mind driving her to work and picking her up. That's no problem. Look, if I was you I'd just let her go and see what happens and then I'd start to worry about it. OK, bye.'

She looked at Will.

'Bloody hell. Tilly wants to get a job living in at some hotel in Bowness.'

'And I take it Lisa doesn't agree.'

'That's putting it mildly. I also got the distinct impression that she doesn't want Tilly to live with us either, if she does get the job. You wouldn't mind, would you? It might stop me dying of boredom.'

Will nudged her in the side. 'Families, eh? Of course I wouldn't, although I kind of understand why Lisa wouldn't want her daughter to live with us.'

Annie looked at him. 'Why not?' She paused then nodded. 'I guess not. She probably thinks she'll be sending her off to join the "serial killers anonymous" group. Which also reminds me – I don't want our baby being dragged into that world either. Do you think everything will be OK? Is it definitely all over with him . . . You don't think he has any kind of revenge plan organised with someone in the event of his death?'

She didn't want to think about him but now Lisa had forced her to.

'I bloody well hope not. Look, he's dead. We know he's dead – I even went to his post-mortem. I didn't tell you because I was still in hospital and you had more than enough to worry about, but Matt sent Stu to come for me. I watched as Matt sliced his body open and removed his internal organs. To be honest I was surprised the man had a heart inside there, but he did. They all got shoved in a plastic bag and sewn back up inside him. Then I watched as he was cremated. I had to make sure he wasn't coming back to get you, to get us. Henry Smith is definitely dead. I promise you, it's over with him for good.'

'Why did you not tell me about any of this before?'

'I let you down, Annie. Twice that man got the better of me and twice you almost died. I wasn't going to wait on the sidelines and pretend it was all OK. I had to make sure it was over, to make sure that I didn't let it happen a third time.'

She reached over and stroked his arm, feeling terrible that he blamed himself when the only person to blame was finally dead and out of their lives.

'None of it was your fault, but thank you, Will. I didn't want to go back to reality just yet – we've only been in England for an hour and boom, back in the room. Thanks a lot, Lisa.'

'I'm afraid so. Never mind, don't worry about her – let her sort her own mess out for a change. How many missed calls have you got off Jake?'

'None. He knew we needed that holiday and a break. For once he hasn't had any dramas that he couldn't cope with himself. I'm beginning to feel a bit redundant.'

'I wouldn't worry about that too much. You know as well as I do Jake will be on fine form. I wouldn't be surprised if he wasn't waiting for us to get back to the cottage.'

She smiled. She missed Jake – although not quite as much now that she had Will – but her best friend was funny, fiercely loyal and a complete drama queen. She was looking forward to catching up with him, his equally handsome husband, Alex, and their gorgeous little girl, Alice. In fact she was going to invite them up to have a meal and stay over, although she'd better clear it with Will first seeing as how he was the gourmet cook. Her burnt pizza was legend amongst her circle of close friends. They could invite Kav, who was more like her dad than a boss and had been the one to give her away at her wedding, and Cathy. They were now in a steady relationship, thanks to Annie throwing them together. They had even gone public, much to her and Jake's delight. If it hadn't been for all of their friendship she and Will might not have been here to tell the tale of what happened at the Lake House six months ago.

'Penny for them?'

'Sorry, I was thinking about . . . you know . . . everything that happened. It was easier to block it out when we were lying under the tropical sun. It was so far away from here.'

Will reached out, squeezing her fingers.

'I know, it was much easier to forget the whole nightmare ever happened. Now we're back here it seems as if it was only yesterday. We need to push it to the backs of our minds. It's over and done; that bloody man is dead and hopefully he went straight to hell – even though that place is far too good for him.'

She squeezed his fingers back.

'Yes, you're right. It is far too good for him. I agree – no more thinking about him or talking about him. Let's concentrate on us and the baby. We need to think of names. It can't come out and be called baby It.'

Will chuckled.

'I'm easy, as long as you don't want to call it Horatio or Ermentrude – whatever you like, I'm sure that I will.'

'Don't you like Horatio? I thought it had a nice ring to it. Horatio Ashworth.'

She giggled and Will smiled. It was his favourite sound in the world. The turn-off for Newby Bridge came into sight; they were almost home. Twenty minutes of some of the most beautiful, lush, green scenery and then they would reach the small lane that led to Apple Tree Cottage. Annie loved her home. She had dreamt about living in a house like it since she was a small child and knew that she was very fortunate that her dream had come true.

'I can't wait to show your dad and Lily the photographs. She'll definitely want to go when she sees how perfect it was.'

'I bet she's already made him book the flights.'

'I bet she has. Your dad marrying Lily was better than any fountain of youth. She keeps him young, a bit like me and you. I'm much younger than you. I hope I have the same effect.'

She winked at Will who laughed.

'I wish I could say you were, Annie, but somehow you seem to be having the opposite effect on me. Have you seen the grey hairs that have come through, and the worry lines across my forehead? You, my little cupcake, are the complete opposite of the fountain of youth. But I wouldn't have you any other way.'

Chapter 5

It was dusky when Jo opened her eyes. The light had faded fast and she was surprised she'd slept that long, not to mention shocked because she hadn't made Heath's tea. Crap, he would go mad with her all over again. He'd made the sandwiches at dinnertime; if he had to cook his own tea she'd know about it. Her head felt a little better but her eye was sore. Throwing back the covers and sitting up she waited a moment, listening to see if she could hear where he was, but there was no noise. The house was completely silent. It was strange; he must still be working. She looked at the clock and almost had a full-blown panic attack. It was quarter to nine; she'd been asleep since two o'clock. She was never going to sleep tonight – that was if he let her off with staying in bed so long in the first place.

Jumping up, she ran to the bathroom then downstairs, relief that the house was in darkness flooding through her. Thank God for small mercies. Whatever he was working on was keeping him busy and for that she was eternally grateful.

She pulled some pots and pans from the rack and thought about earlier when they'd all been moving on their own. *Don't be stupid. He knocked you out cold – it was just a figment of your imagination, concussion.* She carried on chopping onions, garlic, chilli and peppers; she would make his favourite chilli and rice for tea – that would hopefully keep him in a good mood. Before long, the mince was frying and she tossed in everything else whilst waiting for the pan of water to boil. At least it would be almost ready by the time he came back in, so he wouldn't be mad because he was hungry. Her own stomach started groaning. She hadn't eaten much apart from nibbling on the sandwich earlier and for once he hadn't even moaned about her leaving most of that.

Whilst the tea was cooking she went into the living room and switched the television on to his favourite programme. She didn't understand why but she still loved him, even though he hurt her, and she wanted him to be happy – because when he was happy he didn't get as violent. Therefore, as much as possible, she would do things to make him smile. He was so much fun when he was happy; they used to have such good times when they first met. It was just a shame that the anger seemed to be a much bigger part of him now than the love and laughter he rarely showed.

As she turned to walk out of the room the television, which she had just turned on, switched off. She turned around and stared at the black screen, which seconds ago had had Sky News plastered across it. Thinking that she hadn't pressed the on button right in, she walked back and pressed it again – the newsreader filled the screen. This time she got as far as the hallway when she heard the click of the power button being pressed in to turn the screen off. Whipping her head around, the screen was black once more. Jo frowned, wondering if the television was broken – that was all she needed. Apart from taking photographs, the television was his life and he would be in a foul mood if it wasn't working. No doubt he would blame her and then her life wouldn't be worth living.

She strode back in, this time using the control to turn the damn thing on. It came on but this time it was on a completely different channel. It was on one of the documentary channels and there was what looked like a dead body laid out on a steel mortuary table. Jo shivered; she hated these sorts of programmes. A small voice whispered in her head . . . *I'll tell you why you hate them. It's because one day you're going to end up on one if you don't get away from him.* She shook her head, blocking the whispering out that was echoing inside her brain. She pressed the remote to put the news back on but it wouldn't turn over; it was stuck. She shook it then slammed it against the palm of her hand, but nothing. She took the batteries out and reinserted them . . . still it wouldn't move off the damn autopsy programme.

Angry now, she bent down and switched the socket off, so finally the television turned off. Cursing it, she was walking out of the room towards the kitchen to check on the chilli when a loud noise filled the entire house. It was so loud she put her hands across her ears. It was coming from the living room. Her heart raced; she didn't want to go back in there but if he came in and saw that she'd broken the television she would pay for it. Making herself go back into the living room, she stepped into the doorway and shivered – it now felt like the inside of an ice box in there, when moments ago it had been warm. She stared at the black and white fuzzy screen, which was emitting white noise so loud she couldn't hear herself think. Goose bumps broke out all over her arms.

As she forced herself to walk toward the television, she heard a voice call her name. It wasn't his voice. This was a woman's voice and it was coming from inside the television. Her feet did not want to move any nearer to it, but she didn't have much choice; if he heard the racket he would come storming in and go mental with her. Running the last few steps she then yanked the plug from the socket and the room was silent once more. Her hands shaking, she heard the door from the workshop that led into the kitchen slam shut.

'Jo . . .'

She was afraid to tell him what had just happened because he would think she was lying, and if he thought she was lying it didn't bear thinking about what he'd do. Instead she pushed the last five minutes to the back of her mind and ran to the kitchen where she greeted him with a huge smile.

'Are you hungry? Tea is almost ready. Sorry I fell asleep for so long.'

He didn't answer straight away. Eventually he said, 'Have I got time for a quick shower?'

'Yes, I think so. No, you have, you definitely have. I'll just turn the rice down.'

He walked past her and went upstairs for a shower and she breathed out a sigh of relief that he wasn't angry with her for a change. When he came back down they ate in silence and when he told her he was tired and going to bed she followed him upstairs, afraid to be alone downstairs even though she wasn't tired and didn't want to be with him. She had no choice, because she didn't know what was going on and she was terrified of her own house.

Jo didn't sleep all night. She tossed and turned, afraid that if she did doze off the woman from the mirror or the voice from the television would haunt her dreams. Finally, when it was light enough and she couldn't stand listening to him any longer, she crept from the bed and went downstairs; he was still snoring. She picked up the phone with hands that were shaking so much she couldn't press the buttons on the keypad and had to redial twice. There was something wrong with her – ever since he'd pushed her to the floor and she'd hit her head on the concrete yesterday lunchtime, things had been happening to her that had never happened before.

She would make an appointment with the doctor and tell him that she'd fallen off her ladder whilst cleaning the windows. That should be enough to ward off any awkward questions. All she wanted was reassurance that she wasn't losing her mind. Pots didn't shake and televisions didn't turn on of their own accord – well, they didn't before he'd made her lose consciousness, and she wanted to know why they were now. The receptionist was surprisingly helpful, which threw her off course; usually the woman had a brusque manner that made grown men quake in their shoes when they were speaking to her at the desk in the surgery. She couldn't tell Heath she had a doctor's appointment – he would go mad – so she would have to say she needed to nip into the village for some more coffee and milk.

She opened the fridge door, took out the milk and poured some of it down the sink, leaving enough for his cereal but nothing more – at least now she had a good excuse to leave the house, even if she did have to wear sunglasses.

Miss Bates turned to the rowdy group of teenagers, lifting her hands in the air.

'Now I know you are all quite capable of walking through the woods without getting lost; at least I hope you are. I also know that you lot make more noise than a gaggle of geese so if you do get separated from each other we're bound to hear you. But – and this is a big but – look out for each other. This is part of your exam so let's do it right. I hate walking, and if you mess it up and we have to come back and do all this again, I'm not going to be very happy with you all. Understood?'

They all nodded and chorused, 'Yes, Miss Bates.'

'Good, now let's get going. The sooner we start the sooner it will be dinnertime. Scott, I'm watching you and Becky – if you think it's a good idea to have a crafty fag behind a tree and I won't know about it, you're wrong. So don't go sneaking off for one and setting the woods on fire with your dog ends.'

Scott, Becky and Jessica all giggled.

'As if we would, Miss. You know we wouldn't do anything like that.'

Miss Bates rolled her eyes at them but smiled. There was something about the bad kids that she liked. She always had done. Some of the kids in this class had had the worst upbringings imaginable. Most of their parents were addicts, criminals, dealers, or just plain useless and didn't care for their kids. Left to fend for themselves from an early age, at least the kids had one thing going for them – they were self-sufficient and streetwise. She found it far more rewarding working with these teenagers than with the ones in the private school where she'd worked previously, where the kids were rude, arrogant and selfish. These kids might have been dragged up but most of them were honest, polite, looked out for each other and generally did as she told them.

The walk leader nodded and they all heaved their heavy backpacks on and set off walking. Becky – who had decided to wear her new trainers with a thick black heel, the ugliest shoes Miss Bates had ever seen – soon began to lag behind. The ground was soft and the heels kept sinking into the soil.

'Trust you, Becky. Why didn't you put your old skanky trainers on? You're going to ruin them and we're not going to finish until teatime at the rate you're walking,' Scott complained.

'Fuck off with the others then, Scott. No one told you to wait for me. I didn't think it would be like this, did I? I thought there would be a path like the one in our woods back home – not soil, mud and leaves forever.'

Jessica giggled. 'Listen to you both, arguing like some married couple. I think it's really sweet.'

Scott gave her the finger and Becky grinned. They could see a house through the trees.

'Do you think we should go there and ask if we can use the toilet?'

'Are you serious, Becky? We've only just set off, and not only can you not walk, but you want to pee already.'

The rest of the group was already quite some way ahead of them.

'When you got to go, you got to go.'

'What's wrong with squatting behind a tree?'

'Eugh, what's *right* with squatting behind a tree? It's all right for you lot; men can just whip it out and piss anywhere.'

Scott stood shaking his head. As much as he fancied Becky she was a complete pain in the arse. Jessica, who thought the whole thing was hilarious, was still smiling.

'Just go behind that big tree, Becky. I'll stand guard and make sure Scott doesn't try and perv on you. You don't know who lives in that house; it might be some crazy cat lady or a creep.'

Becky knew her friend was right. She broke away from them and headed towards the tree. Scott was shouting something after her and she turned to give him the finger. Missing her footing she fell forwards, landed on the soft ground and dislodged a mound of leaves. She cursed as the sound of her friends' laughter filled the air around her. There was something white sticking out of the ground in front of her. She looked at it, trying to get her mind to process exactly what it was. When it finally decided that what she was seeing was real, she opened her mouth to scream and didn't stop until Miss Bates and the others were standing next to her.

'What on earth is the matter, Becky? Have you hurt yourself?'

They were all too busy looking at her to notice the skeletal hand that was sticking up from the ground. She lifted her finger and pointed to it.

'What is that?' Miss Bates looked down at it and felt her blood run cold. She looked at Scott.

'Is this some kind of joke, Scott? Because if it is, it's not very funny.'

He shook his head. 'No, Miss, I swear down. She wanted a pee and was going behind that tree. I've been standing with Jessica the whole time.'

Jess nodded in agreement with what her friend had just said. The man who was leading the walk bent down to take a closer look, prodding at the bones with a stick.

'It seems real, but how would someone's hand get out here?'

Scott pulled Becky up from the ground and she grabbed onto him.

'Miss, if there's a hand – there might be an entire body under there.'

'Yes, you're right, Scott. There could well be. I think we need to move away now and I'll phone the police. Before I do I'm asking you all one last time – do any of you know anything about this? I'm not angry, but if it's some toy Halloween prop that you got at the pound shop then I need to know because I don't want to look like an idiot and phone the police for nothing.'

Nobody spoke. They all shook their heads at her. Most of them were still staring down at the hand with morbid fascination.

'Right, then I'm trusting you on this – I'll phone the police. I think you should all go over there and sit down. I have a feeling we might be here for a while yet.'

The normally rowdy kids were silent for once and she was glad that she could hear herself think. She walked off away from them so they couldn't hear her conversation with the operator.

Chapter 6

Annie locked the door to the cottage and stared at her car, which she hadn't driven for almost three weeks. Then she decided that by the time she'd driven the short distance into the village of Hawkshead and found a parking place she could walk and still be in time for her doctor's appointment. It was a warm day but there was a gentle breeze, which made it bearable. She walked to the gate and heard the two different voices giggling softly. Looking up at the bedroom window that she'd left ajar she saw the outline of twin boys standing there; she waved, unsure whether they could see her, but they both smiled and waved back. Annie, who had been able to see and communicate with some ghosts after the horrific head injury Mike inflicted on her two years ago, didn't mind her ghostly occupants. They were much friendlier than the woman who'd murdered them back in 1782. Thankfully Betsy Baker was no longer haunting the house, not since she and Jake had dug up her grave in the front garden and, after an awful fight, had managed to bury her in consecrated ground. The boys she could cope with, but that woman had been evil through and through.

Before long she reached the main road that led into the picturesque village. She walked past one of the coffee shops, which had the biggest cake Annie had ever seen in the window, and her stomach let out a loud groan. She rubbed her hand over her bump. *Oh no, you love the look of that cake as much as I do, kid. At last a partner in crime. If I haven't put on three stone in the last couple of weeks when the midwife weighs me I'll treat us both to some.* She walked into the surgery and was surprised to see it so busy. There wasn't a chair free but she didn't mind; she was used to standing up for hours on end whilst at work guarding crime scenes. She booked in at the receptionist's desk and turned around to see a woman, who was around the same age as her, stand up.

'Please, you can take my seat.' The woman didn't make eye contact and kept her head bowed. She did, however, smile.

'Thank you but I'm fine. I can stand for hours – I'm used to it.'

'Oh no, I wouldn't dream of it. Please take it.'

Annie didn't want to offend the small, quiet woman so sat down in the chair. 'Thank you.'

She looked at Annie and nodded. 'You're very welcome.'

The receptionist shouted 'Jo Tyson' and, still keeping her head down, the friendly woman scurried along the corridor towards the doctor's room. Annie picked up the magazine from the table next to her. She had noticed the blue bruising under the woman's left eye and the way she avoided eye contact and kept her head down. It reminded Annie of the woman she used to be three years ago. She shivered. The thought of her dead husband, Mike, and his violent outbursts made her feel ill. She had no idea how her life had changed so dramatically into the one she was living now but she knew it was all thanks to Will. He had stumbled across her when she was at her lowest point and like some scene from her favourite film, *Pretty Woman*, had come to her rescue, falling in love with her when she was battered, bruised and technically homeless.

And now look at her; she had never been so happy. She so wanted to tell that woman that her life could get better if she found the courage to make the break away from her violent partner but it wasn't her place because she didn't know her. Hopefully the woman would realise it herself before her partner hit her too hard and killed her . . .

The midwife shook Annie's shoulder, waking her up from her world of painful memories.

'Sorry, Annie, I called you a couple of times but you were miles away.'

Annie laughed. 'I was. Sorry about that.' She stood up and followed the midwife along to the room that she shared with the practice nurse.

The doctor felt Jo's head, shone a light in her eyes and asked her how many fingers he was holding up.

'Four.'

'Good. I think you might have a slight concussion but everything seems OK. Have you vomited or passed out since?'

She shook her head.

'No, but I've seen things . . . strange things. This is going to sound really crazy but I'm not, I swear I'm not. The pans started to shake on the rack in the kitchen when there was no breeze and I saw a woman I didn't recognise looking back at me through the mirror. She was bleeding from her head. And then the television wouldn't turn off.'

The doctor sat down and began typing on the computer. Jo knew she sounded exactly like she was crazy but she had to tell someone.

'How long was this after you fell and hit your head?'

'Pretty much as soon as I came around.'

'Well, I wouldn't worry too much. I think you must have knocked your head too hard and it messed around with your vision. Concussion can be a strange thing. Now I want you to take it easy for a couple of days, take paracetamol if you have a headache and get plenty of rest. I'm sure you'll be back to normal in a couple of days. If you start to vomit or black out then you need to go to the nearest accident and emergency department as soon as possible.'

Jo nodded. She wasn't about to disagree with a doctor who had spent years at medical school. At least he hadn't told her to wait there while he called for a van and the men in white suits to come and take her away in a straitjacket to the nearest mental hospital.

'Thank you so much, doctor. I'm sorry to have bothered you.'

He smiled at her. 'Just one more thing, Jo. I couldn't help but notice the bruising under your eye. Is everything OK at home? Do you need to talk about anything else?'

She shook her head, standing up. 'Everything is fine, thank you, and no, I don't have anything else to discuss.'

She turned to walk out of the room but he gently took hold of her arm, tugging her back inside and shut the door.

'I know you don't want to hear this but it needs to be said. I've kept quiet about it for far too long. I've watched you come in here the last few years and you hardly speak. What happened to the Jo I used to know? The fun-loving girl who would go down to the pub for quiz night and lose miserably every single week and still have a great big smile on her face? I can't stand to see you like this – it's as if all the stuffing has been knocked out of you and been replaced with cotton wool. When was the last time you went out with your friends to the pub quiz? Do you even have any friends now, Jo, or are you just a dutiful little housewife to Heath? We used to have such a good time all those years ago, and I miss the old Jo. My girlfriend Jo, even though it was only for six months, who once kissed me so hard under the mistletoe on New Year's Eve that I couldn't catch my breath. I still think about that kiss every single New Year.'

Jo looked at him. Her cheeks had flushed red and she felt as if she couldn't breathe. She had fancied him so much when he'd first moved here, fresh out of medical school. In fact, half of the women in the village had fancied him, but he'd turned them all down and had chosen to go out with her for six glorious months – until Heath had come along and blown her away with his charm.

What a complete fool she'd been, giving up Paul for Heath. Christ, she still fancied him – but he was the one who had said it would be far too unprofessional of him to have a serious relationship with his patient. He'd let Heath steal her away from under his nose . . . and now look where she was. What would she give to turn back time and start all over again? Her soul probably. Where was the devil when you wanted to make a deal?

Shrugging her arm away from him she walked away without looking back, not wanting him to see her cheeks, which were burning, and her eyes, which were full of tears desperate to be shed. She didn't want anyone feeling sorry for her; it was her sorry mess and one day she would sort it out – but today wasn't that day.

She walked out of the doctor's room with her head down, not looking where she was going. Annie, who was also leaving, was talking on her phone to Will, telling him about her appointment and wasn't paying attention either. They both reached the main doors at the same time, bumping straight into each other. Jo, who was tiny, lifted off her feet and landed on the floor. Mortified, Annie bent down, reaching out her hand to help her up. Jo began to laugh.

'I'm so sorry. Are you OK?'

'I'm sorry; it was my fault. I wasn't looking where I was going. Are *you* OK?'

'I'm fine. I keep forgetting about the size of my stomach. This bump is made of strong stuff and so am I. I'm Annie, by the way. It's a gorgeous day, isn't it? Do you mind me asking – are you a local?'

Jo took hold of Annie's hand and she pulled her to her feet.

As they walked outside into the warm summer sun, Jo nodded. 'I'm local. I live in a cottage on the edge of the woods. Have done for the last twenty years, since I got married. How about you?'

'Ah, you almost qualify as being a true local. I've only lived here just under a year. We live at Apple Tree Cottage, which borders the woods, but it must be on the opposite side to you.

I've never really got to know anyone in the village because I was always working – well, until I found out I was pregnant that was. Now I'm on doctor's orders not to get stressed, so I'm not at work at the moment.'

She held out her hand and Jo grasped it; her touch was so light it tickled. Annie smiled at her.

'You know I've been fantasising about a slice of that monstrous cake in the coffee shop window. Do you have time for a coffee and cake? My treat. It's the least I can do to make up for almost flattening you into the floor. It's been so long since I sat in a café, I've almost forgotten what it's like.'

She watched as the woman looked down at her watch, biting her lip. Then she looked at her properly, for the first time, making eye contact.

'Me either. You know what, I would love to – but I can't stop for too long. I have to get back.'

Annie didn't ask who, or why the rush. She got the sense that the woman was taking a huge risk by making a decision of her own. They walked the short distance to the café and Annie pointed to a table outside.

'Would you mind if we went inside, out of the way?'

'No, of course not. I'd get too hot anyway.'

They went inside where it was cool and much darker. Annie let Jo pick the table, wondering if she would pick the one at the back in a dark corner, and she did. Annie didn't feel like gloating; she really felt for her. They were like kindred spirits, as if there was some unseen connection between them. Annie smiled. Where was this bullshit coming from? She'd turned into a right soppy wreck since she'd got pregnant. They sat down, chatting about the weather, the village fete that was being held in two weeks' time, and the baby.

'I always wanted children, really wanted children, but my first husband never did and to be honest I'm glad we didn't now. It wasn't a very good relationship. This one was a bit of a surprise but my second husband was delighted when he found out. Do you have any?'

The woman laughed but it was a short laugh. 'No, Annie, we don't and I suppose it's a blessing in disguise. I wouldn't want to bring a baby into my life.' She stopped talking and bowed her head, as if furious with herself for almost letting slip about what a shitty life she led.

Annie changed the subject, feeling embarrassed for her – yet at the same time wanting to hug her and tell her it was OK; her secret was safe with her. But they barely knew each other and Annie hadn't even told her best friend, Jake, about the abusive relationship she was in at the time, so there was no way that Jo was about to confide in her when they'd only just met. They finished their cake and sipped their coffee. Jo looked at her watch.

'Oh gosh, is that the time? I really need to get going, but thank you, Annie. It's been great talking to a neighbour even if we do live a couple of miles in the opposite direction from each other.'

Jo began to dig around in her pocket and Annie pulled out a ten-pound note.

'I told you, this is my treat. I'm so relieved to have some adult female conversation it's the least I can do. You can buy them next time.'

She winked at her and Jo laughed, turning to leave. Annie let her go. She was tired now she'd sat down and that huge slice of cake was weighing her down. Now all she had to do was walk home, or should that be drag herself home. She couldn't stop thinking about Jo and wondered if her husband was a big man like Mike had been – they weren't always. She'd arrested men before who were short and weedy but had fists like bars of steel. Annie knew she should keep out of it, that this was nothing to do with her. But she liked Jo and wanted to help in any way she could.

Chapter 7

Jo hurried home. She'd been far too long and he would be furious with her, but it had been worth it. Annie seemed lovely. It was so nice to speak to another woman. She couldn't remember the last time she had been out for coffee. It felt so civilised and made her realise exactly how crap her life was when going out for a coffee felt like a huge adventure. As she opened her front door she kept her fingers crossed that he wasn't waiting for her. She was in such a great mood for the first time in months. It would be just like him to be waiting behind the front door to spoil it all.

But when she got inside it was almost too good to be true – he was nowhere to be seen and she felt her shoulders relax as she let out a long sigh of relief. Closing the door as quietly as possible she kicked off her shoes and walked into the kitchen to put the kettle on. As she leant over the sink to fill the kettle she saw flashes of bright yellow moving around in the woods behind the cottage. The cold tap squirted water all down her top as the kettle overflowed. She jumped back away from the window, grabbing a tea towel to dry herself.

Her heart was racing. What were the police doing in the woods? She had no idea why she felt so nervous but she did. In all the years she'd lived in the village she could count the number of times she'd seen a police officer on one hand – and now there were at least six of them at the back of her house. Her first thoughts were that he'd done something really bad, but then she scolded herself. He only did the bad stuff to her, didn't he? He was a perfect gentleman to everyone else, especially his clients. He wouldn't do anything to jeopardise what he thought was his perfect life. Why would he? But still she felt uneasy.

She made him a mug of tea, checking in the mirror to make sure she didn't look a complete mess as she walked towards his workshop and knocked on the door. There was no answer, so she knocked again a little louder and this time she heard him swear. The door was thrown open and he looked her up and down in disgust.

'What are the rules, Jo?'

Before she could answer his left hand had slapped her across the cheek, jolting her arm so she spilt steaming hot tea all down herself.

'Never to disturb you when you're working . . . but I think you should know there are a lot of police officers in the woods out the back. What do you think they're doing there?'

His normally ruddy complexion paled – far too quickly for her liking – making her wonder what it was he was hiding, or what it was he did in there when he locked himself away. He pushed past her and ran to the kitchen to take a look outside. She followed him and he leant forward to get a better view of what they were doing. Picking up the tea towel she dabbed at the now tea-stained white shirt she was wearing.

'I don't know what they're doing – what am I, psychic all of a sudden?'

His voice was much quieter and it wavered, just a notch. He kicked his slippers off and pulled on a pair of black wellington boots, grabbing his jacket off the coat peg by the back door. He opened it and went outside. She watched him, intrigued as to why he was so worried. He headed towards the nearest officer and she felt sick. He would be so polite to the policewoman who was standing there. He wouldn't dare to be disrespectful towards her, let alone raise his hand and slap her.

He went out of the back door knowing fine well what they were doing – somehow, after all this time, they had found the grave. He needed to know if they knew much or were just as shocked as he was. He approached them as if he had every right to be there; *never show your fear*, he told himself over and over.

'Excuse me, officer, I live in that cottage there. I was wondering if everything is OK?'

The officer held up her hand to stop him from going any further. 'Sorry, sir, I can't really say – and this whole area is now a crime scene so you'll have to go back inside.'

'No, of course you can't, but can you tell me if I should be worried? Is it bad? I don't want to leave my wife alone in the house if it's anything we should be worried about.'

She looked around to see who was in hearing distance and lowered her voice. 'Well, I'm not supposed to say anything but you'll hear soon enough and officers will want to come and speak to you both anyway. A group of schoolkids out hiking found a skeleton this morning, buried in the woods. We're just waiting for the bosses and crime scene investigators to get here.'

His hand flew to his mouth in what he hoped was a convincing attempt at shock. 'Oh, dear God, that's awful. I can't believe it. Is there anything I can do?'

'Not really. The best thing you can do is to go back inside until one of the detectives comes to see you for a chat.'

'Yes, yes, of course. I can't believe it. If any of you need anything just give us a knock; my wife will be in all day. I might have to go into Barrow on an errand.'

He didn't know whether he wanted to be there when the police came knocking, in case they could pick something up from his body language – like how guilty he was. But he supposed that they would want to talk to him at some point and it might be better to just get it over with and hope that they'd think he was simply shocked at their discovery. After what seemed like forever he turned and walked back to the house. Kicking off his boots he shut the door and turned the key in the lock, shrugging off his jacket at the same time.

'What did she say. Is it bad?'

'She wouldn't say – just said there was a serious incident and they were sealing off the area until CID got there. She said the police will want to come and speak to us at some point.'

'Well, as long as no one has been hurt.'

He looked at her and frowned, staring at the fading red mark on her cheek.

She knew he was hoping it would disappear before the police came knocking on their door wanting to speak to them both. He went back into the workshop, locking the door, and she sat down at the kitchen table, relieved that whatever he was doing meant he was out of her way.

Thirty minutes later he was back. She inhaled and caught a whiff of strong lemon cleaning fluid. She was sitting at the kitchen table reading a magazine and jumped as he walked in, expecting him to shout at her for sitting there wasting time, but he never said a word. He locked up the workshop and went out of the back door to make sure the windows and outside door that led to it were also locked. He came back in and smiled at her.

'Why don't you make us a nice cup of coffee and we'll put a film on? We haven't watched that one with that man you like out of that women's film yet.'

He meant *The King's Speech* and the women's film he was referring to was *Bridget Jones*. She nodded, knowing fine well what his game was. He was playing happy families so that when the police came they wouldn't think anything strange of the married couple who lived in the house near the edge of the woods. If only they knew the truth – but she'd never say anything. She daren't. She hadn't when he'd pushed her down the four steps into the garden; that had cost him a trip to the accident and emergency department whilst her ankle was x-rayed then put into plaster. He'd never left her side the whole time but he needn't have worried; she had nowhere to go if she had asked them for help. She couldn't leave him if she wanted to.

It was almost two hours later that the knock finally came on their front door, and it was Jo who stood up to go and answer it. She could see two men through the small glass pane in the front door. Opening it, she looked at the two men, both wearing suits with ID badges around their necks. She felt drawn to the older, much better-looking one and smiled.

'Hello, sorry to bother you. I'm Detective Sergeant Will Ashworth and this is Detective Constable Stuart Martin. Would you mind if we came in to talk to you?'

She smiled at him. He had such nice, kind blue eyes . . . in fact he had nice everything.

'Of course. This way.'

As he followed her in she got a whiff of his aftershave, which was lovely. It reminded her of Dr Miller. He always smelt good when they'd been dating and whenever she'd gone for an appointment. She led them into the living room, where Heath was in the process of building up the wood burner, even though it wasn't particularly cold. Her eyes looked at the coal dust, which now covered his hands. He never got them so dirty, ever. He was very particular about his hands and always wore gloves when he did anything that might involve getting them dirty.

'This is my husband, Heath.'

Will nodded at the man, and lifted his hand to shake Heath's but then looked at them and smiled. Heath looked down at his hands too.

'Sorry, I'm a bit dirty.'

Will repeated his introduction.

'I suppose you wouldn't be able to help but notice all the police activity out the back. I'm afraid to say there's been a bit of a gruesome discovery in the woods this morning. A group of teenagers found an unmarked grave containing a body – well, a skeleton to be exact – so we just need to ask you a few routine questions.'

Jo gasped. 'A skeleton! Oh, my God – that's awful. Has it been there a long time?'

She was thinking that it might be really old, maybe even a couple of hundred years old.

'We can't really say, to tell you the truth. It's not our field of expertise. But it looks as if it's been buried out there for quite a few years. We're just waiting on the pathologist and a forensic anthropologist who will be able to tell us a lot more. Can you tell me how long you've lived here?'

Heath spoke before his wife could open her mouth. 'Twenty-three years.'

'Have you ever noticed anyone or anything suspicious in the woods out the back?'

'No, nothing at all – but then again, we do have a very limited view. Would you like to come and take a look?'

Heath stood up and Will nodded at Stu to go with him; Will didn't miss the look he gave his wife. He waited until they had left the room.

'I can imagine that this must be a bit of a shock for you. It's not the sort of thing you want to happen near your house, is it?'

'It is . . . I mean, it's terrible. You don't expect things like that to happen right on your own doorstep. The poor thing. How awful being buried out there in the middle of nowhere and left for years. What must the family be going through?'

'It is horrible, isn't it, but whoever it is could have been there a very long time. Do you go out there much?'

'No, not really. I love living here but I don't go into the woods on my own. To be honest I find them a little bit creepy. They're far too quiet for me.'

Will smiled, encouraging her. 'What about your husband? Does he spend much time out there?'

'Oh no, he's far too busy with his work to think about going out and actually relaxing. He spends all his time in his studio.'

Heath walked back in, followed by Stu, and she shut up, not even looking at him – instead she lowered her head.

Will had picked up on the body language as soon as he'd walked in but this just confirmed it – that and the fear that had crept into her eyes. He felt his knuckles clenching. He looked at the man, who was well built but not fat and would make a good rugby player. He took an instant dislike to him. Will hated men who hit their partners with a passion and he would bet a full month's wages that this prick hit the much smaller woman sitting opposite him.

'I'm a photographer so I work long hours; I do a lot of wedding photographs, portraits, proms, school photos . . . that sort of thing. I like to develop them all myself. I much prefer using film than digital, although it does have its uses. Neither of us really goes out into the woods, which is a shame because they really are beautiful and right on our doorstep.'

'Do you remember who you bought the house from? We might need to speak to them, providing we find out how long our body has been buried out there.'

'It was an elderly couple. I'm not even sure if they'll still be alive now but I do have their names and address somewhere. The only thing is it might take me some time to locate them.'

'That's fine. If you could have a look and give me a call when you do, I'd really appreciate it.'

Will was looking at the woman the whole time he was speaking; he pulled a business card from his pocket. The man stepped forward to take it from him but Will pushed it into the woman's hands before her husband could reach it. He let his hand linger on hers for a touch longer than he normally would and then he looked into her eyes.

'That's my mobile number. You can call me when you find them.

Any time, day or night, don't worry about it. If you remember anything or need to tell me something and I don't answer just leave me a message and I'll get straight back to you.'

Stu frowned at Will, not sure what was happening. Then Will stood up and Stu followed. Will turned to the man, whose face was a touch redder than it had been moments ago.

'Thank you for your time. I'm sorry to have bothered you. We won't know for some time yet who it is or how long they've been buried out there, but we'll keep in touch.'

The man nodded and led them to the front door. As they left the room Jo rushed across to the sideboard. Scribbling the number off the card onto a bright pink Post-it note, she then tucked it as far down into the inside of her jeans pocket as it would go. Rushing back, she threw herself onto the sofa, still clutching the business card in her hand. He stormed back in; after snatching it off her, he crumpled it up then pitched it at the fire and she watched as it smouldered and then burst into a tiny ball of flames.

'What a smarmy bastard he was. I hate nosy coppers. If he wants to speak to us he can bloody well come here. I'm not wasting my breath or my money phoning him . . . and what did he think he was doing holding your hand like that? I've a good mind to go out there and knock his head off.'

She flinched at his outburst, waiting for the open-handed slap that would normally accompany such behaviour . . . but it never came. He was far too distracted and stomped out of the living room back to his workshop, leaving her cowering on the sofa, her hand tucked into her pocket protecting the small piece of paper that might just have the answer to all her prayers written across it. That nice detective had sensed something was wrong and he might be able to help her should she need to escape.

As they got outside Stu looked at Will.

'I hope I'm not speaking out of turn, boss, or overstepping my mark – but just what exactly was that? That lingering touch and "you can call me any time you like". I thought you were a happily married man.'

Will stopped dead in his tracks and turned to dead-eye Stu.

'Don't be an idiot, Stu. I can't believe you just said that – in fact, don't even go there. Can't you see the facts when they're right in front of your eyes?'

'What, what facts are you talking about?'

'I don't know what the hell is going on with the skeleton – for all we know that could have been there a hundred years – but I do know that it's pretty obvious that the bloke back there likes to show how much of a man he is by beating his wife.'

'What? How could you know that from the whole ten-minute conversation we had back there? Don't tell me you're a psychic genius as well as your wife.'

'Because of her body language. She practically shrivelled into herself when he walked in the room. Then there was the fact that she had pale blue bruising under her eye, which she'd tried to cover with face powder, and she was terrified of him. When he came back in the room you could almost feel the fear that radiated from her, and she never looked up once when he was in the room or made eye contact with either of us.'

'Really? I never noticed.'

'If there is one thing I hate more than anything in this world, it's weak, pathetic men who feel they have to take their problems out on their wives with their fists. Do me a favour, Stu, and go find someone else to irritate for an hour because I can't be bothered with you right now.'

Will walked away from him, leaving Stu staring after him, shocked at his boss's tantrum. Then, realising he'd been a complete idiot and so wrong it would be hard to put it right, he hurried after Will – trying his best to think of all the ways he could make it up to him.

Chapter 8

Annie walked down the lane towards Apple Tree Cottage and felt her heart fill with joy to see Jake and his adorable baby girl, Alice, playing in her front garden. It never failed to melt her heart – the sight of huge, tough, gorgeous Jake playing with Alice. She opened the gate and Alice squealed with delight at the sight of Annie. She hurried over to scoop her up into her arms and plaster her with kisses. Alice giggled. Lifting her small, chubby finger she twirled it around one of Annie's curls that had escaped her ponytail.

'Well, hello, my adorable Alice. I've missed you so much – did you miss me?'

Alice gurgled at her.

'Yes, you did; I know that you did.'

Jake walked over and bent to kiss Annie's cheek. 'Yes, she did. I cannot lie. The poor kid almost had to go cold turkey off the chocolate buttons because Alex banned chocolate from the house for a week. I missed you as well, though. You look really well. You look . . .'

Annie slapped his arm. 'Don't you dare say that I'm blooming. I hate that expression. I have a bad back, which is keeping me awake at night, can't stop peeing and I still want to devour box after box of Coco Pops.'

'Best not get you started on the haemorrhoids then.'

He laughed. 'Suit yourself – I won't say it then. Tell me, how was your holiday? That's what I've come to see you for. I want to know every sordid detail, every cocktail that you drank and where was the most exotic location you two had sex.'

'I'm not telling you that even though you are my bestie. What's the matter with you?'

Jake pouted. 'Well, did you at least join the mile-high club?'

'In case it's escaped your notice, Jake, I'm six months pregnant – I could only just squeeze myself into the toilet on the plane. There was no room for me to manoeuvre, never mind Will! Come on, let's go inside. I'll make us a cool drink and fill you in on everything.'

'Everything?'

'Well, almost everything – there are some things a lady should never discuss.'

He looked around the garden, 'What lady?'

She ignored him and walked to the front door, passing Alice to him so she could open it. It was cool inside. She hadn't realised how warm it was outside until she stepped onto the cold tiled floor and kicked her shoes off. Jake ducked under the porch and followed her in.

'No sign of?'

He didn't finish it; he knew the rules. Neither of them was to speak about that woman inside the perimeter of the house and gardens.

Annie shook her head. 'No, but I saw those two little boys earlier, looking out of the bedroom window, and I can't help thinking that if she was around they wouldn't be here, would they? They kept their distance when it was all going on and I don't mind kids as long as they're sweet and innocent like Sophie.'

Sophie was the little girl whose soul had been stolen by the shadow man. Annie had never been so scared as the day she had to do battle with the dark entity that collected souls of the innocent and who had wanted Annie's soul. Jake had been there in the church whilst Annie had done her very best to fight the shadow man and send him back to hell; she'd done it with a little help from Sophie and her mum, who had both died in 1984. All three of them had held hands and fought against him, managing to get rid of him for good – or so Annie hoped. She had watched Sophie be reunited with her mum, who she hadn't seen for twenty years, and she'd known then that as scary as her newly found psychic gift was it was also wonderful.

'That's good. In fact it's more than good – it's a huge relief. I mean, you have this fabulous house and it would be terrible if you had to sell it because of its ghostly inhabitants – not that anyone would want to buy it if they knew it was haunted. So come on then, what was Hawaii like? Am I going to want to get the next plane there?'

'Oh yes, it was beautiful and the people were so nice – in fact they were amazing. I would seriously think about living out there if I didn't have to worry about leaving you all behind.'

'See, you're a posh bird now. You've gone up in the world since you married into money. I'm surprised that you still talk to us lower-class heathens.'

'Pfft, Alex is by no means lower class, Jake, and you live in the poshest part of Barrow so stop talking rubbish. Who'd have thought it, though, I mean seriously – you ended up with the man of your dreams, who just happened to be rolling in it with a good job. And I met the man of my dreams, who I had no idea was rolling in it because he kept it so well hidden. I'm not going to lie; it's a lovely feeling seeing the brown envelopes come through the door and not have to worry if my wages will be enough to cover the bills – but if I lost it all tomorrow it wouldn't matter as long as I had Will and the baby.'

'We did all right, didn't we, kid? We've survived some scary shit but we've come out the other side. Bloody hell, we should be drinking champagne not . . .' He took a sip from the tall glass filled with ice and juice that she passed him. 'What is this?'

'A non-alcoholic Pimm's.'

Jake spat an ice cube down the front of his shirt.

'Since when did you drink Pimm's?'

'See, you don't know everything about me. I do have some secrets.'

'You're a dark horse, Annie Graham – I mean Ashworth. I can't get used to calling you that, by the way. You know you will always be Annie Graham to me, don't you.'

She nodded. 'I know.'

'Good, I love my plain old Annie.'

'And I love my red-hot Jake.'

'Calm it down, woman – you know I'm a married man now.'

But he winked at her, relieved to see that for once she had a lovely golden glow, wasn't missing half of her hair, didn't have any black eyes or bruises and wasn't being stalked by a serial killer or a scary ghost. He just hoped that he wasn't jinxing things by being so happy for her. She'd had such a rough couple of years he was amazed she wasn't hooked on vodka and antidepressants. Annie led them into the living room and flopped down onto the sofa.

'You may have to haul me off this thing before you go or, if you can't, hire a crane. I'm so tired all the time. I had no idea it would feel like this.'

'I could haul you off there with one hand. You're not that big.'

'Really, because I feel as if I'm the size of a house. I'm scared to look in the mirror sideways or have a bath when Will isn't here in case I get stuck and can't get out – I don't fancy sitting in a bathtub for hours on end.'

He laughed. Alice was sitting on the soft cream rug by his feet playing with an assortment of toys Annie had brought in from the cupboard under the stairs. They both watched her play and Annie had to stop herself from sighing out loud. She couldn't wait to watch their baby playing with Alice. The ball, which had rolled away from Alice and was too far out of her reach, began to roll back towards her. Annie watched it and smiled. Jake grabbed her arm.

'Did you see that? Jesus, look – it's moving on its own!'

'It's a ball, Jake. They're circular and are known for rolling around.'

He shook his head. 'Not like that.'

It reached Alice and she chuckled, pushing it back away again. Once more it rolled towards her.

'Should I be worried? Annie, I thought you said it was OK here now. What's going on?'

'No, you definitely don't need to worry – it's only Sophie. She's come to play with Alice. Hello, Sophie, where have you been? It's been ever so quiet without you.'

Jake's tanned face turned white, but there was no reply. The room was chillier than before but it didn't feel menacing.

A voice whispered into Annie's ear: 'Hello, Annie, I just brought our Alice to meet Jake's Alice. She's in love with her. You can tell him that his little Alice now has her very own guardian angel because she's besotted.'

'That's lovely. I can't see either of you but I miss you both.'

Jake stared at her. He couldn't hear anyone but Annie. 'Who are you talking to?'

'Don't worry, Annie, we're still around but you haven't needed us as much so we've been keeping an eye on you from afar.'

Annie felt an ice-cold squeeze as Sophie wrapped her arms around her and hugged her. Annie tried her best to hug her back but it was hard to hug someone that you couldn't always see. The baby began to cry and Annie realised that her ghostly friends had left – it made her wonder if little Alice already had a sixth sense because there was no reason for her to be crying. Jake was staring at Annie, who had scooped Alice into her arms. 'Did you like playing with Sophie and Alice? They liked playing with you.'

'What just happened? Was it Sophie? Because I can cope if it's a ghost I know, but I don't want any old ghost playing with my daughter. I'm still not one hundred per cent sure about all this weird stuff, you know.'

Annie laughed. Alice Heaton had died a very long time ago; she had helped Annie to overcome Henry Smith the first time he'd tried to kill her in the derelict mansion in Abbey Wood that her brother Ben had been the caretaker of. If it hadn't been for Alice she didn't know if she would still be here to tell the tale of what happened at the ghost house, as Will had nicknamed it. It was so sweet how Alice and Sophie had both become such good friends and her very own guardian angels.

'Yes, it's all fine. Sophie and Alice wanted to come and see your Alice. They are the kindest, most beautiful souls I've ever met and if little Alice has them watching out for her she will be just fine. They make a pretty good team and they've helped me out more than enough times when I really needed them.'

'Dear God, our lives are never just normal, are they?'

He wasn't expecting a response to that question, because he knew the answer. Normal had left his life when Annie became psychic after the terrible head injury that Mike, her now-dead husband, had inflicted upon her a couple of years ago. She changed the subject. The baby was playing with the gold cross that she always wore around her neck. It had been a present from her friend Father John – who had blessed it after their encounter with that awful woman he'd helped them to bury in the churchyard – and it meant the world to her.

'So what's going on in the busy world of Bowness? I bet you're bored without me. Not to mention skint. Do you have to pay for your coffee now I'm not with you to go inside and get it?'

'Yes and no. It's still free when Gustav is in but he's not been well the last couple of weeks so I had to pay, three times.'

Annie snorted. 'Just imagine how much it would have cost you if you hadn't got all those freebies. Poor Gustav. Do you know what's up with him? I like him. I know he's a big flirt but he's good-hearted and sweet. I'm surprised he isn't married, he's so good-looking.'

'I can tell you why he isn't married. Isn't it obvious?'

She shook her head.

'He isn't married because he sleeps with anything that walks on two legs.'

'I still think he's a sweetie. We all have our faults.'

'Talking about faults, where is your lord and master today? I thought he was off work?'

'To be honest, I'm not sure. He went back to work yesterday and got called into work earlier so I don't know when I'll see him again. You know what it's like. Some job comes in and there's never anyone on to cover. It's getting worse. He promised me he wasn't going to work late today and that he was easing himself back into it, but I should have known better. I wanted him to finish painting the nursery and build the cot.'

Jake chuckled. 'You won't see him again; he probably texted Stu and told him to make a job up, if all you wanted him to do was paint and put together a ten-thousand-part cot. Well, if it was me you wouldn't see me for the rest of the day. There's nothing more depressing than trying to build flat-pack furniture.'

'He wouldn't do that – he likes doing stuff around the house. Doesn't he?'

'Not for me to say, princess, but there are some things a man doesn't like doing no matter how much he loves you. Right, we need to get going. I have loads to do and can't waste all day sitting here with you.'

'Thanks, Jake. I'd hate you to waste your time on me.'

He leant over. Wrapping his arms around her, he kissed her forehead.

'I don't mean it like that. I just have so much to do. Two days off aren't enough, especially not with Alice. I just want to make them count. I had no idea being a parent was so time-consuming, but wonderful. Not long now before you and the man discover this as well – make the most of your freedom because things will change drastically once baby Ashworth arrives. There won't be any of this flying off to exotic locations for long, lazy holidays.'

He stood up. Tucking the baby under one arm, he held out his other hand for Annie to pull her up. She grabbed it and before she could sit forward he'd yanked her to her feet.

'Wow, I'd forgotten just how big and strong you are.'

'See, told you I wasn't losing my touch.'

He winked at her and she smiled, wishing he could stay longer. Being pregnant was the most amazing thing that had happened to her, but it was driving her mad being at home all day. She had never been so fed up. Kissing Alice and tickling her she then stood on her tiptoes and kissed Jake's cheek. They walked to the front door and she led them outside, watching Jake buckle his bundle of love into her car seat, then walk around and get into the driver's seat.

'See you soon, my friend.'

'I hope so Jake, because I miss you.'

He blew her a kiss then reversed out of the drive. Annie watched him until the tail lights on his car disappeared from sight, then she turned to go back inside. She would finish the painting and build the cot herself if Will wasn't man enough to say he didn't want to. At least that would pass the time until he was back with her.

Doctor Paul Miller sighed as his last patient for the day left his office. He had the rest of the day to himself, which was a nice change. He had been planning on going fell walking but all he could think about was Jo Tyson. He'd never liked Heath since the day they'd fallen out over Jo – she never knew about the big argument they'd had, which had turned into a fight. One that Paul had won in the physical sense because he'd hit Heath so hard he'd fallen back, hitting his head against the slate wall in the darkened car park of the Queen's pub, which knocked him out. It had been the one and only time Paul had ever fought over a girl in his life.

He might have won that fight but he lost the prize. Panicking, he'd sat with Heath until he'd regained consciousness and apologised profusely – he'd told Heath that he'd won. He could keep the girl. Paul wouldn't bother either of them again as long as Heath didn't report him to the police. Heath had agreed, although Paul had a feeling that he wasn't the sort of man who would go running to the police anyway, but he had too much to lose. He couldn't afford to be arrested for grievous bodily harm; it would have ended his career if he had. So Jo had gone off into the sunset with Heath. He'd told Jo the next time he saw her that he couldn't really get involved with her; he had to think of his career. She'd always been gullible and she'd cried a few tears but then had gone running straight into Heath's arms and, oh, how that had hurt.

Watching them at the pub hurt so much that he'd stopped going down there for the quiz. In fact, he'd pretty much stopped going anywhere apart from fell walking. He liked that – being on his own, out in the open with just his thoughts. He wondered how Jo felt now. He wondered how long it had been before she'd realised what a huge mistake she'd made leaving him for Heath. He didn't like the fact that he knew Heath hit her on a regular basis. But there was nothing he could do about it – because Heath knew Paul wouldn't report him, as much as he wanted to.

In fact, what he wanted to do was to make Jo see sense and leave Heath for good and come back to him, because he was so goddamn lonely. He was good-looking and could have any woman he wanted if he tried but most of the women in the village and surrounding areas were his patients. This bloody code of ethics was a complete pain. If Jo did come back to him he would make her sign up to the doctor's in Bowness and no longer be her GP. It was his turn to live happily ever after . . . well, it would be once they figured out how to get Heath out of the equation.

Chapter 9

He had been very quiet since the police arrived and it made her wonder what he was trying to hide, because something was wrong. She knew he had nothing to do with the body outside – that was ridiculous. Yes, he was violent and a bully, but he'd never brought women home or done anything that had aroused her suspicion. He spent all his time cooped up in his studio or workshop, then seemed to do nothing but complain about the women he photographed, saying they all expected him to be a miracle worker. They didn't just want a portrait – they wanted to look thinner, younger, prettier, sexier. Jo had sniggered the first time he'd started to really rant about his clients. She had never sniggered again after the beating she got for it. He was a good photographer, though, and she couldn't take that away from him. She supposed it was his calling; where some people wrote books, danced or played the drums, he was very good at taking photographs.

She wondered what she was good at and realised that at the moment her best virtue was making cups of tea and having great stamina for taking a beating. She sighed. Maybe she should join the secret service and go undercover somewhere exotic; anything would be better than this non-existent life. The door banged as he came in, looking as if he'd been caught with his hand in the biscuit jar.

'Would you like anything to eat or drink?'

He shook his head. 'No, I think I'm going to lie down. I don't feel well.'

'OK, I hope you feel better soon. I'll make sure I don't make any noise and disturb you.'

He looked at her but didn't really look at her. Something was bothering him and she did her best to look concerned, but inside she was gloating. It made a change for him to be ill; normally it was her having to go to bed because the punch he'd thrown at her had given her a migraine. He turned to go upstairs and she turned on the kettle – if he wasn't going to talk to her she might as well take some drinks outside to those poor police support officers who had been standing there for hours. At least she could strike up a conversation with one of them for a little while and they might be able to tell her a little more about what was happening.

Will had spent all afternoon on the phone, trying to push what had happened earlier at the Tysons' house to the back of his mind, but he was still annoyed with what Stu had said. As if he'd been coming on to that woman in the cottage. Why would he, when he had everything he ever wanted waiting for him back at his own house? It was careless remarks like that which started gossip, and the station was rife with rumours about affairs. Hell, he'd been the source of most of them for a few years, but not anymore. He'd changed, and Stu should have realised that before he opened his mouth.

He'd spoken to Matt, his friend who also happened to be the pathologist for the South Lakes, and requested his assistance. Then he'd spoken to the detective chief inspector, who just happened to be at headquarters in a meeting – he'd told Will to do his thing until he could get there. Will had told him no problem, relieved because his boss was a pain in the backside anyway. He would flounce in and take control, giving out orders that had already been actioned, only to leave once the weather turned chilly or dark, whichever came first. He dialled another number and held the phone to his ear.

'Hello, gorgeous. I'm just ringing to say I'm going to be late home.'

'Oh, is everything OK?'

'Not for whoever's skeleton some kids stumbled across this afternoon it's not.'

'Oh no, that's terrible. Really? Where at?'

'Not far from our house, actually – a mile and a half in the other direction. It's out the back of a cottage on the outskirts of the village. In a secluded wood, which is why it's stayed so well hidden for such a long time.'

'Aw, that's so sad.'

'I know; that's why I want this doing right. We need to find out who it is and, more importantly, who buried them there.'

'Well, you're the right man for the job. If anyone can send them home, you can. I love you, Will.'

'I love you more, Annie. I'll probably be late so don't wait up if you're tired. I've got a key and don't worry about food. I'll grab something when I get home.'

He waited for Annie to end the call. It was tradition that she ended it first and she knew how much he hated cutting her off. It had turned out he was a lot soppier than she'd ever given him credit for.

Annie wandered into the kitchen and smiled at her pale pink Aga; it had the same effect on her each time she walked in and saw it sitting there. Jake had come through with his part of the bargain – when she'd confessed to him how much she wanted one, he'd told her Will would buy it for her and he'd been right. It was the only concession to pink in the house, which was mainly white, pale green and grey. Unless of course they had a baby girl, and then pink would be everywhere. She rubbed her hand across her swollen belly. Then she thought about the skeleton that had been found in the woods – for a small village, there sure were a lot of dead people hidden around it in gardens and woods. She shivered so violently her teeth clashed together. Something wasn't right. She felt as if she was being watched and knew that someone was standing behind. Her heart raced as thoughts of Betsy Baker, the woman whose name she would not speak out loud in her house, filled her mind.

Please God, don't let her have come back for round two. I'm not up to it and I don't want to be scared out of the house I love.

Annie turned but there was no one behind her and she breathed out a sigh of relief. It wasn't Betsy because if it had been she would have let her presence be known. The woman had been hanged as a witch, but Annie knew she had been a cold, callous, calculating killer and nothing more. But something was wrong – there was a spirit around; she could tell by the sudden change in the atmosphere and the fact that her built-in psychic sensors had kick-started themselves. It was then that she saw the face of a young woman staring at her through the kitchen window.

Annie squealed, jumping back, but the face didn't move or smile. She was painfully white, with black smudges for eyes. Straggly long blonde hair hung down in rat's tails on her shoulders, and on the left-hand side of the girl's face was a horrific head wound that looked as if it was alive with maggots and worms moving around inside of it. Annie scolded herself. No matter how many times she saw a ghost, for want of a better word, it nearly always had the same effect on her. Sophie and Alice were the exceptions, but even they could sometimes startle her. She forced herself to walk towards the window.

'What do you want? Can I help you?'

Her voice wavered and the words felt heavy, as if they were floating in the air. It was so quiet the huge American-style fridge, which Will had insisted they had to have, had stopped its humming. There wasn't a sound in the house except for her breathing, which seemed to be far too loud in her ears, and the pounding of her heart. The face never moved or changed its expression – it just stared at her. Annie walked up to the glass window and could feel the drop in temperature. The kitchen now felt like the inside of a fridge. The girl had something clasped in her hand and Annie recognised the curled-up white edges of an old Polaroid instant camera photograph. She lifted her hand, pressing the picture against the glass, but it was so old and faded all Annie could see was yellow and grey shapes where the images had once been. She shook her head at her.

'I can't see anything. What is it?'

But the girl's image quivered – as if she couldn't make herself stay visible any longer – and then she was gone, taking her picture with her. Leaving Annie wondering what she had been trying to tell her.

When she tried to tell Will about it when he got home, hours later, she found that the only way to describe the woman was that she looked haunted. She knew how corny it sounded because she was dead, and wouldn't we all look haunted if we were dead and still wandering around, but the woman looked distressed, which had then made her feel upset for her. She'd spent the rest of the night upstairs in bed reading on her Kindle with the television on in the background so the house didn't feel so big and empty, hoping that Will would be home soon to tell her she was being ridiculous and there were no dead women staring in through the kitchen windows, and that it was just her overactive imagination.

1995

Heath went out for a walk in the woods to check if the grave he had dug lay undisturbed. He had taken some of the soil in a wheelbarrow in the middle of the night and put it into his recently built rockery outside his back door, then covered the grave with stones, moss and branches from nearby so it didn't look fresh. It was just as he'd left it. Then he made his way to the village hall, where he offered to take some of the flyers that had been printed up and post them through letterboxes. The woman who was in charge was brusque with him; in fact she was downright rude, and he had wanted to tell her to go fuck herself. But he hadn't because she was the doctor's receptionist and he never knew when he might need an appointment – not to mention the fact that she was a gossip. He'd smiled, nodded and taken his flyers like a good boy.

There were a few mothers, friends of the family and teenagers there, everyone feeling hopeless – all wanting to help find Sharon Sale. Most of them knew that by now things weren't looking good and the chances of her turning up alive were slim. In fact they were zero to none, but he couldn't tell them that. He just had to carry on like a concerned villager and hope they all lost interest soon. He hadn't taken any of this into consideration before it had been too late and she was lying on the couch in his studio, very much dead. Already the police presence had been scaled down from what it had been the first five days. Now there were just a couple of officers sitting at a table at the far end of the village hall with a clipboard each and huge, steaming mugs of tea.

He didn't like the police, never had done since he'd been a boy and his mother had scared him to death with threats of taking him to the nearest copper if he was naughty. He never understood why parents would do that to their children. Surely if your child was lost or in trouble you wouldn't want them to be terrified of asking for help from the people who were meant to provide it. The woman called Jo, who lived opposite the post office, made a beeline for him and he was glad of her conversation to make him look like he was part of the community and not some oddball loner. He chatted with her about the weather, how awful it was that they hadn't found poor Sharon. He nodded. It was a bloody miracle that they hadn't found her but thank Christ they hadn't or he wouldn't be standing here today to tell the tale. They both walked out of the hall and into the village together, ready to begin knocking on doors and posting the flyers.

It only took him thirty minutes and he was done. It was such a warm day and he wanted to go home, lock his door and have a cold shower. Jo came strolling back towards him.

'I was wondering if you fancied a cold drink from the pub? I think we've earned it, don't you?'

'I'd love one. That might be the best idea I've ever heard.'

They'd gone to the pub where they'd sat outside under the shade of a wonky umbrella on a creaky old picnic table and had spent the next hour chatting about poor Sharon, their lives and the locals. Heath knew he wasn't interested in the woman opposite him, apart from the fact that he'd seen her with the doctor a couple of times at the pub quizzes he'd forced himself to go to so he looked like part of the community. He also knew that she could provide him with great cover and alibis because at the moment he looked like a complete loner and he didn't want anyone starting to gossip about him – that strange man who lived near the woods who liked to photograph women for a living. If he had a girlfriend he wouldn't stand out so much, and it would be a challenge to steal her away from the new doctor who thought he was better than everyone else, but who Heath knew wasn't. So he turned on the charm he normally kept reserved for his clients and plied her with it until she'd agreed to come to his house for a meal the next night.

She had dithered for around ten minutes before agreeing and he'd smiled; the fact that it was quiz night tomorrow hadn't escaped him. The doctor would be sitting waiting for her and wouldn't realise that she was hopefully with him – if she didn't chicken out. He would cook her a perfect meal and ply her with alcohol, then take her to bed and show her such a good time that she'd never want to look at Dr Miller ever again.

Chapter 10

2015

Will pulled up outside the house and stared up at their bedroom window. The dull glow from the bedside lamp was the only light on in the entire house. He couldn't wait to see Annie, hold her in his arms and tell her how much he loved her and the baby. Murder cases made him appreciate the good things in his life more than usual; when he had been single it hadn't been so hard on him – his relationships were never serious and none of them ever meant anything more to him than a quick leg over with preferably no strings attached. When he wasn't in a relationship it would be a few Jack Daniel's chasers in the Black Dog with the rest of the team, then he'd go home and drink some more until he'd blacked it all out, falling into a drunken stupor until it was time to go back to work and find the bastards who committed such heinous crimes.

Now, it was much harder to block it out – and it hit home how much he had to lose. He was too scared to count just how many times it had almost been taken away from him in the blink of an eye. He didn't know what had happened to change the infamous bachelor boy Will Ashworth, but he was grateful that something had . . . actually, he knew it had been Annie. That day he'd seen her at her Ben's farmhouse at Abbey Wood wearing the blue woollen beanie hat, even though it had been a warm day, had been the day he changed and somehow the spell had been cast. He'd found he couldn't stop thinking about her, every minute of every day.

He got out of the car, careful not to slam the door too loud in case Annie was asleep, and went inside, kicking off his shoes. The house smelt of vanilla and lime air freshener but he could also detect a hint of Chanel No 5. He considered pouring himself a large whisky to help him sleep but he didn't want to go to bed smelling like he'd been down the pub. He was hungry, although not enough to eat a full meal, so he walked into the kitchen and poured himself a bowl of the chocolate cereal that she'd bulk bought last time they went shopping. He would forever associate Coco Pops and Chanel perfume with his wife.

His mind wanted to flash back to the photographic stills of the skeleton, which he'd spent hours staring at this afternoon, but he forced it to think of Annie and their baby; hell, even Jake's face was a better option than that desolate, open grave. When he'd finished he rinsed his bowl and spoon, putting them on the sink to drain.

'Is that all you're having?'

He started at her voice, not expecting her to still be awake. He strode across the room to where she was standing, pulling her close. She smelt of the expensive body lotion he'd bought her for her birthday.

'God, you smell so good.'

'Yep, even I can't stop sniffing my arms. Was it really bad?'

He nodded.

'They're all bad but there was something so . . . so desolate, sad.'

'Yes, I can imagine. How awful to be murdered then buried where no one except your killer knows where you are – until someone stumbles across your grave years later. Whoever it is, their poor family must have gone through hell. All the years of wondering why and where they'd gone. It makes me feel cold to the bottom of my feet.'

Annie squeezed him tighter; kissing his cheek she let go and grabbed his hand.

'Come on, I'll run you a nice hot bath and if I can bend down I'll even scrub your back.'

Will laughed. 'How is our bump today?'

'He's been off on one all day, so restless – I'm tired just thinking about it.'

'Well, she might take after her mother; she never does know when to quit.'

Will rolled his eyes at Annie but squeezed her hand tight and let her pull him towards the stairs.

'You'll see. I'm positive it's a boy.'

'And I'm positive she's a girl.'

'Are we placing bets, Mrs Ashworth?'

'No, because you always win.'

She tugged him towards the bathroom.

'You go back to bed. I'll have a quick shower. I don't want you getting yourself into any compromising positions whilst trying to scrub my back.'

He pulled her close, kissing her until he could think of lots of ways to take his mind off work. She shoved him towards the bathroom.

'Go get your shower. I'll go warm the bed.'

Will dived into the bathroom, leaving her grinning at the top of the stairs. As she turned to go back into the bedroom she caught a glimpse of the woman from earlier at the bottom of the stairs. Annie felt her heart racing as she went into the bedroom and shut the door. She wasn't about to let her in her bedroom; some things were sacred. It bothered her that this woman had latched on to her, yet wasn't saying anything. Tomorrow she would sit down and try and speak to her. She didn't look scary like— Annie almost said the forbidden name and stopped herself just in time. The woman looked shocked, like she needed help – maybe she had only recently died and didn't know what had happened to her. It happened now and again. Annie often wondered if she gave off some kind of psychic radio waves that told the recently departed that she could see and hear them, because they seemed drawn to her.

Will came in, a short towel wrapped around his waist, and she soon forgot about her ghostly visitor. His tanned body looked good; even though the scar that ran along the side was impressive, it didn't take anything away from how amazing he looked.

'Do you still like what you see, even with this big old scar ruining my six-pack?'

She threw the duvet across and patted the bed next to her. 'Yes, I like very much – and that scar just makes you look even sexier.'

They both laughed and he ran and jumped onto the bed, careful not to land on the bump, which was even more impressive than his scar.

He pulled her close and she kissed him, long and hard.

1995

Since the day they'd met handing out the flyers they had pretty much been inseparable. For some reason she was besotted with him; he knew he was a complete charmer when he needed to be and with Jo he'd turned it on full force. Yet she was just a convenience for him – it drew the villagers' attention away from the single male who lived near to the woods now he was in a relationship. Yes, he did like her and she wasn't bad-looking. She had nice, pale green eyes that matched her auburn hair and she was pretty good in bed, but the one thing he did hate was her laugh. It was so loud and unladylike. If he spent enough time with her he would change that. After spending time with him, she would be meek and mild and not dare to answer him back. She would be there to answer his beck and call whenever he wished. If she didn't comply then she would become another photograph in his very special album, which was locked in the small safe in his workshop. It was covered by a table that had a long, white cloth on it, out of sight should the police have reason to come snooping around.

It had been almost three months now and everyone had given up hope of finding Sharon, which was a relief. The general consensus in the village was that she had run away. Her parents didn't believe it, but the police did – and the people were keen to point fingers. All sorts of accusations had been flying around but the one that seemed to stick was the well-known fact that her parents had been far too strict with her and she'd run off. He couldn't stop thinking about how much he wanted to do it again; he didn't enjoy the killing so much – that part was far too messy. What he did like was having the perfect model to pose for him for hours, even days, without having to worry if they needed the toilet or something to eat. It was wonderful being able to take your time; in fact, he was pretty sure if other photographers realised how wonderful it was they would all be doing it for the sake of their art.

He wasn't sure why people had lost interest in photographing their dearly beloved once they had departed from this earth. It could make a huge comeback and he'd even thought about offering his services as a post-mortem photographer, but something had stopped him. People would call him weird and start talking about him; the thought made him angry so he'd kept quiet, deciding it was far better to be able to create his masterpieces in death alone, taking as long as he wanted. There was one thing he was sure about: his photographs would go down in history once he decided to share their beauty with the world.

Tonight he was going to ask Jo to pose for him, see if she would after he'd made her a romantic meal and plied her with a few glasses of red wine. Once he had her naked and under his lens he would be able to blackmail her in the future should the need ever arise. He knew she was pretty much hooked by his kind, selfless ways. He might even propose to her – a wife would be very handy, then he'd also have a permanent alibi and they could live happily ever after until it was time for him to kill again. He'd gone back into his studio without even thinking about it, pushing the table to one side so he could open the safe for another peek at his ever-so-perfect pictures. It was like an addiction. He loved the feeling of power, knowing the girl was dead.

One day he would enlarge his favourite shot and frame it to hang on his studio wall, see if anyone noticed how dead his model was. They wouldn't unless they stared at her hands, which were slightly darker than the rest of her, but he didn't think they would because she was so beautiful in death that she looked more alive than ever. The telephone jolted him from his fantasy and he rushed across to pick it up before it stopped ringing.

'Hello, Star Style Photography.'

There was a slight pause on the other end of the line.

'Hello, erm, I was wondering if you did photoshoots that would be suitable for a portfolio?'

'As a matter of fact I do. I'm doing a lot more of those than I used to – they seem to be becoming very popular with all the teenagers. Are you wanting to become a model?'

The girl giggled. 'Well, I would like to, but I'm not too sure if I have what it takes.'

'Why don't you let me be the judge of that? I bet you do. When would you like to come?'

'I'm off work all week so whenever you can fit me in would be great. My parents are away on holiday so I can use their car to get to you.'

He smiled – this was perfect, too perfect.

'How about tomorrow at three? It will give you a chance to get here because if you've never driven before you need to allow around forty minutes. I prefer to work in the late afternoon, early evening. You'll be my last client so we won't have to rush. Oh, and what's your name?'

'Sorry, I'm Wendy Cook and that would be really great. Thank you. Can you tell me how much it will be?'

'The sitting is always free. If you like any of the photos you can order them and pay for as many or as few as you like. Don't worry about the money, Wendy; you won't need any tomorrow – just bring yourself and any clothes you want to wear. Do you know how to find me? I'm afraid my studio is a bit off the beaten track?'

He rattled off directions to her, knowing fine well it was far too risky and too soon, but who was he to turn away such a good opportunity? He doubted anyone would know where she was – if she brought a friend along she would live another day, but if not, and he quizzed her a little to make sure she hadn't told anyone where she was, it would be perfect. He replaced the receiver and went for a shower before Jo came around, needing to cool himself off because he was more than a little excited at the prospect that tomorrow could bring him a fresh model.

Wendy Cook stared at herself in the mirror, pouting then turning from side to side. She had a good profile. Her friends had always told her she was pretty and skinny too. Never having to worry about her weight, always eating whatever she wanted. She knew it was a stupid daydream wanting to be a model, but if she didn't try she would never know what could have been. There was no way she was telling anyone about the photoshoot, though, because her friends would take the piss out of her for months about it. She piled her long, blonde hair on top of her head, holding it with one hand and pulling her slouch top down over one shoulder, exposing the bare flesh.

As long as the photographer wasn't one of those perverts who were always on the news she should be OK, and she doubted he would be. He worked in a studio in Hawkshead, for God's sake, one of the quietest Lakeland villages. It was hardly the place to run a seedy, back-street pornography ring from, and besides, she could look after herself. She hadn't been going to karate since she was four not to be able to kick the shit out of someone should the need arise. He had sounded nice and sincere on the phone, not to mention helpful. She couldn't wait.

The doorbell chimed and she let her hair loose, pulled up her jumper and ran down the stairs to open the front door for one of her best friends, Susie. It was funny Wendy hadn't been to Hawkshead before, even though Sharon – who was both her and Susie's friend – had lived there. Wendy wondered where on earth Sharon was; it was as if she had disappeared off the face of the earth. She had been so shocked when she and Susie had got to college that day and the police were waiting to talk to them. All three of them went to the same college at Kendal and, although they were all on different courses, on the very first day they had sat together on the bus that travelled from Barrow through to Kendal picking up an assortment of teenagers on the way – and they had made friends.

Sharon had never told them she had a boyfriend but then again that didn't mean anything; they'd only known each other a year and out of them all she was the quietest. Susie was the loudest and she was the prettiest, although she didn't brag about it because she didn't want to upset her friends. Even so, Wendy hadn't mentioned anything to Susie about wanting to be a model because Susie was the biggest gossip in Barrow and by bedtime tonight would have told everyone she knew. Susie walked in carrying two frozen pizza boxes and handed them to her.

'I thought you might need a little sustenance because I know I do. I'm starving to death. Can you cook pizza?'

'Aw, thanks, Susie, that's very kind of you – and do you know what? I can even turn the oven on by myself and cook anything that comes out of a packet, as long as it has instructions on it.'

'No need to be sarcastic – I was just checking. Not all of us are blessed with cooking skills. So what have you got planned? Should we have a party now that you've been left home alone? Invite all the guys around and get drunk?'

'No, we should not have a party, as much as I'd like to. If anything got broken or wrecked my parents would go mad and never let me stay at home on my own again. Besides, I'm not in the mood for a party. I'd rather watch a film.'

'Just as well I stole my brother's pirate copy of *The Terminator* then; that Schwarzenegger guy is gorgeous even if he is a murdering robot.'

Wendy giggled. 'And how did you manage that?'

'He's too interested in the Frank Bruno fight that's on television later. It's all he keeps talking about.'

They went into the kitchen where Wendy proved she could turn on the cooker and heat up two pizzas. She also managed to turn the radio on. They both squealed and danced around the tiny kitchen to 'The Sunshine After the Rain'; picking up a spatula and fish slice they sang the words to each other down their makeshift microphones. Wendy knew that one day she would be famous for either being a supermodel, although she wasn't quite tall enough, or a singer in a pop band. It didn't matter, as long as everyone loved her and her face was plastered all over the latest magazines.

Chapter 11

2015

Jo was restless. She had fallen asleep a couple of hours ago but hadn't been able to get comfortable ever since. She was not quite awake but not asleep either; images kept filling her mind and she had no idea what they meant. As she lay there next to Heath, listening to his heavy breathing, she found herself in his studio – somewhere she hadn't been since the early days, not long after they'd first met, and she'd got drunk, letting him take those awful photos of her that she'd made him promise to burn.

In the half-dream, half-vision, she felt like she was waiting for Heath to come in, and began to look around. As she turned to the back of the room she looked into the huge mirror, which covered the entire wall, and she jumped. As well as her reflection staring back at her there was a girl who didn't look as if she was eighteen yet, although the underwear she was wearing was more suitable for a much older woman. The girl was pouting at herself with the deepest red lips Jo had ever seen, and she had ice blonde long hair. The girl shivered then looked down at her arms. The smooth, tight flesh was now covered in raised bumps that made her look as if she had the skin of a freshly plucked chicken. There was a silk dressing gown on the floor and the girl picked it up, wrapping it around herself to keep her warm. Then she turned back to stare at herself once more, turning from side to side, admiring the view.

Jo stepped back, near the door that led from the house into the studio and into the shadows; she hadn't wanted to be there and knew he would have gone mad with her if he caught her. What was that saying Jo's mother used to say to her when she was that age? Something about vanity being a sin? It was that long ago she couldn't remember, but whoever this girl was she loved herself; that much was clear. The door banged, making her jump as he walked in, his camera dangling around his neck. He smiled at the girl and nodded. Jo watched as she slipped the silk gown from her shoulders, letting it fall to the floor. She didn't want to be a part of this but she couldn't stop thinking about it and instead she had to watch him smile in appreciation at the gorgeous young thing standing in front of him. Lifting his camera he began to click away, walking around her.

'That's it, don't pose. You look much sexier when you're not trying too hard.'

After a few minutes he crossed the room towards her; grabbing her arm he tugged her towards him. Jo wanted to scream at him to let go of the girl, but she couldn't find her voice. A spike of dread lodged in the base of her spine, so cold it made her want to pee it was pressing down on her bladder so much. He yanked the girl's arm and she was standing so close to them she could feel the heat from his body.

'You are the most beautiful woman I've ever photographed.' His hands reached up and he tousled her long, blonde hair with his fingertips. 'There, now you look as if you've just been taken to bed and shown a good time.'

He stepped away again, and Jo noted the redness creeping up the girl's cheeks – she was so young. What on earth was he doing taking these sorts of photos of a young girl? It wasn't right;

it was indecent.

'Perfect – you are so sexy yet demure. You must drive all the boys mad.'

The camera continued clicking away for another few minutes and then he stopped.

'I think that's a wrap; you can get dressed now.'

Jo felt her whole body relax.

'Really? Wow, that was so fast.'

'It's easy when you're working with someone so naturally beautiful. There was no having to work miracles to make you look presentable. You're a natural at this.'

The girl smiled, her cheeks burning, and walked across to where she'd folded her clothes into a neat pile. She tugged on her jeans, not paying any attention to what Heath was doing at the other side of the studio. A door banged as he walked out to where his darkroom was and Jo made her move. She knew she had to get out of there before he came back in and caught her, but she couldn't remember anything else. What happened next? Where was that pretty girl now? She drifted off to sleep only to have the most awful nightmare where someone was choking Jo whilst the girl from her vision was the one in the dark, watching. She felt as if she was choking and flailed around on the bed. The door flew open and light bathed the room. The invisible grip on her throat relaxed and she could breathe once more. He was standing there, staring.

'What's the matter with you? Are you having some kind of epileptic fit?'

She sat up gasping and shook her head. 'I couldn't breathe. I felt as if . . .'

She didn't finish her sentence. She couldn't say she thought he was trying to kill her when he hadn't even been in the same room.

'Never mind – it was just a horrible dream.'

He nodded and shut the door behind him. Getting out of bed, she went into the small bathroom and turned on the light.

Expecting to see red marks around her neck she lifted her fingers to check, but there was nothing there. How could a dream like that be so real? Her mind must be playing tricks on her. She couldn't shake the feeling that it had been far more than a dream. Was that how that poor woman died out in the woods? Had Heath brutally killed and buried her out there? How did she know about that young girl in the studio? It was the first time Jo had ever thought about it. Had she seen him doing something bad all those years ago or was she letting her imagination run wild?

Scolding herself she cupped a handful of water, sipping it to quench the dry feeling in the back of her throat. She didn't want to speak to him or see him and if she went downstairs it was inevitable. Instead she went back to bed, pulling the covers up because it was freezing cold in the bedroom. So cold that her teeth began to chatter. Afraid to turn off the light, she left it on. She was also afraid to go to sleep but she was so tired; she felt as if she'd been fighting for her life.

He went back downstairs, puzzled as to why she had looked at him as if he were a ghost. He knew deep down that she hated him now much more than she loved him and he didn't care, but he'd never seen her openly show him such contempt. If the police weren't sniffing around he'd have given her a good slap, but the last thing he wanted was that smarmy copper coming back and seeing her with a black eye. It would arouse far too many suspicions. They had to look like they were a happily married couple. He'd heard talk in the village of the police bringing in highly trained sniffer dogs to scour the woods and make sure there were no more bodies buried out there and he was nervous. He had no idea if a dog was clever enough to sniff out a corpse from twenty years ago or not, but if they did find the other grave it wouldn't look good for him – especially living on the edge of the woods. But surely they would think he wouldn't be so stupid, and there was no evidence to tie him to the bodies except for his photographs. He had long since burnt the clothes he'd worn when he'd photographed the girls and dug the graves. He'd worn gloves and a hat; the only evidence they would find would be circumstantial, not forensic.

As long as they couldn't trace those girls to having visited him before they disappeared off the face of the earth, everything would be OK. He would just have to play it by ear, keep his cool and not get worked up by that; his hands involuntarily clenched into tight fists. Just the thought of that policeman, blatantly squeezing Jo's hand right in front of his eyes, made him feel violent. He punched the wall – *fuck* – skinning his knuckles in the process before he'd even thought about it.

Chapter 12

Will reached out his hand to feel for Annie but the bed was empty. He opened his eyes, squinting at the clock on the wall, and jumped out of bed. He'd thought that he would be plagued by nightmares, but he'd slept all night and as far as he could remember he hadn't dreamt once. Pulling on a pair of boxers he went to the bathroom; as he opened the door, a whiff of grilled bacon filled his nostrils and his stomach let out a groan. He was starving this morning, which wasn't surprising considering he'd hardly eaten anything yesterday, relying on cups of strong coffee to keep him going. By the time he went downstairs Annie was plating up his cooked breakfast; he walked behind her, wrapping his arms around her.

'That smells divine. It doesn't even smell burnt.'

'Cheeky – I can cook a little, just not to your standards.'

He kissed her cheek then took the plate from her and pulled out a stool from underneath the breakfast bar; he watched as she made a pot of coffee and a bowl of cereal for herself.

'A good old bacon and egg sarnie would do you the world of good, set you up for the day. You look like you need feeding up a bit – that cereal isn't exactly good for you.'

'Make me throw up for the rest of the day more like; just

cooking it makes me feel sick.'

'Aw, you shouldn't have bothered. Sorry.'

'Don't be daft – I'm not a complete wimp. You're going to be busy all day and I wanted to make sure you had a good breakfast in case it's hours before you get the chance to eat again.'

He blew her a kiss. 'You're the best. What would I do without you?'

'Probably have a stress-free life.' She winked at him but they both knew she meant it.

'What are you going to do today? Have you got any appointments?'

'Not today. I'm probably going to be bored out of my tiny mind. I know you hate me working, but I can't stand being at home on my own all day. Can I not at least come with you and do some house-to-house inquiries or paperwork in the office?'

'Annie, as much as I'd love you to come in to work and help out, you and me both know that neither Kav nor Cathy would allow it. You're on the sick for a reason. I don't want your blood pressure getting any higher – and trust me, a day working with my team and it would be through the roof.'

'Bollocks.'

'Ever the lady . . . Why don't you go and see my dad? Get Lily to take you shopping. I'm sure there must be a baby outfit somewhere in the North West of England that she hasn't already bought.'

Annie grinned at him. She loved Lily but she didn't want to talk about babies all day. Soon enough she would have her very own baby and, as much as she couldn't wait, she would rather spend what little free time she had before its arrival doing the stuff that she enjoyed and that included her police work.

'It's OK, thanks – I can't take a day of shopping. I hate it at the best of times and combined with hours of baby talk it might just send me over the edge. I'll find something to do. Did I tell you about the woman I met at the doctor's?

He shook his head, not wanting to talk through a mouth full of bacon and egg.

'It was so embarrassing – I actually knocked her over with my humongous stomach, but she was so nice we got chatting and I took her for a coffee to apologise. I might go and see if I can find her this morning. I'm not sure where she lives but it can't be that hard to find her and I imagine Marge at the post office will know who I'm talking about. She knows everything about everybody.'

'Yep, you should definitely do that. Did you check her credentials first, though? I mean you're not a very good judge of character, are you?' He smirked at her and she flipped him the finger. Will laughed. He felt bad for her – he knew it was killing her being stuck at home, but it was as if a giant weight had been lifted from his shoulders knowing that she wasn't out on the streets putting herself at risk. Annie had the worst track record for attracting violent men into her life, worse than anyone else he'd ever known.

'I'm sorry, I'm only joking – I know that you're fed up. How about you come into the village and see me at dinnertime? I've asked if we can use the village hall as a temporary base whilst everything is ongoing. I'll even take you out for your lunch – my treat.'

She smiled at him. That was something – at least he wouldn't be working far from her should she need him. In fact, as sad as it was for whoever's body they had discovered in that grave, it was good for him – no long drive to work and five minutes from home.

He mopped up the rest of his egg and shoved the slice of toast in his mouth. 'I'd better get going. The sooner we crack on the better.'

She nodded, staring at his lack of clothes. 'Are you going to get dressed first? I mean, don't get me wrong, there is nothing more beautiful than the sight of you dressed only in your tight white boxers, but I don't know if the rest of the village is ready for such excitement.'

'Of course I am. You don't think I'd go out looking like this, do you?'

'Nope, probably not, but you just never know.'

He turned to run upstairs to get dressed. He always wore a suit to work – the suits that he knew she secretly loved to see him in but would never admit it – more often than not teasing him about them.

He kissed her before he left and she pushed him away laughing. 'Go before I make you stay with me and finish building that cot.'

Will decided that skeleton in the woods was a much better option than trying to decipher the instructions that had come with the cot. He knew he should have insisted on buying one ready built, but Annie would not waste money – which was sweet, but on this occasion he really wouldn't have minded paying the extra. He got into his car and backed out of the drive; every time he left this house he felt as if he was leaving a tiny piece of himself behind, he loved it so much.

It struck him that maybe that was how ghosts came to be, leaving so much of themselves behind that when they died they stayed in the place they loved. Then he told himself to man up. Annie being pregnant was turning his brain to mush. Before he knew it he'd be wandering around barefoot writing poetry and hugging trees. Although somehow he didn't think his tough, funny wife would allow that. Because of the scrapes she'd got into the last couple of years he had also become much tougher; he had been ready to kill Henry Smith with his bare hands and he had felt no regrets, questions or doubts about it. Before he'd stepped into that kitchen at the lake house he'd felt a calmness descend on his entire body like no other. It had been a blanket of white. No rational thoughts could infiltrate it, and he often wondered late at night when he couldn't sleep, thinking about what had happened, if this was how all people felt before they committed murder; if the bubble they wrapped themselves up in turned off all of their emotions.

Of course his bubble hadn't lasted long because Megan had literally burst it with a six-inch carving knife that had gone right through his kidney. The calmness had soon been replaced with white-hot pain – pain that had seared his entire body, making him collapse before he even got to face Smith. He turned the car into the car park and wondered how the hell he had got there. He had been so deep in thought the car must have driven itself, because he didn't remember anything other than leaving the drive. *Shit, pay attention, Will. You could have killed someone or crashed and what good would you have been then?*

He jumped out of the car and strode the short distance across to the village hall. He hoped Stu was not going to act like an idiot all day because he really couldn't be bothered. He wanted everyone focused and ready to go out and find some answers. The hall looked like the old major incident room back at the station. The tables had been set up into small workspaces and there were two laptops, a printer and endless coffee cups and scraps of paper strewn across them. He smiled then stopped as soon as he saw the detective chief inspector and the chief super come out of the kitchen with mugs of coffee and deep in conversation.

A voice whispered in his ear: 'Sarge, I think you might want to come and take a look at this before those two tossers do.'

He turned to see Stu, who nodded at him.

'They got here ten minutes ago and have done nothing but talk about who is putting in for the inspector's exam and moan about the fact that there are no decent biscuits.'

'Wankers.'

'Tell me about it. I've been doing some research on missing persons in the area and in 1995 there was a local girl, Sharon Sale, who disappeared off the face of the earth. She was only seventeen, but on her missing person's report it was written down that most people thought she ran away because her parents were too strict with her. Both parents had no trace on the system and neither of them had ever been in trouble.'

'Brilliant, Stu – it's possible it could be her. Do her parents still live in the village?'

'I sent Tracy and Sam to go and knock at their old address and see if they did. They should be back soon.'

Stu pointed to the image on the computer screen of a very pretty teenager who was trying her best not to smile for what could have passed as her passport photograph. Will felt his heart skip a beat; he didn't know whether he wanted the body to be her so her family could have closure or whether he didn't want it to be her so they could believe that she was still out there somewhere enjoying the morning sun on her face and living her life to the full. Fuck, he loved his job but at the same time he also hated it.

He turned to see the PCSOs walk into the hall joking with each other. They took one look at the two chiefs standing near the kitchen and stopped. Will crossed the room towards them, smiling, and nodded for them to follow him outside. He had no idea why he didn't want the bosses to hear this conversation but he didn't. He disliked the chief super because of the way he treated Annie's inspector, Cathy Hayes, who also happened to be his ex-wife. He also didn't like the way he would crawl into an investigation, not do very much, and then take all the credit away from Will's team, who worked very hard to find the offenders and bring them in for questioning.

'Are we in trouble, Will?'

'As if. I just don't want those two to know anything until I'm good and ready to tell them. You know what they're both like.'

'Unfortunately, we do. Stu asked us to go and check this address to see if the parents of the girl who went missing still lived there, but they don't. The woman at the shop said they moved away about eight years ago, but she thinks she might have their address back home. She said she'll go and check on her dinner break and come and find us if she does.'

'That's a shame, but thank you both. Would you do me a massive favour?'

'Scene guard,' they both said at the same time, their smiles turning into grimaces.

'No, I need you to help me today; the others can scene-guard. You're now officially honorary members of CID. Could you start some house-to-house inquiries in all the local shops? Ask if anyone remembers the family. Was anyone friends with Sharon Sale or her parents? If you find anyone, get their contact details so either me or Stu can go and talk to them.'

'Erm, I'm not entirely sure we want to be in your team, Will, but can we get a decent cup of coffee and some cake from that café that has those Guinness Book of Records-sized cakes in the window?'

'If you find me someone who knew the family I'll buy you the coffee and cake. Deal?'

They both laughed. 'Sounds like a deal to us.'

'Good. Can you start now – and if those two ask what you're up to, don't tell them anything except you're doing the house-to-house and it's negative.'

They nodded. Sam leant close to Will. 'I wouldn't tell those two that their hair was on fire. I don't trust either of them – and besides, they won't speak to us, it's below them.'

She raised an eyebrow at him and they turned and walked off back in the direction of the village and the cake shop. Will had no idea why he didn't want to share any information with his superiors just yet – call it a hunch or whatever – but he just knew that for now he was keeping everything close to his chest. He'd figure out the why part later. He went back inside and pulled a chair over to where Stu was still doing a Google search on Sharon Sale, printing off whatever newspaper articles he could find in case they named friends or neighbours who might be able to shed some light on the case. After twenty minutes, Will's phone vibrated in his pocket; he pulled it out.

'You owe us two lattes and two slices of death by chocolate cake. So you better pay up, Ashworth.'

Will laughed. 'Bloody hell, you don't mess around. What have you got?'

'Come up to the café – we're standing outside – and we'll tell you.'

He stood up, looking around the room at the various officers, PCSOs and bosses. 'Be there in two minutes.'

He nodded at Stu. 'Come on, I'll buy you a decent cup of coffee. Shut that down, though.'

He pointed at the laptop, which Stu had already begun to log off from. Then they both walked out into the warm summer sun. There were plenty of tourists watching the village hall with the assortment of marked police cars parked on the double yellow lines outside it and he felt as if he'd suddenly grown another head as a group of tourists stopped to stare at them.

'I love the summer. It just makes you feel better.'

'It does Stu, it really does.'

'But I love cake more. What's up with you this morning? You're not only in a good mood, you're also wanting to eat cake?'

'Are you saying I'm not always in a good mood, Stuart?'

'No . . . but . . .'

'But what?'

'Forget it. I suppose if I'd been through the crap you had I wouldn't have much to smile about.'

Will frowned – as much as he liked Stu, he said the strangest things. He waved at Sam and Tracy, who waved back, and they went inside the café.

Will looked at the huge chocolate cake in the window and smiled as Stu's mouth dropped open. They went inside to the small table near the back where Sam and Tracy were already sitting and in the process of removing their body armour.

'Well, my two favourite PCSOs – spill the beans, the suspense is killing me.'

A waitress came over to take their order; if Will had to guess her age he'd say she was about thirty-five. He was normally quite good at ageing people, and underneath her apron was a faded Stone Roses concert T-shirt. As she turned to the side he could see the list of tour dates on the back.

'Will, this is Susie. She used to be friends with Sharon Sale before she went missing. She was also very good friends with a girl from Barrow, Wendy Cook, who also went missing about a month after Sharon. They all used to sit together on the bus that took students up to Kendal College every morning.'

Will stood up and held out his hand to shake hers. She blushed and took his hand, shaking it gently.

'I'm Detective Sergeant Will Ashworth. Would I be able to talk to you when you've finished work? I gather you've heard about the body found in the woods yesterday?'

She nodded. 'I did, and it's so sad; do you think it could be Sharon or Wendy?'

'I can't really say at this moment – it's a possibility, but as soon as they've been identified I'll let you know immediately. Is that OK?'

She nodded. 'Yes, that's fine, thank you. It's been such a long time since I saw them both, but at the same time it feels like it was only yesterday. I never understood how two of my best friends could just disappear without a trace. I always assumed that they'd run off together, even though they lived twenty miles apart and were on different courses at the college. To be honest I've spent the last twenty years totally pissed off that they never asked me to go with them.'

'Which college was that again?' Stu was taking the notes, letting Will do what he was so good at – he had a knack for making people feel at ease so they didn't feel as if they were being interrogated.

'Kendal. I did hairdressing with Sharon Sale, and Wendy Cook did catering. We used to take the mickey out of her all the time. She used to say she would open up her own business – Cook's Catering – and then we'd see who had the last laugh. It was only before Christmas that I tried to find them. I did loads of searches on Facebook, Snapchat, Twitter, Instagram . . . you name it and I tried it, but I couldn't find either of them. That was when I sort of wondered if something bad had actually happened to them all those years ago.'

Will had never heard of either girl before this morning. Their names had never been mentioned once since he started working at the station – but then again, he didn't suppose there was any reason for them to be. He needed to check the records but if they were both down as missing persons, after a year it would be old news. By the time he'd started, years later, no one would have remembered except whoever took the missing person's reports at the time.

'Stu, I need you to pull both girls' files; see what's in them. I also need you to find out who dealt with the cases. I doubt they still work at the station but it's possible. Thanks, Susie. If I need to speak to you again what's the best number to get hold of you on?'

She reeled off her mobile number. 'I'm here every day except for Sundays. My mum owns the shop. We always used to come here when we were little. I love this area. She bought it for something to do now she's retired but she hasn't been well so I've had to come and help out, which I don't mind – I love it here. So if you can't get hold of me by phone, because you know what the signal is like around here, then come to the shop. I live in the flat above; the door's round the side.'

'Thank you so much. That's brilliant. You've been a big help.'

'Now what can I get you?'

'Four coffees and three slices of chocolate cake, please.'

Sam looked at Will. 'Are you not having any cake?'

'No, I had a cooked breakfast not long ago. This six-pack doesn't survive off cake.'

Both women giggled.

'What six-pack? We won't believe you until you show us.'

'Steady on, ladies, I'm a married man. You'll just have to take my word for it.'

He winked at them both, setting them off into fits of laughter.

Stu dead-eyed him and he smiled. Poor Stu was still jealous of his success with women, which was a much politer way of saying it than how Stu had once worded it. He didn't intentionally flirt with them; it was just how he was. It was his personality. Once upon a time he'd used it to sleep with a fair few women, but he looked down at his wedding ring and thought about Annie and how much he loved her. Stu was also looking at Will's left hand, as if to remind him he was married, and he made a note to have a word with Stu about his sudden change in attitude the last couple of days whenever Will spoke to any women. He wondered if he was having problems at home with his wife, Debs; yep, he definitely should take him to one side to try and find out what was going on before the end of the day. If there was a problem at home that he was bringing to work Will needed to know about it. He needed Stu focused. They had to find out who it was that had been buried and left in the woods.

Susie brought over a tray with four huge mugs of coffee and slices of cake so big he didn't think that any of them would be able to finish them. He thanked her and passed her one of his business cards. 'You can reach me on either of those numbers should you need to.'

She nodded and tucked the card into the pocket of her jeans, then went off to take some more orders, leaving them in complete silence whilst they dug into their mountains of cake. Will sipped his coffee, his mind working overtime thinking about Wendy and Sharon. Where were they now? Would both of them have run away and not told their best friend? It didn't make sense. Teenage girls were generally not known for keeping secrets from their friends. If the body belonged to one of them, then there was a good chance the other wouldn't be too far away – and if that was so, who had killed them and put them there?

Chapter 13

Annie left the house and for a split second debated about driving into the village, but then told herself off for being lazy. It was another gorgeous day and the exercise would do her good, so she set out on the familiar walk – or waddle, as it was fast becoming – up the narrow lane that led onto the main road into the village. She felt restless. She couldn't settle in the house and had phoned Jake to see if he was at work, hoping that he would be able to find an excuse to come and see her, but he wasn't on duty until two and she would drive herself mad if she stayed in the house on her own until then. She would see if she could find out where the lovely but slightly mysterious Jo lived and invite her out for coffee. She needed to do something to keep herself busy.

As she got to the village she saw Will's car and her heart skipped a beat; she had never known she would love someone so completely. She had scoffed when watching love films back in the day when she was married to Mike, not believing it was possible to care about another person so much. It made her wonder how many people actually married partners who weren't *the one*, or how many actually managed to find *the one*. Maybe it was a complete fluke that she and Will were so compatible and they were the exception to the norm; although, he did drive her mad with his almost permanent state of happiness. He rarely sulked, but he did like the ladies – or should she say, he *used* to like the ladies. He'd never cheated on her, but she still found it hard to believe that he had managed to stay so faithful considering his track record.

As she turned the road into the village she saw not only Will, Stu and a couple of PCSOs coming out of the little café she loved; she also saw Jo walking up the small street past the village hall.

There was one advantage to living in a place so small – you couldn't help but fall over everyone. She watched Will run across the road to speak to Jo, gently taking her arm and pulling her to one side away from the others, and for one insane moment she felt a spark of jealousy ignite inside her. One that she tried her best to dampen before it had chance to take hold. Stu and the others wandered back in the direction of the village hall, leaving Will and Jo in deep conversation. Annie walked as fast as her stomach would let her, the whole time telling herself to behave because she was being completely irrational. It was Jo who spotted her first and waved at her, pulling away from Will and walking towards her. Will saw Annie and smiled; it didn't look as if he had anything to be feeling guilty about.

'Annie, how lovely to see you. How are you today?'

'I'm great, thanks. I was just on a mission to find you and see if I could tempt you into sharing some cake.'

'I'd love that; you don't need me, do you?' Jo turned to Will, and Annie noticed the woman had her fingers crossed behind her back.

'No, I don't, but if you think of anything at all you'll give me a ring, won't you?'

His tone of voice wasn't his usual one and Annie opened her mouth, about to ask him what was up, when he shook his head at her.

'Morning again, how are you getting on?'

She had no idea what was going on but if he thought he could give her the cold shoulder and pretend he didn't know her then two could play that game.

'Oh you know how it is, officer – I'm lonely being stuck on my own all day and wondering what on earth is happening and what exactly my husband is up to while he's at work.'

'That makes the two of us then. I have no idea, either. Enjoy your coffee, ladies.'

He turned and walked away and for the first time in forever Annie actually felt angry enough with him that she could have run after him and wiped the smile from his face. He had his head bent and was busy texting on his phone. Instead of running after him she forced herself to turn away and smile at Jo. The bruising underneath her eye had faded to a yellow colour and was harder to detect than it had been yesterday, but the point was it was still there, and it very likely hadn't got there through any fault of her own.

'I don't like this. It's scary – all these policemen and women are everywhere asking questions. Have they been to your house as well?'

'Erm, yes, sort of. I already know him.'

'Do you? He seems very nice. He came to my house yesterday with another detective because we look out onto the woods where that body was found. It's so horrible thinking that all this time someone was buried behind my house. I couldn't sleep last night thinking about it – gave me the shivers it did.'

Annie's phone vibrated in her pocket. She took it out.

Forgive me, don't be angry. I'll tell you everything later, but can you try and get as much info out of her as possible? She won't speak if she knows you're a copper and I'm your husband. I'm worried about her. Love you xxx

Annie didn't know whether she was even more annoyed with him after that text or not. She tucked the phone back in her pocket. She had no idea what was going on, but it didn't seem as if Jo knew him very well so maybe she should stop being so paranoid.

'Sorry, Jo, what did you say?'

She laughed. 'I was just saying that he's a bit dreamy, isn't he, so good-looking – a bit like that guy off *The Mentalist*. Have you ever watched that? I love it. It's my favourite television programme. But he's married. Not that I'm interested, you know. I don't want you to think I'm a terrible person, but he kept playing with his wedding ring when he was at my house yesterday so it was kind of hard to miss.'

'Oh, yes, he is married. I know his wife as well.'

'Really, what's she like? I bet she's drop-dead gorgeous. I can't imagine how nice it must be waking up to him every morning. Some women get all the luck.'

Annie laughed. 'Yes, it would be rather nice, wouldn't it? What's your husband like?'

The woman's cheeks flared red and she lowered her head. 'Busy, he's always busy. We don't see a lot of each other really, considering he works from home.'

'What does he do?'

'He's a photographer.'

'Does he do portraits?'

'Oh yes, he does all those sorts of things – he has a lot of wealthy older women coming in, wanting him to make them look beautiful.'

Annie laughed. 'That must be a nightmare. I've been thinking of getting a portrait done – well, not so much of me because I hate having my picture taken – more of my bump. You know, to have as a keepsake.'

'He's done lots of mother and bump photoshoots, right through to baby's first birthday portraits. They seem to be all the fashion now along with those baby showers. I can't believe how Americanised this country is getting.'

'I might come and speak to him about it then, see if he can fit me in before my stomach explodes. That is, I would if I knew where to find him.' Annie winked at Jo who blushed. They reached the coffee shop and Annie pushed the door open for Jo to go through.

'I'll give you a business card with our address and phone number on, but he's really very busy. He might not be able to fit you in. There's another photographer in Bowness who might be more suitable.'

Annie wondered why Jo didn't want her to meet her husband or have him take her photo; not that she had any intention of letting him photograph her, but she wanted to see what he looked like. See if he was similar to Mike. Annie knew she was getting too involved. She hardly knew Jo, but she knew she wouldn't be able to stop herself now even if she tried. They both smiled at the woman behind the counter and sat down ready to order. Annie thought about Will's text – what did he want to know about the woman next to her? She spent the next thirty minutes trying to coax out how long Jo had lived in the village, where she was originally from and if she was happily married. Every time Annie asked about her husband, Jo would try and change the subject, so she tried a different approach and didn't mention him at all, hoping it would make Jo feel comfortable enough to relax. She did finally, until she looked at her watch.

'Oh my God, is that the time? I've been ages. He'll kill me.' She stood up and pulled a ten-pound note out of her pocket.

Annie waved her hand at her. 'Put that away – you can pay next time. I was the one who dragged you in here. I hope I haven't caused you any trouble at home?'

Jo looked at her and opened her mouth to say something, but thought better of it and closed it again. 'Are you sure?'

Annie nodded. 'I'm positive. Take care, Jo. Oh, do you have that business card?'

Jo passed her a crumpled one from the bottom of her handbag. 'Thanks, Annie, I will. You look after the both of you.'

Annie watched her scurry from the café back in the direction of the village hall and the army of police officers; once she made it past them she would have to face her bully of a husband. Annie wanted to ask her if she was OK and how bad it was at home, but she couldn't. She knew from past experience Jo would deny anything was wrong. Women like her always did and that included Annie herself. How many times had she gone to work wearing enough make-up to cover the bruises, the long-sleeved tops in the summer? It all seemed as if it was in another lifetime, not three years ago.

She would try and broach the subject with Jo, just to let her know that she got it. She understood the pain and embarrassment, the living in constant fear – it was no way to live. Annie also made up her mind to visit Jo's husband to see what he was like. She would go while she was already in the village. She hadn't bothered asking Jo if she could go back with her because she hadn't wanted to put her in a difficult position. But if she turned up unannounced then Jo wouldn't get in trouble with her husband, fingers crossed. Annie already had an image of him in her mind and she bet it wouldn't be far wrong. She had no intention of paying him to photograph her, though; the thought of him looking at her naked stomach made her skin crawl, but she did want to know more about him so she could pass it on to Will.

She went to the counter and paid the bill, then decided to have a wander around. As she walked outside she bumped straight into Sam, who was talking to an old woman. Sam grinned at her and Annie smiled back; no doubt she would catch up with all her friends over the next few days. A familiar car drove into the village. Inspector Cathy Hayes was her boss and friend so Annie waited for her to park up then walked towards the car. She reached the car and leant inside the window.

'If it isn't Annie Ashworth in the flesh – I was thinking about you this morning. I just said to Kav that we all needed a catch-up. How are you?'

'Fed up. I can't stand being at home doing nothing. There are only so many times you can hoover in one day. It's funny you should say that about a catch-up because I was saying the same to Will. How's my favourite sergeant doing? I hope you're not wearing him out.'

'As if. That man has found a new lease of life since he's had the pleasure of my company. He's like a lovesick teenager with a permanent erection.'

Annie laughed so loud a group of tourists turned to look at her. 'You're awful. Talk about lowering the tone. That's just far too much information – you know he's like my dad, don't you? How about you?'

'Me, I'm fabulous, thank you. I forgot how good it was to have a big, strong man to keep you warm at night and put the bins out every Wednesday morning.'

'Do you and Kav want to come for tea on Saturday night if you're not working? I was going to ask Jake and Alex as well.'

'Are you cooking?'

Annie chuckled. 'Definitely not.'

'In that case we'd love to. It's our weekend off. Jake is on a late but I'll change his shift when I get back to the station. Aw, it'll be like a reunion – you haven't got any bad news to tell us, have you? Because I could get used to this, having a quiet life. I haven't had heartburn for ages or any blinding headaches since you've been off sick.'

'Nope, I just miss you all.'

'Bloody hell, are you ill? I think this pregnancy lark is messing with your brainwaves. But thanks, Annie, I'm looking forward to it already.'

She got out of the car.

'I see the tosser is already here.' Cathy's head moved in the direction of her ex-husband's navy blue Range Rover parked across the street.

'No show without fucking Punch is there. I bet he's sat around drinking coffee and chatting shit – that's about the limit of his usefulness – in fact it always was. He's never been much good for anything.'

Annie shrugged. 'I can't help you with that one but I suspect you're right. See you at six on Saturday, and you can both stop over if you want, then you can have a bottle or two of wine and not have to worry about driving home.'

Cathy stuck her thumb up at her, then answered a call on her radio with a 'You have to be fucking kidding me'. Annie smiled to herself. Cathy never changed. She walked in the direction of the house on the front of the card that Jo had given to her. She wanted to make sure her new-found friend was all right and she also wanted to meet her husband – and make an appointment that she wouldn't keep, just to see what he was like.

Chapter 14

Tilly got off the bus and the first person she saw was her Aunty Annie walking along the opposite side of the street just past the bus stop. Her heart racing, she went into the whitewashed public toilets to wait for a few minutes until she was out of sight. Of all the times for her to bump into her, now was not a good one. She never bumped into her in Barrow town centre, which was far busier. This was just her luck. Annie would want to know why she was here in Hawkshead instead of in Bowness and she didn't want to have to explain it all to her, even though she knew that Annie was far more accepting and not judgemental like her mum. But what if she offered to go with her for the photoshoot? She would be mortified. Posing was something she did in front of the mirror in her bedroom on her own. It would be bad enough having a complete stranger taking the pictures, never mind Annie sitting on a chair watching her – she'd die of embarrassment.

After five minutes she stuck her head out of the entrance to the toilets; there were an awful lot of police cars and coppers wandering around and she wondered what had happened. Typical – any other day this place was probably dead to the world, but not today, when all she wanted to do was go and have her photos taken then get back home without anyone being any the wiser.

She had already typed the address into Google Maps so she wouldn't get lost; she put her earphones in, took her sunglasses from her oversize bag and put them on. As she reached the village hall she saw Annie bending down speaking to someone in a car. Scurrying past as fast as she could, she followed the directions that the voice in her ear was telling her. She reached the cream-coloured cottage and walked around to the side where he'd told her the entrance to his studio was. She looked around. There was a copper standing some distance away in the woods at the back of the cottage but they had their back to her. She walked up to the brown wooden door and lifted her hand to knock but it opened before she had the chance.

The man standing there smiled and she felt all the anxieties she'd had about this melt away. He wasn't very old – maybe in his late thirties, early forties – and wasn't bad-looking. He was a big bloke, but he didn't look like a pervert. She had expected him to be in his fifties with grey hair and big thick glasses.

'Come in. That was good timing, wasn't it? I was just going to nip to the village shop for a bottle of wine for later, but I can go after.'

'Oh don't let me stop you. I don't mind waiting.'

'I wouldn't dream of it. I'm not desperate – I've already got some but was just going to get another bottle in case I needed it.'

'Is that in case I'm terrible and you need to blot it all out, drown your sorrows?'

He laughed and took hold of her arm, leading her into the studio. 'No way. I think you're going to be a complete natural at this. You're so pretty, it will be the easiest session I've had all month.'

Tilly felt a burning sensation creeping up her neck. She liked him; he seemed very kind. She'd always wondered what it would be like to go out with an older man. She hated the boys her age – they were so immature. Annie had met Will, and Tilly had been gobsmacked the first time she'd set eyes on him because he was so good-looking. In fact, the first few times she'd met him she'd had to excuse herself because her cheeks would turn bright red and it was wrong to fancy your auntie's boyfriend . . . but he was so cute. She'd managed to cure herself of that little crush when she'd seen how happy Annie was – how happy Will made her. She didn't know all the details but she knew that Mike, Annie's first husband, had hurt her a lot and she deserved to be happy. Snapping herself out of her daydream she smiled at him.

'Sorry, I hope so. I'm so nervous about this, you wouldn't believe it.'

'You have nothing to be nervous about. I promise you'll love it. Now, should we take some shots of you just as you are, so that you don't feel uncomfortable, and let you get used to the camera? Then we can progress from there?'

He walked away, shrugging off his jacket, which he slung over a chair, then he picked up a camera that was on the long bench at the back of the studio in front of a full-length mirror and turned towards her.

'Now if you just stand in front of that screen we'll do some test shots.'

Tilly felt sick as he led her across the room to the huge white screen. She was so embarrassed. What if she looked like a whale in the pictures? What if he thought she was a complete freak? She smiled at him and, feeling stupid, let him walk around her snapping pictures. After five minutes he stopped.

'I'll take a look at these and we'll go from there. You know you don't have to be so nervous. I promise I won't bite.'

'Sorry, I just feel so stupid.'

He smiled at her. 'I understand – most people do, but you'll get used to it. How about a nice cold glass of wine to put you at ease? It works wonders; obviously only the one because it's no good if a model is too drunk. It makes them harder to photograph if they can't stand still and are falling all over the place – but just a small one might help you feel a little bit better. Or I have vodka if you prefer?'

'I don't know. I don't really drink wine, to be honest; I don't like the taste. Maybe a small vodka, if that's OK?'

He grinned. 'Of course it is. You won't get the best shots if you're too wound up like a coiled spring. You need to be relaxed. You wouldn't believe how many bottles of vodka I've gone through this year.'

He opened a small fridge and pulled a bottle of vodka from out of the freezer compartment; she recognised the bottle straight away – it was the really expensive one that was so strong you only needed a couple of shots before you were drunk. She watched him pour out two shot glasses and carry them over, handing one to her.

'I will if you do. How about that? Although I can only have one – I don't want to take any fuzzy photos of you.'

He winked and she took the glass from him. Before she could think about it he downed his and coughed.

'Gets me every time.'

She laughed. Following his lead, she threw her head back, swallowing it in one. It burnt the back of her throat and she also began coughing. Her eyes watered and she felt his warm hands patting her back.

'Are you OK?'

She couldn't speak but stuck her thumb up.

'I'll give you a couple of minutes whilst I check these and get my other camera, then we'll try again.'

He walked out, leaving her alone. She hadn't noticed the drops of liquid that he'd slipped into her glass. He knew this was far too risky, but he couldn't help himself. No one knew she was here – even the police hadn't noticed her coming, because he'd been watching her from the upstairs bedroom window. The whole time, the officer out the back hadn't turned around once. He wouldn't be burying this girl out in the woods because that was too dangerous, but he did have his morgue fridges in the garage, which were perfect. Once she was dead he could put her into one of them until he was ready to take his photos for his special album – and the beauty of it was he could keep on doing it again and again as long as he kept the heating off in the studio and didn't keep her body out for too long.

Tilly began to feel light-headed. The room was swimming and she stumbled to her bag to pull out the bottle of water she had in there and her phone. She didn't feel well at all. There was no way one shot of vodka would do this to her – she was used to drinking it, although normally only the cheap stuff from the corner shop. Trying to sit on the stool to steady herself she completely misjudged it and slid to the floor. Her mind wasn't working like it should and she felt as if her head was disconnected from her body. The thought that he'd drugged her screamed into her brain, but she didn't want to believe it. Why would he want to drug her? He was so nice. She pressed the buttons on her phone, trying to find Annie's number. Annie would know what to do, but Tilly couldn't see the screen – everything was blurred. Holding the home button down she tried to speak into it, 'Phonnnne Argnie.'

'I'm sorry, I didn't get that, Tilly.'

She tried her best to speak clearly but her tongue felt as if it was far too thick for her mouth and was sticking to the roof of it. 'Call Annnie . . .'

'Calling Annie.'

And then the room went black.

He got his camera from the garage and went back in to see her slumped on the floor. Her eyes were unfocused but she had her phone in her hand. His heart began to race; fuck, had she had time to phone for help? Snatching the phone he saw that she had indeed called someone called Annie, but there had been no answer. He couldn't think what to do first. He needed to get rid of the phone, but where? Not in the village, because the police would be able to trace it. It was an iPhone so it probably had that 'find my iPhone' app on it. He turned the phone off and slid it into his pocket; she had mentioned that her family thought she was going to Bowness. He needed to dump it in Bowness somewhere, now – before anyone noticed she was missing.

His heart was beating so fast he thought he might be on the verge of a heart attack. It wasn't supposed to be like this. Shit. He didn't have time to do anything with her now; instead, he grabbed hold of her arms and dragged her from the studio out into the workshop where his darkroom was. Taking a rag from the bench he tied it around her mouth as tight as it would go and then he took some of the washing line he had used on the others to tie her hands and feet together. He didn't care if she suffocated – it would save him the job – but he needed her to be secure until he'd disposed of her phone and whilst the village was flooded with coppers. This would give him some much-needed time to figure out what he was going to do. When his head was thinking straight he could decide how long he was going to keep her for. He pressed two fingers to her neck; she still had a strong pulse. Turning off the light he shut the door and locked it, then dragged a heavy bench over just in case she managed to escape somehow.

'Heath, sorry to bother you, but are you busy? There's someone here who would like a word,' her voice called through the studio door and his heart sank to the bottom of his shoes. Who the hell wanted a word? If it was that smarmy copper he'd be fucked.

'Be out in a minute.'

He knew that his voice sounded different. It had almost quivered when he'd spoken. The sweat was pouring from him and he ran across to the sink and splashed handfuls of cold water all over his face, hands and hair. He checked the door to the darkroom, then turned the light off in the workshop and locked the door behind him. Her phone felt like a brick in his pocket and he couldn't wait to get rid of it. As he walked into the kitchen he saw a heavily pregnant woman sitting on one of the chairs sipping from a glass of water.

'This is Annie. She lives in the village on the opposite side of the woods, and would like to have her baby bump photographed.

I told her how good you were at taking photos, but she knows that you're also very busy.'

Heath was furious with Jo for bringing this woman into their kitchen unannounced. Annie? That was twice he'd heard that name in fifteen minutes, but if she lived in the village surely she wouldn't know the teenager he'd drugged up who was from Barrow. It must be a coincidence. What was wrong with Jo? At least she was trying to fob her off, but he would need to show her what a huge mistake she'd made later on – after he'd disposed of the phone in his pocket.

He forced himself to smile at Annie. 'No problem – I do lots of them. When were you thinking of getting it done? And do you want a family portrait or just you?'

He was trying his best to talk normally but his hands were shaking and he couldn't stop the fine film of sweat that was forming on his forehead. He was so hot, it felt as if the phone in his pocket was burning his leg off. Yet he'd turned it off. He didn't understand what was wrong with him.

'Just whenever you can fit me in, and to be honest I'm not too sure – I haven't thought about it a lot.'

'Well, have a think and let Jo know. I'm really booked up at the moment, but I'll see if we can sort something out. I need to go into Barrow for some bits. Do you need anything, Jo?'

He looked at his wife, hoping she hadn't noticed the change in his demeanour. She shook her head, no doubt relieved to be rid of him for the couple of hours it would take him to get to Barrow and back, which was at least forty minutes each way – depending upon the traffic.

'Nice to meet you, Annie. I'll see you later, Jo.'

He walked out; the phone in his pocket was feeling heavier by the minute. He couldn't breathe and when he got outside and into his car he wound the window down and sucked in a huge gulp of air. He'd totally screwed up and he knew it. Then he realised that the girl had left her handbag on the chair. Damn it, it was too late now – he couldn't go back in. He was acting like a complete head case and Jo was sure to notice something. He knew that she wouldn't say a thing to him, but there was nothing stopping her talking to that copper from the other day. He started the car and drove towards the village. He had no intention of driving to Barrow. Instead he would get the ferry over to Bowness, park up and think about where he was going to dispose of a phone in broad daylight without attracting any attention.

As he turned into the village the sight of the many police cars and uniformed officers made his stomach lurch and he had to force down the vomit that was threatening to rise up his throat. He smiled at two female officers who were standing outside the village hall and they smiled back, then he turned and drove towards the ferry, wondering if by the time he came back they would all be waiting outside his house to arrest him.

Chapter 15

Annie finished her coffee and stood up to leave.

'I'd better let you get on. Sorry, Jo, I've taken up quite enough of your time today.'

'Don't be daft. You have no idea how good it is to be able to talk to someone else. Let me know about the photos and I'll see if Heath has a slot available to book you in.'

'I will, as soon as I've spoken with my husband. Thanks.'

Annie walked to the front door and let herself out. She waved at Jo and began the trudge back to the village hall to see if Will was still around. She was still mad at him, but if he offered to cook for everyone on Saturday night she'd forgive him – as long as he told her what was happening.

She couldn't make her mind up about Jo's husband. He hadn't looked a bit like the ogre she had imagined him to be; in fact, he had been quite the opposite. But – and it was a big but – there was no discounting the bruising under Jo's eyes and the way she seemed to get all fretful whenever she talked about him. Which in a way made it even worse. Mike had looked like a thug but Heath didn't, which made it harder to believe. Now she knew where Jo lived she would keep popping in and checking on her, let him know that she knew without saying anything. It might make him stop, or at least think about it. There was one thing, though; she didn't think she'd be having her photograph taken any time soon.

She rounded the corner and walked towards the hall. As she walked in, she sighed – the air was much cooler inside. She saw Will sitting in the corner typing away on a laptop. Stu was on the one next to him and they both looked as if they were on a mission. Will looked up and smiled at her and she felt the last bitter pieces of anger from earlier disperse. Damn it, how did he manage to do that? She could never stay mad at him for long, even when she wanted to. He stopped what he was doing, locked the computer and strode across the hall to kiss her on the cheek.

'I've been waiting for you. I'm starving.'

'Sorry, I got carried away.'

'Come on. Stu – I'll be back in an hour. I'm taking my beautiful wife for lunch.'

Annie punched him half-heartedly on the arm. 'Stop that, you idiot, you're so embarrassing at times.'

He rubbed his arm, but didn't stop smiling as he reached out for her hand and pulled her towards the exit. Once they got outside he turned to her. 'But you are my beautiful wife, and I'm just winding Stu up. He's in a right funny mood. Every time I speak to another woman he keeps staring at my wedding ring and reminding me I'm a married man. It's really odd.'

'Well, would you be flirting with these other women?' She arched one eyebrow and looked him in the eye.

'No, of course not . . . well, not the sort of flirting that you mean. You know how much of a charmer I am naturally; I'm afraid it's something I can't help. Well, he seems to have taken a big objection to it all of a sudden.'

Annie laughed. 'It's a bloody good job I trust you, Will Ashworth – and love you – but no wonder you're getting on his nerves if you're always so full of yourself and talk that much crap. You can tell me what you meant about Jo earlier on. What was that all about? Pretending that you didn't know who I was – that wasn't very nice, you know. And by the way, she's the woman I met yesterday at the doctor's. How long have you known her?'

'Sorry about that. I just wanted to see if you could get anything out of her – and if she'd known you were my wife she might have clammed up. I only met her yesterday. We went to her house because it backs directly onto the grave in the woods and I wanted to speak to them. Did you notice the bruising under her eye? She was terrified when her husband walked in and I knew then that he was too handy with his fists for his own good. All I did was pass her a card with my number on in case she wanted to talk when he wasn't around – about the grave or her situation – and Stu thought I was asking her out on a date.'

She laughed again. 'What are you like? You're such a gentleman at times and I think it's really sweet that you tried to help in your own little way. You're a good man, Will, even though you're slightly vain and delusional – but I'd never hold it against you. You'll be pleased to know that she thinks you're really quite dreamy. As if your head needs to swell any more than it already has, but I do agree with her. You are dreamy, and I also think that you are a complete sweetie for caring about her. I've just been to her house and met her husband – he seemed very nice, and he wasn't what I was expecting at all, but you can't judge a book by its cover. I should know that better than anyone.'

'Really? He was nice to you? Because he was a complete cock when we were there yesterday.'

'Yes, but you're a man, stepping into his world and with a badge of authority. He would perceive you as a threat and it's pretty obvious he's going to be wary of the police, especially if he's beating the crap out of his wife.'

They went into the pub, which was full outside, and Annie went and sat down on the last empty table that was tucked into a corner. She was glad to be out of the sun and in the shade; this being pregnant business was much harder than she'd ever imagined and she was tired now. After lunch she was going home to lie down for a couple of hours to recover from all her exertions. Will came over with two glasses filled with ice, lime and lemonade and she took one off him, drinking half of it in one go.

'Thirsty?'

'Yes, but I'm starving even more.'

'I've ordered two jacket potatoes with tuna and salad – is that enough or did you want a bowl of chips?'

Annie ran her hand over her bump. 'Nope, that sounds fine. He doesn't need any extra today after all the coffee and cake.'

Will sat next to her and she inhaled his aftershave, which wasn't as strong as when he'd left this morning, but still smelt good. She leant her head against his shoulder.

'I wish you could come home with me and we could go back to bed.'

He spat the mouthful of cold lemonade all over the front of his suit. 'Steady on, I thought pregnant women were supposed to go off sex? You're turning into a nymphomaniac. Not that I'm complaining.'

She nudged his side, forgetting about the scar until she'd done it. 'Oh God, I'm so sorry. Did I hurt you?'

'No, I'm good. You know how tough and brave I am.'

'I didn't mean I want sex; I just want you. You know, at home with me bored out of your head as well. The last few years have been so hectic, I'm not used to living a completely normal, sane life and I have no idea what to do with myself.'

'Well, you'd better get used to it, because I love it – knowing that the worst thing you can do is hit your thumb with a hammer or drop a paintbrush on your toe. You have no idea how stressful it's been watching you get hurt over and over again.'

The waitress brought their cutlery over and Annie lifted her head and smiled at her. She was the same age as Tilly, which reminded her that Tilly was going for that interview today. She pulled out her phone and saw that she'd missed a call from Tilly, but when she phoned back it went straight to voicemail. Bugger, she'd wanted to wish her good luck. At least if she got the job she could come and stop with her and Will for a bit and give her some company.

She typed, *Good luck, you'll be fine. Ring me when you're done. Xxx*, and sent the message, hoping she would get it before the interview. The food came moments later and she forgot all about her niece and Jo, and even the relentless boredom, as she tucked in.

Heath drove to the car ferry and joined the queue, hoping he would get on it this time. It held eighteen cars and took ten minutes to cross the lake – he didn't want to be stuck here hanging around. He looked at the clock on the dashboard; it had only been an hour since she'd knocked at his door. It was highly unlikely anyone would be missing her so soon; hopefully he had a few hours yet before any alarm bells began ringing. He'd felt sick when he saw the number of police milling around outside the village hall. He was pretty sure they didn't have a clue – or so he hoped – but it *was* him they were all looking for, after all.

What the hell was he thinking, drugging that girl when the village was full of more coppers than Japanese tourists? He was cracking up. Still, it was done now and the only thing he could do was damage limitation. He was confident they wouldn't be able to trace the bodies – if and when they found the other one – back to him, but it all depended upon how good Mr Smarmy really was and for all he knew he could be shit-hot.

The cars began to load onto the ferry, until the one in front of him stopped. Groaning, Heath turned his engine off – it would be another twenty minutes now. He thought about launching the phone into the lake whilst he was waiting, but a car pulled up behind him, followed by another, and some cyclists rounded the bend. So that put paid to that idea. He didn't have a clue where to dump the phone. He pulled it from his pocket to take a look; he had no idea how to get the battery out or even if you could.

Taking a chamois leather from the glove compartment he wiped it down, getting rid of his fingerprints. When he was happy it was clean he wrapped it in the leather cloth and put it on the seat.

He might dump it in the church grounds; it was the only place he could think of that might be pretty quiet this time of day. It was tourist season, though, and they were bloody everywhere, like swarms of flies. He wiped the sweat from his brow. What was he going to do with the girl when he got back? He might have to toss a coin: heads she lives, tails she dies. He couldn't let her live, though, could he? Not now. She would go straight to the police and it would all be over. She would have to die.

They left the pub hand in hand. Annie was stuffed and could hardly walk now that she'd been sitting for a while. She was worn out.

Will looked at her. 'You're tired. Did you come in your car?'

She shook her head.

'Right, well, I'm going to drive you home – no arguing. I can even take you up to bed and tuck you in. I don't want you tiring my daughter out too much.'

He winked at her and for once she didn't argue with him. She felt exhausted.

They walked past Stu who was outside the hall having a heated conversation on his phone, which reminded Will he needed to speak to him and see if everything was OK back home. By the sound of his raised voice it clearly wasn't. They reached Will's car and he opened the door for her to climb in. He ran around to his side of the car and jumped in with a bit more energy than Annie had.

'What's up with Stu?'

'I don't know but he doesn't sound too happy.'

'I'll ask Jake. He'll know if there's any gossip on the home front – you know what he's like.'

He drove the short distance to their house and she waited for him to open the door and haul her out, which he did without even thinking about it.

'Do you want me to come and tuck you in?'

She thought about it for a split second – yes, she bloody well did, but she also wanted him to stay with her. *These hormones better do one when the baby is born or I'll be a gibbering wreck,* she thought. His phone rang. As he lifted it to his ear it didn't take a genius to figure out what this conversation was about.

'How far from the other grave? Is the dog sure – I mean, we've been here before, haven't we?'

She watched him nodding his head.

'Right, well, you'd better call everyone out and have Dr Matt on standby. I'll be there in ten minutes. Have you cleared the area?' He ended his call.

'Have they found another body?'

'The dog handler thinks so.'

'Do you think it's those two girls who went missing?'

'Your guess is as good as mine, but probably. At the moment I haven't got a clue what's going on. When you've had a rest, do you want to do some digging around on the internet for me, see what you can come up with? I need you to look for any info on a Wendy Cook or a Sharon Sale. Stu's good but his mind isn't on it today.'

'I'd love to. Do you think that's who the bodies belong to? Who are they?'

'A couple of teenagers who went missing in 1995. Because they were from different towns nobody seems to have made any connections, but they were both friends. The waitress in that coffee shop knew them and was friends with them. She thought they'd both run off together to find fame and fortune.

'Really? That's so sad. Thank God for the technology we have – it would be flagged up now, wouldn't it? It's such a shame. If it is them they had their whole lives ahead of them until some sick bastard decided to take it all away. I'll have a look and see what

I can find; at least it will give me something to do for a couple of hours. I'll phone you later.'

He kissed her cheek and grinned. 'I love you, Annie.'

'I love you more, Will. Be careful. I have a bad feeling about this.'

He chuckled. 'You always have a bad feeling – and besides, this is an old case. Whoever was responsible probably moved away or could even have died years ago, and to top it all off you're not involved in the investigation on a professional level so what could possibly go wrong?'

He got into his car and drove away, leaving her watching until she couldn't see him through the trees.

Annie finally went inside. She kicked off her shoes then went upstairs to put her pyjamas on. She might as well be comfortable and she wasn't expecting any visitors. The house was silent, peaceful, and it was heaven. No one was there who shouldn't be. She came back downstairs to get the laptop and thought about sitting at the desk but it wasn't comfy. Taking a bottle of water from the fridge she went upstairs to her bedroom and the bed that Will had picked – and boy had he picked the right one. Positioning the pillows she lay down and opened the laptop, beginning a search of the two names the waitress had given Will.

When Heath finally got to the other side of the lake, he decided to drive around for a bit and see how busy it was. He'd already put his baseball cap and sunglasses on, and he was wearing a black T-shirt and black cut-off cargo shorts. He looked so nondescript not even his own mother would have noticed him. All the usual places were busy: the coffee shops, pubs, cafés. He carried on driving up the main street until he reached the church, which was past the police station. There weren't any police cars outside, which he took as a good omen. There was no one around by the church; in fact it was perfect.

After parking his car on the opposite side of the road he took the phone and slid it into his pocket. There were lots of old graves and bushes; he wandered around pretending to be interested in them, reading a couple of headstones, and after five minutes of no one coming into the church grounds he walked across to some bushes behind a grave and shook the phone from the cloth he'd wrapped it in, letting it fall underneath them. He stayed another couple of minutes just in case anyone had been watching, but no one came. So then he casually strolled across to his car.

He didn't look strange or out of place but his hands were so slick with sweat that he couldn't grip the handle of his car without wiping them on the side of his shorts first. He drove off in the opposite direction, not sure where the town's CCTV cameras were, continued up through Windermere then on to Ambleside where he would go around the lake and make his way slowly back home.

Chapter 16

Tilly tried to open her eyes but they felt as if they had been glued shut; in fact she felt as if she'd been drinking shots all night and was absolutely hammered. The vodka . . . she remembered him passing her a shot glass of vodka and they'd both drunk them down in one, but he wasn't lying here almost comatose, or was he? She wondered why she couldn't move her hands to feel around then realised they were tied together. Opening her mouth to scream she felt the thick material of whatever it was that was wrapped around her mouth stopping her and she gagged. Trying to roll to one side her head swam and she sank back into the darkness.

Stu was still outside the hall when Will got back; he was no longer on his phone but he was pacing up and down, looking so angry that even Will felt uncomfortable just watching him. Will parked the car and walked across the road to him.

'What's up, Stu?'

'Nothing.'

'Nothing? Sorry, I'm not buying that. You haven't been yourself and I couldn't miss the shouting down your phone before. Look at the state of you. What's got into you? You're scaring all the nice tourists.'

'Look, it's got nothing to do with you – Mr Perfect, "look at me my life is so fucking wonderful" – you wouldn't know a bad day if it bit you on the arse.'

Will flinched. 'Bollocks, my life hasn't exactly been wonderful now, has it? My wife was almost killed and I nearly died three months ago. Why don't you stop feeling sorry for yourself, snap out of it and start acting your age, Stu?'

Fuming, Will walked away from him. What Stu had said burned inside his chest, though, and he questioned himself. Had he done nothing but brag about how wonderful his life was? No, he knew that he hadn't because bragging wasn't Will's style – in fact, he was the complete opposite. He'd never told anyone at work about his dad or his wealth. Annie only found out by accident and that hadn't gone down too well. Stu had always been jealous and he'd known that but he hadn't realised he was that upset about his whole situation. He walked back to his car and drove back to the woods, where the dog handler was waiting for him and the DI to turn up at the possible new gravesite. He parked his car and phoned Stu.

'Take the rest of the day off, go sort your head out and I want you back in work tomorrow first thing, in the right frame of mind, or you can go work someone else's department because I haven't got time to put up with your childish rubbish. When you decide that you want an adult conversation about your situation then I'm here for you, Stu, and you know that.'

'Yes, boss.'

'And Stu, if something's wrong at home and you don't tell me, how am I supposed to know?'

'Yes, boss.'

Will ended the call, then rang Jake next. 'How's it going, big man?' Will asked.

'Who told you?'

'Told me what?'

'That I'm a big man.' Jake laughed and Will smiled.

'You have a filthy mind. Listen, have you heard anything about Stu and Debs? He's acting really weird and I didn't know if something had happened at home I should know about.'

'What would you do without my amazing head full of gossip? I have heard a rumour that Debs has been seeing that new boy in CSI and Stu caught them in bed together. New boy is currently sporting a black eye and broken nose by all accounts. Oh, and Debs has kicked Stu out – he's supposed to be sofa surfing on Smithy's couch. Bit of a mess if you ask me.'

'Shit, really? He looks like such a kid. No wonder Stu's pissed off then; it all makes sense now. I can't believe that Debs would cheat on him, though. How come I haven't heard about any of this? Is the new boy not pressing charges then?'

Jake snorted. 'Apparently he's saying he fell down some steps when he was drunk, and are you being serious, Will? Stu isn't exactly Mr Personality, is he?'

'Well, maybe not, but I always thought they made a good couple. You just never know, do you? How's things? When are you all coming to visit? It might cheer Annie up if you come and see her. She's so bored.'

'Life's too normal for our Annie, finally. I'm off this weekend. I'll see if Alex has anything planned and if not we'll come up Saturday night. Annie already texted to see if we were doing anything so I hope that you're cooking, because I love her but not enough to eat her food – and I mean that in the nicest possible way. Take care, my friend – I hear you're up to your neck in skeletons.'

'Haha, did she really? Yes one body up to now but the dogs have found another potential gravesite. Thanks, Jake, I'll speak to you later.'

He put his phone away. Poor Stu – he might be a pain, but he didn't deserve this. It wasn't until there had been a misunderstanding between him and one of his own colleagues that it had sunk in just how hurtful it was when you thought your partner was cheating.

Annie opened her eyes; the room was much darker than when she'd come upstairs. She felt around for the laptop and looked down to see it was upside down on the floor. Bugger. She leant over, picked it up and pressed the button. It powered on and she shut it down again. She'd found some bits and pieces on the missing girls and sent them downstairs to the printer before she'd dozed off. Her stomach let out a loud groan and she smiled to herself. Hungry, son? She got off the bed and was about to go downstairs when she noticed the young woman standing outside on the landing. Annie felt her heart skip a beat. No matter how many times it happened it still scared her.

'Look, I can see you and I want to help you. What do you want? If you don't tell me I can't help you.'

'He's at it again.'

'Who?'

'The man who killed me. He's got another girl and you need to help her.'

'Who is he? Where is he?'

'I don't know his name, but he lives near the trees. He likes to keep pictures of us.'

The house phone rang and the woman disappeared. Annie's arms were covered in goose bumps. What was going on? She had a sinking feeling in the pit of her stomach that this was all to do with the skeleton that had been found. But what did that mean? That after all this time he was still out there killing? How many bodies might there actually be in those woods? It had been twenty years since the two girls went missing. What if he'd carried on killing every year? That would be at least twenty bodies. She shivered and made her way downstairs to answer the phone, which rang off just before she got to it. She turned to go to the kitchen and it started ringing again. Picking it up she heard her sister-in-law's frantic voice on the other end.

'Thank God! Where have you been? I've been ringing your mobile for the last hour.'

'Asleep. Why, what's wrong?'

'Have you heard from Tilly? I can't get hold of her and she should have been home by now.'

'I don't know, I've just woken up, Lisa. Let me go and find my phone, then I'll ring you back.'

Annie put the receiver down. That was all she needed – Lisa freaking out over nothing. She went into the living room and picked up her mobile from the coffee table. There were ten missed calls from Lisa, the earlier missed call from Tilly and a text message from Jake. She dialled Lisa's number, which was answered before it finished ringing.

'She rang me at one but I missed her call and when I tried to phone her back it was switched off. Her phone's probably died. What time was her interview?'

'Twelve-thirty, so she rang you after it. She didn't bother to ring me. Bloody typical.'

'Have you spoken to Ben? Did she ring him?'

'Yes, and no she hasn't; she only called you. She might be stranded in Bowness somewhere.'

'Does she have any money on her? She is capable of getting a bus or a train; she could probably even use a phone box at a push, Lisa. Give her some time. She might have gone for a wander around. I'll have a drive over and see if I can spot her.'

'Would you do that? Ben's not home yet. He said the same as you, but he's got the car or I'd have had a drive around myself. I can't drive his pick-up; it's far too big and a bloody disgrace.'

'Yes, I'll text her now and go and see if I can find her.'

'Thank you.'

'You're welcome.'

The phone went dead and Annie groaned. Lisa was such a nuisance. She wouldn't be surprised if Tilly had decided to make the most of a chance to spend time on her own doing her own thing. She went and got dressed, grabbed a bar of chocolate and a banana, and got in her car to begin the drive to the car ferry. She passed a car coming into the village, driven by Jo's husband, and she wondered what he'd been up to. He'd told them he was going to Barrow, which was in the opposite direction to where he'd come from. Maybe he was having an affair; she wouldn't be surprised. Mike had been popular with the women even though he was a thug and he'd cheated on her a few times, which never even used to bother her because it meant he'd leave her alone while he had some other poor bugger to mess around with.

Annie was in Bowness before long and she drove as slowly as she could, seeing if she could spot her niece along the pier or near the coffee shop. She carried on through the small town to the police station where she worked. It was much quieter up here. No sign of Tilly; she could be anywhere and Annie knew this. She was more than likely sitting on the bus back to Barrow and Lisa was making a fuss over nothing. Annie turned the car around and drove through the back lanes and small side streets. As she came to the road that led back out towards Newby Bridge, instead of turning off for the ferry she decided to drive along it to the A590 just in case Tilly had decided to walk to the bus stop near the main roads.

By the time Annie got there and then drove back to Hawkshead and her house it was getting dusky. As she passed the village she could still see a couple of police cars outside the village hall. Will's car had gone and she hoped he was waiting at home for her. As she reached the gate to the cottage she sighed; his car wasn't there so that meant he was probably down in Barrow. She picked her phone up and rang Lisa. It was Ben's soft voice that answered.

'Tell me she's home safe and sound – false alarm.'

'I wish I could, Annie, but she's not here. I've phoned the bus company, then I phoned the hotel she was going to for an interview. They haven't heard of her and there were no interviews today. We don't know where she is and she hasn't answered her phone for hours – it keeps going to voicemail.'

'Jesus Christ, where the hell is she then?'

'I don't know. Lisa is talking to a police officer now. They've been very good and came not long after Lisa phoned it in. I told her not to, in case Tilly has just gone off to meet some boy and wanted some space, but you know what Lisa is like. She was frantic with worry and at first I wasn't too worried – you know what it's like being a teenager – but now I am. It's not like her; she's a good kid. Even if she hated living here, she wouldn't run away.'

Annie didn't know what to say. It wasn't like her niece at all. She was a good kid, but Lisa was a nightmare to live with and Annie couldn't blame her if she'd run off.

'Have you phoned her friends, looked at her Facebook?'

'Annie, I can barely use a mobile – I haven't got a clue about Facebook.'

She pushed away the short, panicking breaths that were threatening to make her start hyperventilating, and inhaled slowly. 'I'll do the computer stuff – I'll get a list of her friends and we can start making our way through them. Ask the officer who is taking details to ring me when they get a minute so I can talk to them, and make sure you get their collar number in case they forget so I can ring them. Ben – we'll find her; she can't be far. I'll be in touch soon and if she turns up in the meantime, ring me straight away.'

'Yes, will do. Do you think she's OK?'

He whispered the last words so his wife couldn't hear; Annie knew her brother so well, even if they didn't see a lot of each other.

'Of course she's OK. She's probably with a friend somewhere having a good time and it hasn't even entered her head to ring you.'

She put the phone down and breathed out – this wasn't good. It wasn't good at all. Moving as fast as she could, she went upstairs to get the laptop from the bedroom. It was freezing cold upstairs but she was so hot and flustered that she didn't notice. Grabbing the computer off the bed she went back downstairs to the kitchen where she sat down at the table and fired it up. Opening one of the drawers she took out a notepad and pen ready to write down a list of the friends Tilly interacted with the most. Annie just hoped her niece had been naïve enough not to change her profile settings to private. It was unlikely, as most people never considered the implications of the whole world being privy to some of your most personal information.

As she loaded Facebook and typed her niece's name into the search bar she felt a sharp pain in the back of her head as her name came up with a thumbnail image of Tilly. Clicking on the picture she smiled to see her niece's face appear in front of her; she was such a pretty little thing. When she clicked on her privacy settings she was relieved to see they were public, but also mildly annoyed and made a note to have words with Tilly about it when she next spoke to her. Head bent she began to list the friends she seemed to talk with the most and jumped when her phone rang next to her. Grabbing it she pushed her pen behind her ear and smiled to hear Will's voice.

'Sorry, I had to come to Barrow. Look, I think that Stu has split up with Debbie. They were arguing when I arrived back here earlier and he's in a foul mood. Should I tell him I know or ignore it and hope it will all blow over?'

'Will, have you seen the logs?'

'Not today, why?'

'Tilly hasn't turned up at home yet. Ben rang the hotel – she didn't have an interview there at all. Lisa rang the police and there's an officer with them now.'

'Jesus, where is she?'

'Wouldn't we all like to know. I wasn't worried at first when Lisa rang earlier, but I've had a drive all around Bowness and didn't spot her anywhere. I'm scared. I know she doesn't get along with Lisa but she wouldn't do this to Ben.'

'Or to you. She's not a bad kid, Annie, and she knows you're pregnant and the first person that her mum is going to ring. I'll take a look now and go and speak to whoever is dealing with them.'

'Thanks, Will. I have a list of her friends here off Facebook. I'll email them to you and you can give a copy to the officer in charge.'

'She'll turn up, Annie. Try not to get yourself all upset and worked up. I know you must be worried sick but Tilly isn't stupid. There's probably a very good reason she hasn't come home.'

Annie put her phone down, blinking back the tears that were filling her eyes. Being pregnant was making her an emotional wreck and she hoped with all her heart that Will was right.

Chapter 17

Heath drove home, the bile threatening to rise up from his stomach. The village was crawling with police. He was off his fucking head thinking he could get away with this. What had he been thinking? Clearly not very straight. At least he had the fridges to keep her body in. They would mask the smell of decomposition. As he reached his cottage he saw the words 'POLICE DOGS' in big black letters on the side of the police van, which was parked nearby. He thought he was going to faint there and then in his car as his whole world went foggy. He parked behind it and got out with shaking legs. He forced them to walk one step in front of the other to his front door. Glancing into the van he saw it was empty and scurried the rest of the way. He heard dogs barking in the distance and wondered just exactly what they were doing.

He went into the house and the smell of fish made him gag. It didn't help that his stomach was already in knots and churning. The last thing he wanted was to eat fish, but she wasn't to know and normally he enjoyed a piece of haddock. He avoided the kitchen and went back outside to go to his workshop from the side entrance. He just hoped the dogs weren't out there because dogs made him nervous anyway. Combined with the sickness he felt and the cold sweat that had formed on his brow he might as well write 'Fucking Guilty' across his forehead in big, black marker pen for them all to see and go hand himself in. He opened the door and was relieved to see the dogs were in the distance, busy with what looked like his second grave.

Blocking it from his mind he opened the door and crept inside; he couldn't think about what they were doing out there because he had no control over it whatsoever. He did have control over what was going on in here, though, and he needed to think it through. She couldn't die yet. What if those were cadaver dogs specially trained to find dead people? He'd read all about them in an article online and apparently they could sniff out a skeleton that was twenty-five years old – it was incredible. They would probably smell her dead body from miles away, so he needed to keep her drugged up and tied up until the police had stopped hanging around the woods – he just hoped it wouldn't be weeks.

Annie was so engrossed searching through Tilly's friends on Facebook that when the hammering on the door started she jumped up, startled. Her heart began to pound. Who would be banging on her door at this time? She walked across to the utility room where the computer monitors linked up to their CCTV cameras, and looked at the one on the front door. Slumped against the door was what looked like a very worse-for-wear Stu. She tutted and went to open it. As she pulled it open he stumbled into the hall; the smell of alcohol hung around him in a thick haze.

'Sorry to bother you, Annie. Is the boss man here?'

'No, Stu, he isn't. Where have you been to get in this state?'

'That pub in the village. Can I come in and wait for him? I don't want to go home just yet – well, actually I have no home to go home to and no way of getting to it if I did.'

Annie grimaced but she had no choice. She couldn't let him go out in that state – anything could happen. He didn't know the area and he could end up falling in a stream or passing out along one of the narrow lanes where there were no streetlights.

'Come in. I'll get you a strong coffee. Have you eaten at all today?'

'Not a bite since this morning. Don't want coffee. Have you not got anything a bit stronger?'

'Sorry, we haven't bought any alcohol since I've been pregnant so it's coffee or water – your choice.'

That technically wasn't true. They had a fridge full of wine in the utility room but he wouldn't know that. She walked to the kitchen, leaving him to follow her. She looked on the table for her phone so she could text Will and tell him to come home, but it wasn't there. It had been there less than five minutes ago, so where the hell had it gone? She cursed under her breath. Now was not the time for any of her ghostly friends to be playing games. She turned to look at Stu who had managed to drape himself onto the kitchen chair that she'd been sitting on. He was staring at her, making her feel uncomfortable, so she turned away from him and made him a mug of coffee and popped some bread into the toaster.

'You're so lucky, aren't you?'

She turned to look at him. 'Yes, I suppose I am, but I know that, Stu, and I thank God every day for everything I have and for just being alive after everything that's happened.'

'Bollocks.'

Annie didn't need her sixth sense to tell her that Stu was looking for an argument. Hadn't she spent years living with a man who acted exactly the same whenever he got drunk? She looked at the telephone in the hall and wondered if she should use that to phone Will, seeing as how her mobile had disappeared. She put the coffee and toast on the table in front of Stu, who pushed the mug away, splashing coffee all over. She grabbed some kitchen roll and began to mop the spillage up. As she reached across, Stu grabbed hold of her wrist.

'What is it about you, Annie Graham, that has turned men into killers and my boss – the man who used to be my all-time hero – into a complete fucking wimp?'

She pulled her hand away from him and backed off. 'Will is on his way home; he'll be here soon. Why don't you ask him?'

Her heart was racing; she knew that on a normal day she could handle Stu, but she was pregnant and he was drunk. Men were a lot stronger when they weren't thinking straight. She backed away from him, thinking if she left him to it she could go and lock herself in the bathroom and hope she found her phone on the way up.

'Don't be shy – you can tell me. Is it all that money he has stashed away in the bank, or is he really that good in bed? Or is it you? It must be. You must be a really good fuck if men go weak at the knees for you and throw their whole lives away wanting to kill you. How about you show me just how good you are? Will won't mind; he likes the women, does our Will – you wouldn't believe how many he's had over the years since I've been working with him.'

Annie's heart was hammering in her chest. It was like listening to Mike all over again. She kept on walking backwards towards the stairs, frantically scanning the room for her missing phone. Stu pushed himself up from his chair and stumbled a couple of steps towards her.

'Come on, what do you say? You and me, we can have a bit of fun before Will gets home. You might like it better with me than you ever did with him; you never know.'

Her skin was crawling and she wanted nothing more than to walk over and boot him in the balls so hard that he'd need plastic surgery to remove them from his backside – but she didn't want to get violent unless she had to, because it might make him worse.

'I'll tell you what, Stu, why don't you take yourself and your foul mouth out of my house and wait outside on the porch for Will to come home – because you're not welcome in here. How dare you speak to me like that in my home. What do you think Will's going to say when I tell him?'

As soon as she said those last words she knew she shouldn't have, but it was too late. She'd spoken them without thinking about the consequences and the look of anger on his face warned her to move fast. She turned and ran for the stairs, hoping that because he was so drunk he wouldn't be able to catch up with her. She made it to the top step before she felt his hand lunge for her ankle. Kicking out at him she felt her foot connect with his head, but it didn't stop him. He roared in anger and grabbed it. Using all his strength he dragged her back down the stairs and she felt herself losing her balance; twisting herself so she didn't land on her stomach she fell onto her back and bounced all the way down.

Before she knew it Stu was on top of her thighs, straddling her. His hot, beer-drenched breath in her face, she tried to twist away from him. If she hadn't had her bump she would have nailed it in one – and him at the same time – but all she could think about was protecting her baby. The front door slammed against the wall and she felt Stu's weight being lifted off her as Will threw him against the wall and pinned him there. His elbow was pushing hard under Stu's neck, choking him so much that his face went beetroot red and he spluttered.

'What the fuck are you doing to my wife?'

He looked across at Annie. She shook her head.

'I'm fine, Will; I am honestly. Just a bit winded.'

He could tell that she wasn't fine at all and he drew his fist back and punched Stu in the face, making Annie wince as his nose exploded in a bright red mess. She pulled herself off the floor and ran towards Will, dragging him off Stu before he really did some serious damage.

'Leave it, Will, he's not worth it. He's drunk – he doesn't know what he's doing.'

Stu, who had fallen to his knees and was whimpering, kept on crying, 'I'm sorry, I'm sorry.'

Annie felt a searing pain in her stomach and bent over, both arms wrapping protectively around her baby. She heard Will on the phone to someone asking for an ambulance and then it all went black as the pain in her head and stomach combined, pushing her into unconsciousness.

1995

Heath was pacing up and down, not sure whether it was his nerves or excitement. More than likely a combination of both. He wanted to have another model to photograph. He'd had to bury the last girl because the electric had gone off in a power cut and the freezer didn't work properly. The smell had been horrendous that day when he'd lifted the lid – it had made him throw up all over the garage floor and he'd had to bury her that same night. He'd have enough money one day to buy a couple of those fridges they used in morgues and then it would be better. Much easier to pull them out on a tray than to try and heave them up. It was amazing how heavy even the slightest build of girl was when they were dead; he'd never expected it.

Today he was going to take photographs of this one alive then do exactly the same after she was dead, sort of a comparison experiment to see whether death made them more beautiful than life. He would put them all into his special book. One day he would be famous for his studies of beauty in death; he had no doubt about it. He checked his cameras once more, impatient for her to arrive. At least she wasn't from the village this time. It would be far too risky for that, but Barrow was a good distance away so hopefully the coppers wouldn't put two and two together – luckily they were so stupid it was unlikely. They weren't exactly known for being brains of Britain, just drinking cups of tea and watching the football.

The doorbell rang and he smiled to himself. At last she was here – now the fun would begin. Checking his reflection, he decided he didn't look too bad even if he did say so himself. He opened the door and smiled at the girl standing there. His nerves disappeared as he slipped into his professional mode.

'You found me then?'

'I did. It took a bit longer than I imagined. I'm not very good on these twisty roads and my sense of direction is terrible.'

He laughed, which made her smile and instantly put her at ease; charm was one thing he'd been blessed with, even if a conscience wasn't.

'Come in then. Let's get started. Are you nervous?'

Wendy Cook nodded.

'Don't be. I promise once you get used to it you'll love it, especially when you see how beautiful you look through the lens of my camera.'

He led her through to his studio, which was brightly lit; picking up his camera he put it around his neck. A lot more confident than the last girl, she smiled and stood with her hands on her hips. He nodded. 'Gorgeous.'

After thirty minutes he told her he needed to nip to the toilet. She'd posed on the chaise longue, on the back of a chair and on the floor. That was enough for him; he couldn't wait any longer – he was desperate to see how beautiful she looked when she was dead. He came back in. Walking over and turning the chair to face the wall, he told her to sit on it so he could get some pictures of her from behind. He snapped a few then walked over to her and placed his hand on her shoulder.

'You know you really are beautiful, such a natural. Just stay that way a couple of minutes more and then I think that's a wrap.'

She stayed facing the wall. He had to go to the toilet again he was so nervous, and he left her for a couple of minutes. When he came back in he felt the bile rise as he touched her shoulder and she slumped forward. There didn't seem to be as much blood this time, for which he was thankful. It made him feel faint and it ruined his beautiful photographs; the smell of it was enough to turn the hardest of men's stomachs.

She was all his now. He put his hands under her arms and lifted her onto the floor. He didn't want her falling off the chair and scraping her face before he'd taken his photographs – making it worse than it already was. He was going to have to clean the head wound up and use some of the theatrical make-up to try and cover it up as best as he could. At least she had long hair, which would help to cover it. He hated sloppiness and this had been rushed; there was no doubt about it. He should have taken his time to kill her and not made as much of a mess. But there was no rush now; she was all his and he could take his time.

Making sure she was dead, he pressed two fingers against her neck. She was still but her eyes were wide open and the tiny blood vessels inside them had burst with the pressure of the rope around her neck. He was furious. Now he was going to have to glue her eyelids shut because she didn't look beautiful with bright red, bloodshot eyes as well as a huge gaping wound in her head. He felt in her pocket for her car keys; he was also going to have to take the car and dump it somewhere away from here. Taking the tube of super glue from his toolbox in the garage he went back in and carefully spread a thin line of glue across each eyelid. Using the blunt end of a screwdriver handle he held them together until they wouldn't open. Then he threw a sheet over her and locked the studio, turning off the lights.

Her car was outside his house and he just hoped that no one had really taken much notice of it. By the time he got back her eyes would be set and the blood should have dried up. This one was going to be a challenge but it was worth it – or should he say, the finished result would be worth it. No one should be remotely interested in her car because there were often different clients' cars parked outside his studio. He got in and drove away. Taking it to Newby Bridge he parked it in the big car park of the Swan Hotel and left it there, right at the back in the far corner next to a huge conifer that hid it from view. Going inside he ordered a pint of lager and sat at the bar drinking it slowly. After a while he got up to use the payphone and rang Jo.

'Hello, would you do me a huge favour?'

'I'll try. What is it?'

'I've had a meeting with a client at the Swan. Would you pick me up? I've had a drink and don't fancy walking back.'

'Course I will. I was going to ask you if you wanted to come for tea?'

He swore under his breath. He wanted to go home to Wendy and have some fun but it was going to look strange if he didn't go to her house after he'd dragged her to collect him. He would just have to pretend he didn't feel well and go home after an hour.

'That sounds perfect. I can't wait to see you.'

She laughed. 'I'll be there in ten minutes and I can't wait to see you either.'

'Thank you.'

Before he could say anything else he heard the pips, signalling he was about to be cut off, so he put the receiver down and finished the last of his pint before moving to a table outside to wait for her to come and collect him and give him his alibi.

Chapter 18

2015

Kav and Cathy arrived before the ambulance. Will had phoned Kav after ringing for an ambulance – he didn't know what the hell to do with Stu, and Kav told him he'd been on his way to pick Cathy up from work so they weren't too far away. Will had Stu handcuffed to the front porch and was sitting holding Annie's hand, who he'd managed to put into the recovery position. Kav sprinted from the car, took one look at the mess in front of him and ran his hand over his shaved head.

'I bloody knew this was too good to be true. I was just thinking how wonderful it was – this peace and quiet. What's his excuse?'

Kav nodded in the direction of the drunken, mumbling Stu who was muttering apologies to the wooden porch he was handcuffed to.

'I lost it and hit him; I was so angry. I came home to find him straddling Annie, who was lying at the foot of the stairs. I didn't know if she'd fallen down them and banged her head or whether he'd done it. What the fuck was he thinking?'

Will turned to face Stu and shouted, 'What the fuck were you thinking?'

He couldn't say any more because he was scared to speak the words out loud, but if the idiot had hurt their baby or badly injured Annie then he wouldn't be responsible for what would happen to him. They heard the sound of sirens in the distance; Annie blinked and opened her eyes.

'Don't move, sweetheart, the ambulance will be here soon.'

She clasped his arm. 'The baby.'

'Don't you worry – the baby will be just fine, and so will you. Just let them take you to get checked out and don't argue. Stu, on the other hand, is not fine because I'm going to fucking kill him.'

His voice got much louder when he mentioned Stu's name. Cathy, who was standing at the gate waving the ambulance down the narrow lane, stared across at Kav who shrugged his shoulders. They watched as the paramedics loaded Annie into the back of the ambulance and Will jumped in with them. Kav went to shut the doors.

'You take care of Annie; I'll take care of Stu. We'll take him to Windermere. Can't have him booked into custody at Barrow. Someone from Kendal can come through to deal with him once he's sobered up. Do you know what you want him charged with?'

'To be honest, I don't know what's happened, Kav. Apart from seeing him sitting on top of Annie I have no idea.'

'Right, well as much as I'd like to arrest him for being a prick it won't wear with the custody sergeant. Assault for now, then we'll work on the fine print once we know.'

Will looked across at Stu, who was snivelling and crying to himself. This would be the end of his career if they pressed charges. He wasn't himself but it was no excuse for whatever he'd been about to do to Annie. Kav slammed the door shut and the paramedic drove away. As they reached the top of the lane Will took his phone out and rang Kav.

'Just take him somewhere for now to sleep it off and tell him not to move an inch until I've spoken to Annie and seen what she wants to do.'

'Your choice, my friend, but he's not coming to my house in that state – and Cathy is shaking her head with extreme vigour. Where do you suggest?'

'Take him back to Debs. Tell her the least she can do is keep an eye on him until tomorrow. This mess is partly her fault so she owes it to him this one last time.'

'Roger that.'

Will ended the call and looked at his wife who, despite having a golden suntan, was paler than he'd seen her look in a long time. He closed his eyes and prayed that she would be OK and the baby would be fine. They had to be, because they were his whole world. The ride to the hospital wasn't a pleasant one, the roads narrow and twisty, and by the time they arrived Will felt even sicker than before. This time it was a different hospital, but the same all over again – some idiot had hurt Annie. When would their lives be free from all the hassle? Annie would laugh and tell him probably never.

He went to the reception desk and booked her in once more. He didn't want to have to do this again, except for when she went into labour – then he would make an exception. His phone vibrated in his pocket and he didn't have to look to know that it would be Jake having a panic attack and wanting to know where they were and should he come. He sent him a text message telling him: no, it was fine, he would call him if he needed him. Before he got the chance to go and sit on one of the hard plastic blue chairs, a nurse came out looking for him. He followed her in, his heart beating so fast he could hardly breathe. The nurse pointed to the curtain, which was drawn, and Will pulled it to one side and felt a whole lot better to see Annie awake and holding a cardboard sick bowl.

'Sorry.'

'What are you sorry for? You've done nothing wrong.'

'I let him in. I knew he was drunk – he smelt like the slop bucket from the Black Dog. Urgh, just thinking about him makes me want to throw up.'

Will couldn't help but smile. 'I need to know what happened, even though I don't really want to think about it.'

'He started to talk really rude. He was feeling sorry for himself but then he got offensive and obnoxious. He has a huge problem with you. I had no idea he was so jealous of you.'

'What do you mean, really rude? I always sort of knew he was a bit envious; he seems to have got worse the last twelve months, though. Always getting sly digs in when he could, but I never really took them to heart. What exactly did he say?'

Annie laid her head back and closed her eyes. She had that sharp pain in the side of her head again. It was so intense it made her eyes screw up, even though they were shut.

'What's wrong?'

She shook her head. 'I don't know . . . my head, it really hurts.'

'Did he hit you?'

'No, he grabbed my ankle as I was running upstairs to lock myself in the bathroom and ring you. He tugged me too hard and I lost my footing. I bounced all the way down the stairs on my backside so that should be hurting, not my head. I didn't even bang my head.'

Will placed his hand on her stomach, spreading his fingers as wide as he could over the bump. 'Did he hurt the baby?'

'No, he didn't. He sat on my legs not my . . .'

She squeezed her eyes shut again as another wave of pain blasted through her head. This time it was accompanied by the image of the girl she'd seen in her house. It was only a fleeting glance but the girl was standing in front of her with blood dripping down the side of her head. That image was replaced with one of the woods where a man was digging a grave. Then it all went blank and she knew there was some connection between the pain in her head and how the girl died, but she needed to make sure it wasn't because she was going mad or hallucinating. If the doctor said everything was OK then she would tell Will what was going on; it might even help him identify the girl whose body had been discovered.

Will pressed the orange bell for the nurse, who appeared within seconds. 'Something's wrong. She keeps getting pain in her head.'

The nurse felt her pulse. 'The consultant is on his way. You're lucky – he was just going home before you arrived. He's going to scan the baby and then he'll take a look at your head. He won't be long. Have you any pain in your stomach?'

Annie shook her head.

'Good. I'll go and get everything ready.'

She watched the nurse disappear behind the faded orange curtain and turned to Will. 'Where is he?'

'Kav's taken him to Debs for the night until we decide what to do about him.'

'Oh my God, what a day it's been. Has Tilly turned up?'

Will didn't want to upset her any more than she already was, but she wasn't stupid and he knew she would soon find out.

'No, she hasn't. I spoke to Smithy who went to take the missing person details. I'm sorry, Annie, but she's almost eighteen. I know you're worried about her but she'll turn up. What would you be like if you had to live with Lisa?'

'I know she's a nightmare but it's not like Tilly not to even tell Ben. They're really close.'

The consultant walked in and introduced himself. He was followed by the nurse with a portable scanning machine. 'Now let me check on that baby of yours, just to be on the safe side. Have you had any pain in your stomach?'

'Just the one. It was like cramp but it hasn't happened since.'

'How long ago was this?'

'Just after I'd fallen down the stairs on my bottom, but that's OK – there's plenty of padding on that.'

The consultant laughed; squirting a large dollop of the cold gel onto her stomach, he began to move the Doppler around until he had a clear picture of the baby. They could see it moving around and its tiny heart was beating away. Will squeezed her fingers. No matter how many times he saw it, he couldn't believe that the small black and white shape that resembled an alien more than a human was their baby. After a couple of minutes the consultant passed Annie a handful of green paper towels.

'Perfect – your baby doesn't seem any worse for its tumble. However, it would be really great for the both of you if you could refrain from such strenuous activity. Now, the nurse said your head is hurting – did you bang that on your way down?'

'No, not this time, but I've had a few accidents in the last couple of years that have resulted in quite serious head injuries.'

'Now why doesn't that surprise me?'

Annie smiled at him as she felt her cheeks burn.

'To be fair neither of them were my fault. My ex-husband hit me over the back of the head with an empty champagne bottle, which knocked me out and left me needing thirty staples across the back of my head. Then last year my car went off the road and crashed into an oak tree. I was in a coma for a couple of days.'

'Really, is that it? Blimey, your poor head, it must be made of tough stuff. Did you black out earlier?'

Will answered. 'Yes she did, for fifteen minutes. She regained consciousness just before the ambulance arrived.'

'Yet you didn't bang your head, is that right?'

He shone his torch into the back of her eyes and held his finger in front of her eye, moving it from side to side. 'I think we'd better admit you and see what's going on – although there's nothing I can do tonight. But I can tell you the neurologist, who I work closely with, is on in the morning and she's excellent. She'll be able to tell you what's happening without a shadow of a doubt.'

'How do you know? They might not be able to?'

'Oh, I can vouch for her. She's my wife and she is very persistent.'

He winked at Annie and she smiled.

'Do I really have to stay here? I'd rather go home.'

'Well, I can't stop you from leaving, but then you'll just get an outpatient's appointment, which might take weeks. If you stay here and have bed and breakfast, then I'll tell my wife all about you when I go home – so she'll come see you first thing in the morning. How does that sound?'

It was Will who spoke. 'She's staying. Thank you, we really appreciate it.'

'No problem, it's the least I can do for our law enforcement officers.'

Annie shut her eyes. She was quite capable of speaking for herself, but Will was right. She should just stop here; at least that way she'd get seen quicker. If there was a problem with her brain she'd rather know about it now and get it sorted out. The consultant left them alone. He nodded at Will on his way out.

Will didn't care if she was angry with him; she wasn't going anywhere until they knew she didn't have any life-threatening injuries or diseases.

'Pass me your phone, please?'

'Why?'

'I need to speak to Ben and see if she's come home. Will, I'm worried. What if something bad has happened to her?'

'Come on, Annie, you know that apart from the disasters that happen to us it's pretty safe to live around here.'

'Do you really think so?' Annie pictured Henry Smith, the man who had stalked her then tried to kill her in the cellar of the abandoned mansion in the woods near to Ben's farmhouse, and again after his escape from the secure mental hospital. In her honest opinion she didn't think that living in South Cumbria had been particularly safe up to now; she just hoped she hadn't attracted some other psychopath who had decided to kidnap Tilly just to get to her. What if Henry had more than one helper and they were carrying out his final wishes? She wouldn't put it past him to have had a backup plan should the worst happen to him. In fact, it would make perfect sense. She was about to tell Will this when Ben answered the phone.

'No, she's not home. Lisa is in a state. I'm going to drive up to Bowness and see if I can spot her.'

Annie didn't tell him it was a waste of his time and effort; that he would be better off at home waiting for her. She knew that she would be doing exactly the same thing.

'OK, look, I've had a bit of an accident. Nothing serious but I'm in the hospital and they want me to stay overnight, otherwise I'd come with you. I'll be out in the morning so I'll ring you and hopefully she'll be home by then and oblivious to the fuss she's caused.'

'Oh, Annie, please tell me you're both fine. I can't believe it. What happened?'

'Nothing – a stupid misunderstanding – and I fell down some stairs. Look, the only thing that hurts is my pride. Don't worry about me, Ben. Please be careful and ring me as soon as she turns up.'

'Will do, and Annie, just for once, do what the doctors tell you.'

He hung up and she felt terrible for him; he didn't need to be worrying about her as well as his daughter.

Will's phone vibrated in his pocket. He took it out to see who it was.

'You should go; there's nothing you can do here. I'm fine, and I know you have a lot on at the moment.'

'Are you sure? You have no idea how much I hate walking away from you whenever you're in hospital.'

She nodded, her eyes threatening to fill with tears. She wanted to walk out with him, but she needed to rule out what was happening with her head. Tomorrow, if Tilly hadn't turned up, she could go home with a clean bill of health and try and figure out what was happening. Will bent down and kissed her lips; she inhaled – he smelt so damn good. She kissed him back then pushed him away.

'Go, work some of your magic and make everything right.'

Will didn't smile this time. She could almost see the weight of the case and worry about Tilly pressing down on his shoulders. Not to mention wondering what to do about Stu. She felt terrible.

'I truly wish I could, Annie, but sometimes even I just can't fix everything.'

He turned away from her and walked towards the exit. She had to blink back the tears that filled her eyes. Why was her life so bloody complicated? It never used to be like this. A nurse and a porter appeared at her bedside.

'Right, you're off up to the ward – even got your own little side room so at least you can have a sleep. That will be nice, won't it?'

Annie looked at the nurse, who was just trying to be friendly, and wondered if she even had the slightest inkling of what a fucked-up life the woman on the bed in front of her led. A nice peaceful sleep would be wonderful, but it was very unlikely – it would be filled with the strange sounds of patients on the ward and the snatches of sleep would only come between the worry for her niece and trying to figure out who this latest ghostly visitor was. Who was she talking about when she said he was at it again? Annie needed to figure it out, fast.

'Yes, it sounds wonderful.'

Annie lay back and closed her eyes as they wheeled her bed out of the cubicle and down towards the corridor that led to the lifts and the wards.

Chapter 19

Will walked out of the hospital. He had so much to do he wasn't sure where he should start and he was so tired of all this. He wanted to speak to Smithy again. Annie was right to be so worried about Tilly. As far as teenagers went she was a good kid; she didn't go out and get drunk or take drugs. She idolised Annie and there had been a few times she had mentioned joining the police. Will had laughed at her, telling her there was no way he could babysit two Grahams and do his own job, but he had been secretly pleased that she wanted to do something with her life. Tilly even looked a little like Annie; she had the same thick, black curly hair – although she straightened hers to within an inch of its life – and she had Annie's kind eyes.

Oh God, what if somehow Henry had made the connection and had arranged for one of his sick friends to pay her a visit? The thought made his stomach lurch and he tasted stale coffee in the back of his throat. His phone rang and he answered it to a breathless Kav.

'The stupid fucker has run off. We can't find him anywhere.'

'Where are you?'

'At the playground near to Biggar Bank Beach. We were taking him home, but he wanted us to pull over. Said he was going to puke, so I got out of the car with him . . . The next thing I knew, he'd booted me in the balls and was running away.'

'Jesus Christ, maybe he'll make his way home anyway.'

'I doubt it. He's never stopped crying the whole way here and mumbling to himself. The tide's coming in, Will. Cathy and I have looked all over and been shouting him for the last five minutes. It's so windy I can't hear a thing. I've had to get back inside the car to phone you.'

'Jesus, have you phoned it in?'

'Cathy is on the phone now to call Handling, and officers are on their way. Sorry, Will, I had no choice. What if the stupid bastard runs into the sea?'

'I'm on my way.' He put the phone down. No need to ask where exactly they were as the circus of blue and white flashing lights should give it away by the time he could get over there. He started the car and swore.

'Come on, someone give me a break. I've had enough of this shit to last me a lifetime. No more, please.'

He drove way too fast, but he didn't care; there wouldn't be anyone to pull him over because hopefully they would all be over at the beach searching for Stu. He made it across town and over the bridge in record time. There were a couple of police vans already parked up. It was so dark – the sky was full of black clouds and there was no sign of the moon. None of the streetlights were working because the council were in the process of replacing all the ancient ones with new ones. Only the bright blue lights illuminated the inky night sky.

He got out of his car and ran across to where Cathy was standing with her arms wrapped around herself, talking to the duty sergeant. A couple of officers were down at the shoreline, walking along with one of the bright dragon light torches and scanning the beach, shouting Stu's name. Will cupped his hands to his mouth and shouted, 'Stu, Stu, come out – it's OK, we can sort this out. It's just been a misunderstanding. Come and talk to me, buddy.'

Will's words were carried away by the wind and he just hoped that wherever Stu was he heard some of it. Sirens and lights filled the air as more patrols drove along to the stretch of road where they were standing, to join in the search. It was cold tonight. If he curled up and fell asleep behind some bushes or a rock he'd get hypothermia and die – that was if he hadn't already thrown himself into the sea.

'I don't think he's chucked himself into the sea – for one thing it's too cold, and Stu's a bit of a wimp.'

Kav took the words from Will's mouth; Will nodded in agreement.

'I think you may be right; that means he's probably hiding somewhere. We need a dog.'

Cathy nodded. 'There's one on the way. Shite, we should have just locked the stupid bugger up. We try and do him a good turn and this is how he repays us. I sure as hell don't want him doing any harm to himself, even if he is number one on my hit list.'

Will took out his phone; it was almost dead. 'Has anyone phoned Debs? He might be making his way there.'

There was an almighty screech as the panda car that was driving round the corner at high speed slammed its brakes on. They all turned in time to see Stu, who had stumbled across the road from wherever he'd been hiding, as he hit the bonnet of the car. His body flew up into the air and landed with a sickening thud in the middle of the road. Will ran as fast as he could towards the lifeless form, dread forming in the pit of his stomach. All he kept saying under his breath was 'please God, please God'. He reached the bloody, crumpled mess that was his colleague and knelt down, pressing two fingers against his neck for a pulse. There was a lot of blood but there was also a pulse and he felt a sigh of relief escape his lips. Within no time at all an ambulance arrived and he felt himself being lifted up by Kav's strong arm and led away.

'Let them do their stuff, Will. He'll be fine eventually. It might take a little while – but you never know, that knock to the head might just give his brain enough of a shake to do him some good.'

Will looked up at Kav's grim face. He wasn't smiling; in fact he looked grey in the blue-tinged light. Cathy was standing with her arm around the officer who had been driving. He looked as if he was going to pass out.

'I didn't see him; he just stumbled out. I swear to God I didn't see him.'

'Son, we all saw him stumble into the road. None of this is your fault, but we have to go through the procedures – you know how it is. There was nothing you could do. Do you understand that?'

He looked at Cathy.

'I repeat, this isn't your fault. Stu was the worse for wear. He's been drinking a lot and was hammered; he wasn't thinking straight. Say it after me, "This wasn't my fault."'

'This wasn't my fault.'

'See, I told you it wasn't. It's a complete mess – I'm not going to deny that – but you can stop blaming yourself right now because it wouldn't have mattered who was driving; the outcome would have been the same. If some idiot is going to throw themselves in front of a fast-moving car they're going to come off a lot worse than they ever imagined.'

There was some heavy banging and clattering as the lift was lowered from the ambulance. Will felt guilt weigh heavy in his heart. This was all his fault – if only he hadn't been so angry with Stu. Kav looked at his friend.

'Will, you'd better stop that now or I'll set Cathy on you as well.'

'But this is all my fault.'

'How is this your fault? Did you tell Stu to go and get so steaming drunk that he thought it was a good idea to go to your house and assault your wife?'

'No, but . . .'

'But what? The only person who is at fault here is Stuart, and I'm afraid if he makes it then he's going to have plenty of time in hospital to mull over what a fucking prick he's been.'

'I just feel responsible.'

'Well, stop it. You have enough to worry about. How's Annie?'

'She's fine. They're keeping her in overnight for observations.'

'And she agreed? There's a first.'

Will smiled at this. The ambulance drove off with the unconscious Stu and he watched it leave. He wanted to go with it but the duty sergeant had gone instead. A car pulled over and the duty inspector got out. He pulled his cap on, which was immediately blown off by a gust of wind. Will stopped it with his foot then bent down and picked it up, handing it to him.

'Sir.'

'Will, how is he?'

'A mess.'

'Jesus, what a night to pick to swap my shift. I should have known better. There are plenty of witnesses to say that this was all his own fault – is that right?'

Kav nodded. 'Yep, there are.'

'Dare I ask what he was doing in a car with you and the inspector?'

'He turned up at Will's house in Hawkshead very drunk just as we were leaving; we offered him a lift home. He said he was going to be sick so I pulled over and he ran off.'

The inspector nodded his head. 'Bloody idiot. Has anyone called Debs?'

Will showed him his phone that was still in his hand. 'I was about to when he ran into the road. I think you'd better send an officer around to be fair. I know they've split up but she's still going to be upset.'

'If I can find an officer who isn't involved in this mess then I will; crash scene investigation are on their way. We'll sort something out. Can you all get your witness statements to me by tomorrow night and I'll pass them on?'

Will nodded. He walked back to his car, which was inside the perimeter of the cordon of blue and white police tape, which was whipping itself into a frenzy with the wind. Thank God he was parked behind where it had happened so he could leave – he needed to get out of here. He felt as if he should be the one to go and speak to Debs. He jogged back to where the inspector was talking to Kav and Cathy.

'I'll go and speak to Debs, let her know in case she wants to go up to the hospital.'

'If you're sure, that's much appreciated.'

Will wasn't sure, but it was the least he could do. She would have been expecting Kav to be dropping Stu off half an hour ago and news travelled fast. He didn't want her reading about it on the internet. The officer standing at the end near to where he was parked lifted the tape up for him to drive through and he waved his thanks. The radio was playing George Michael, singing about how he needed faith, and Will had to admit that at this moment in time he needed a whole lot more than faith.

The thought of passing the news about Stu on to Debs made him feel even queasier than he already was. For the time being he forgot all about Tilly being missing; he even forgot that he'd had to leave Annie in hospital once again. All he could see was the image of the crumpled, bloodied mess that was Stu.

Chapter 20

It was getting dusky. Heath looked out of the window to see a solitary police van parked near to the woods. It still made his heart race, despite the fact that he knew they couldn't be any closer to finding the killer or else his house would have been crawling with police. There would have been a welcoming party waiting for him earlier with Tasers and the full works, but it didn't stop the bitter taste in his mouth. What was he going to do with the girl? She couldn't die just yet; he was going to have to keep her alive and run the risk of his wife hearing her – or even worse, the police.

He wondered how long she would last in one of the morgue fridges, if he turned them off at the mains so she wasn't slowly frozen to death. Even if he only put her in it for a few hours at a time – as long as he remembered to take her out, feed and water her. It might just work; they would be pretty soundproof and the dogs wouldn't be able to smell her inside one of those. If she did suffocate then he'd just switch it on at the mains and freeze her. For the first time in hours he smiled to himself; it sounded like a great idea. Jo had gone upstairs for a bath, telling him that she felt unwell and wanted an early night. He'd waited for her to go then he'd scraped his fish straight into the bin, covering it up with some kitchen roll. The smell was offensive, but at least that would throw the police dogs off kilter as well. He made a couple of sandwiches and took two cans of cola from the fridge. He would go and sit with her. Make her promise not to make a noise so he wouldn't have to hurt her.

He carried the food through into his studio then locked the door behind him. Pocketing the key, he did the same with his darkroom door, glad he had spent a full afternoon installing a lock now. He listened at the door before opening it; there was no movement inside so he opened the door and stepped into the narrow room. Placing the sandwiches and drinks on the counter he locked this door as well, just in case she felt brave and tried to escape. He tugged on the light pull so the single bare bulb spread some light onto the floor. She was lying on her side in a different position to when he'd left her. Kneeling next to her, he listened to see if she was breathing. After what seemed like forever she let out a small sound and her chest rose and fell again. He nodded in approval, then he shook her arm to try and rouse her. She didn't respond so he shook her even harder. He lightly slapped her cheek and she let out a small groan. One eye opened and she stared at him for a moment before the realisation of who he was struck fear into her and she flinched away from his touch. He smiled, then tucked both his hands under her arms, pulling her up into a sitting position.

'Come on now, there's no need to be so stubborn, is there? I thought you might be hungry and thirsty, so I've made you a sandwich.'

He picked up the plate to show her. She shook her head and muttered something into the gag that was tightly bound across her mouth.

'Sorry, I didn't catch a word of that. Now, if you are a good girl, I'll remove the gag for a while so you can eat and drink, but if you make a sound I'll kill you.'

He didn't shout or speak in a menacing tone; he just stated the facts and Tilly found this far more scary than if he'd been in her face threatening her. He bent over her and undid the knot at the back of her head, pausing before he completely removed it.

'Did I make myself clear? You do understand that if you make a sound I'll strangle you with my bare hands. I've done it before, so bear that in mind, should you think I'm full of shit.'

She nodded her head – anything to get this foul-smelling rag out of her mouth. Her jaw was aching she had been clenching against it so hard. The release as he pulled the material from her mouth was wonderful and she found herself yawning and stretching her lips. He lifted a finger to his lips and she nodded, which in turn sent a wave of nausea running through her body. He offered her a drink of cola; she shook her head, afraid he was going to drug her again. But he popped the tab and opened it in front of her eyes and she felt the cold spray as some of the brown sticky liquid hit her cheek. Once more he offered it and she nodded; her mouth was so dry that her tongue was stuck to it. She took a sip, managing to dribble some down her chin, and he paused; lifting his sleeve, he wiped it clean.

'Take your time, there's no rush. Neither of us is going anywhere tonight.'

He lifted it again and this time she gulped it greedily; she hated fizzy drinks but this tasted divine, her mouth was so dry. He put the can down and lifted a small triangle of a sandwich to her lips. She wanted to tell him to fuck off and shove it where the sun didn't shine but her stomach betrayed her, letting out a loud growl. She didn't know what was going on, but she did know that she needed to keep her strength up if she was going to find a way to escape from here. If she acted like some hero and went on a hunger strike, by the time she had an idea of what she was going to do to escape it wouldn't matter; she wouldn't make it a hundred feet and would end up collapsing on legs that were too weak to support her body.

She slowly chewed the ham sandwich, all the time trying to take in her surroundings. She noticed the lock on the door with no key and realised that he must have it in his pocket. He kept feeding her and she felt more helpless than she'd ever felt as a child, even when her mum had suffocated her with her bossiness. At least she'd known deep down that the woman was trying her best to look after her. Tilly wasn't stupid. She knew that this man was holding her a prisoner for some ulterior motive and she also knew that it didn't seem as if it was going to end all that well unless she did something to stop it.

Until she could think about what to do she needed to be good and do what he told her. She didn't know how angry he could get, or how violent. She ate the sandwich and whispered *thank you*.

He nodded his head in approval; at least she was polite. He'd never kept one alive this long before so it was a learning curve for both of them – he'd been expecting her to become all feisty with him and start screaming. After a few minutes he leant over and retied the gag.

Tilly knew why they were called gags now – because this one made her want to retch. She let out a small cry but stopped herself from making any more noise. The room swam once more and she knew that somehow he'd managed to drug her again. As the blackness took over she felt herself sinking to the floor. He caught her before her head hit the cold concrete, but she wasn't aware of that because her world had turned silent.

He gently laid her down on the floor then, prodding her with his foot to make sure she was unconscious, he stood up and opened the door.

Across the room he could see his bank of fridges. He went and opened the door to one of the lower ones and slid out the gurney that was attached to the rails inside. Going back into the narrow darkroom he struggled to pick her up but he managed it. After throwing her over his shoulder he carried her across to the open fridge and manhandled her onto the tray. He slid the door shut, locked it and grabbed the cans and plates from the darkroom; he needed to get rid of the evidence.

He had almost made it to the kitchen when he remembered he hadn't switched off the electricity and he ran back to pull the plug out. Stupid – he could have killed her. And then he laughed to himself. Well, wasn't that the whole point?

Chapter 21

Will had hugged Debs long and hard before he'd left her in the hands of her sister. She'd been unable to stop sobbing and was blaming it all on herself and he felt like crap. If only he'd handled it better, maybe none of this would have happened. He got in his car, but couldn't go straight home like he wanted to, like he knew he should.

It had been a long time since Will had been to see Annie's brother, who lived in the farmhouse where it had all begun in Abbey Wood. He no longer had to worry about leaving his car and parking at the bottom of the long woodland path that led to the house. The huge wooden gates had caused no end of trouble getting access to the farmhouse and the abandoned mansion in the woods near to it when Henry Smith had been killing young women and stalking Annie. Jake had put an end to them the night he and Kav had driven through them at full speed to come and rescue both him and Annie. Will shivered. He tried to repress the memories of the night and most of the time he succeeded but tonight they didn't want to stay hidden. Maybe it was because of the time of night; it was almost midnight and the moon was hidden behind the clouds, making the woods behind the shiny, new automatic gates look ominous.

He got out of his car and pressed the number on the keypad to open them; by the time he'd turned around and climbed back in they were almost open. He nudged his car through and carried on driving up towards the house, not having to worry about fiddling with the old rusty chain and multiple padlocks that used to adorn it. With his car headlights on full beam he concentrated on the narrow road; he didn't look into the trees just in case he caught a glimpse of white. Although he hadn't personally met the ghost of Alice Heaton, Annie had and Alice had come to Annie's rescue a few times when Will hadn't been able to. Although if you had asked him if he believed in ghosts he would have laughed it off, he knew from Annie's experience that they did exist. And Will would always be indebted to Alice and little Sophie who had been there for him not that long ago when he'd been stabbed and left to bleed to death by Megan Tyler at the lake house. As he took the right-hand fork, the farmhouse – which was illuminated from almost every room – beckoned him, drawing him in. He parked next to Ben's battered pick-up and Lisa's shiny white Mercedes; as he slammed his car door shut, the barking began and the kitchen door opened. The black bundle of fur came racing towards the gate just as Will stepped through it. She took one sniff of Will and rolled onto her back for a scratch.

'I don't know, Tess. I see your guard dog skills haven't improved any since we last met.'

The dog lay there, her tail wagging, letting Will rub her belly.

'Tess, come on, girl.'

Ben appeared at the door. He looked haggard and Will noted his red eyes.

'I hoped you were bringing her home.'

'Sorry, Ben, I should have rung to let you know I was coming. I just wanted to see you both. See if there's anything I can do.'

'Don't worry, it's not your fault. Thanks for coming, Will; I appreciate it. How's Annie?'

'Oh, you know your sister. If there is the smallest chance of a bit of drama there she is.'

They both laughed and Ben clapped his arm around Will's shoulders.

'At least she's getting our money's worth from the NHS.'

'I think she's getting half of Barrow's money's worth, if you ask me. She's fine. They'll let her out in the morning after she's seen a consultant.' Will didn't want to worry him more than he already was, so didn't go into detail.

'There's been an incident over on Walney with one of our officers so I haven't been able to speak to Smithy yet to see where he's up to with his inquiries.'

Ben arched an eyebrow.

'Sorry, I meant Officer Smith who came to speak to you earlier.'

Ben led him into the kitchen where he went to the fridge, took out two bottles of lager and offered one to Will, who took it without a second thought. He unscrewed the cap and almost downed it in one gulp.

'It's been that sort of day, eh?'

Will nodded, watching Ben as he fiddled with the cap of his, peeling the silver foil from the lid before twisting it off and taking a sip.

'Can you tell me what Officer Smith did and said before he left?'

'He said that he wasn't unduly concerned about Tilly; that she was almost old enough to do her own thing anyway and that she'll probably be home tomorrow without even thinking of all the fuss she's caused.'

Will sucked in his breath. What an idiot. How much more insensitive could Smithy have been – honestly, some of the coppers in that station wouldn't know how to hold a conversation or be tactful if their lives depended upon it.

'Tell me what you think, Ben; you are the closest person to her. Do you think that she would do this without a second thought for your or Lisa's feelings?'

Ben shook his head. 'No, she wouldn't, Will. She's never been like that. It's not as if she had any reason to lie. I don't understand it. I mean, I know Lisa is a lot more controlling than I am but still there was no reason for her to lie about where she was going. It doesn't make sense.'

'No, it doesn't. I completely agree with you. I'll arrange to have her phone traced and see if we can get a location on it. If she didn't go to Bowness for a job interview where do you think she could have gone?'

'I don't know. I haven't got a clue.'

'Can I have a look around her bedroom? There might be something in there I can find to give us a bit more information than we already have.'

'You can but Lisa has already rooted through her drawers and wardrobe like a demented woman. It's a mess; there's clothes everywhere. Tilly will go mental when she sees it.'

'Where is Lisa?'

'She passed out about thirty minutes ago. She'd already had almost a full bottle of wine by the time I came home and then she started on the gin. By the time she took two sleeping tablets she couldn't string two words together.'

Will knew that Lisa liked to drink but tonight he couldn't blame her. Maybe she was hoping by the time she woke up tomorrow, Tilly would be home and they could all carry on with their lives. Hell, he was wishing that was going to happen but there was a gnawing feeling inside his stomach telling him something was wrong, badly wrong. Will left Ben, who was now sitting at the kitchen table, staring at the bottle of lager in front of him. He went upstairs to the room he knew was Tilly's because that was the room that Annie had slept in when she had been house-sitting.

The light was already on and he pushed open the door. Lisa had almost ransacked the room; it looked as if burglars had been in. Underwear was strewn all over the bed and floor, the make-up that was on the top of the dressing table was spilt all over the place. He turned and checked that Lisa or Ben weren't behind him; the landing was silent. So he pulled out a pair of blue latex gloves and stepped inside; if there was a diary or something personal he knew from past experience that teenagers could be good at hiding things from their parents.

He pulled each drawer out and felt underneath to see if there was a book taped to the underneath. Then he lifted the mattress and bed up but there was no diary. Putting the bed back down he noticed the stack of *Vogue* magazines on the floor by the bedside table. He picked one up and flicked through the pages; there was nothing in it but adverts for expensive designer clothes and accessories, not to mention stick-thin models. Lily, his dad's wife, always had copies of this and other similar magazines lying around their house – but she could afford to buy the expensive stuff they were advertising. Ben and Lisa weren't short of money but they weren't exactly rolling in it either.

He looked around the room to see if Tilly had lots of designer stuff; she had a pair of Ray-Ban sunglasses on her bedside table, which were next to a Michael Kors watch – these were pricey, but affordable; they weren't Chanel or Gucci.

Will looked in the wardrobe and checked inside the handbags that were on the back of the door, but they only had half-eaten packets of chewing gum, hair bobbles and some bus tickets. He went back down to speak to Ben, who was still staring at his bottle of lager.

'I couldn't find anything.'

Ben laughed. 'That's maybe just as well – if I told Lisa you'd found Tilly's diary that she couldn't and I let you take it away, I think she would kill me. In fact I know she would kill me – no doubt about it – and then she would kill you. She can be a psychotic bitch at times, as much as I love her.'

'Does Tilly like expensive designer stuff? I noticed the stack of *Vogue* by her bed.'

'Only what most of her friends have, although Lisa would be able to answer that question better than me. I wouldn't know my

Chanel from Primark; it's all the same to me. That's why I drive a battered shit heap and Lisa has a Mercedes.'

Will smiled. 'It's just you don't get many girls her age reading *Vogue*. I always thought it was for older, rich women.'

Ben shrugged.

'I'll get going. First thing in the morning I'll review what's been done and I'll be in touch with you. If you think of anything ring me, OK?'

'I will. Thanks for coming – I know you already have more than enough on your plate. I saw the paper tonight. It said you were in charge of investigating the skeleton that had been found. Then our Annie and her addiction to hospitals – oh, and you never said, how's the officer that was in the accident earlier?'

Will had no idea how Stu was; he was waiting for a text from the duty sergeant.

'He's not good, stumbled in front of a police car.'

'Shit, really? Oh that's bad for whoever was driving. Do you know the injured officer?'

'I do. I work with him almost every day.'

Ben nodded. 'Life is truly shit at times.'

'You can say that again, but he's in good hands. Tomorrow my main priority is finding Tilly and bringing her home.'

'Thank you, Will.'

Will left. Tess was in her dog bed next to the radiator fast asleep. He smiled. She was a good dog even if she was the world's worst guard dog.

By the time Will arrived back at their cottage he was exhausted; he'd had to drive with the radio at full volume and the windows down so the fresh air blasting his face had kept him focused on the narrow, winding roads that led to Hawkshead. He pulled into the drive and checked his phone; he had three messages from Jake asking if he wanted to stop there, how Annie was, if they'd found Tilly, and was it true Stu had thrown himself in front of a moving panda. He replied.

No thanks I'm home now. Annie is fine. No sign of Tilly and yes Stu has managed to splatter himself all over Biggar Bank.

As he got out of the car he rang the duty sergeant to get an update on Stu; he was told that he was alive, but in a bad way. He was still in the resuscitation room but was due to be transferred to intensive care soon. Will turned his phone onto silent; he'd had enough of shit news for one night. If Annie needed him she could ring the house phone. He walked inside and shut the door. The house was so quiet without Annie; he'd got used to her being at home since she'd gone on the sick and it felt strange not to hear her constant chatter. He kicked off his shoes and made his way upstairs to the bathroom. He needed a quick shower because he was convinced he had Stu's brain matter splattered all over his jacket and hands, even though he'd wiped them several times with the hand gel he kept in the glove compartment of his car.

He got into bed and reached out to pat Annie's side. Pulling her favourite pillow towards him, he stuffed it under his head. He could smell the faint, lingering notes of her perfume. He turned on his side so he was facing the window and didn't see the faded outline of the young woman with long hair and blood dripping down her head who was standing on the landing watching him.

Chapter 22

Tilly couldn't move. Her head felt too heavy for her shoulders to support. She blinked a few times then opened her eyes. It was pitch-black. She had no idea what time it was – in fact, she had no idea where she was. She knew he'd moved her from the cold, concrete floor she'd been lying on, but she felt like she was lying on some kind of trolley. Hope filled her heart; maybe she was in the hospital – he might have changed his mind about whatever he had been going to do and phoned an ambulance. She moved her hands what little she could and they immediately hit a cold metal wall; she bent her elbow and that hit the metal wall on the other side. She couldn't see anything, she couldn't move anywhere, and it was so cold. Trying to kick out her feet, she didn't have to move them far before they made a dull thud as they hit another wall.

A chill spread over her. She still couldn't see very well, but her eyes had adjusted slightly and she realised she was in some kind of container. Panic filled her chest as she wondered if she was already in a coffin. Had she died? Is this what happened to those people you heard about on the news? Everyone thinks you're dead when really you're wide awake inside your own coffin with no one to hear or help you. Tears fell from her cheeks but then she realised that coffins weren't generally made of metal or had metal trolleys inside them to lie on. The reality of where she was hit her and she tried to scream but the stupid, stinking gag in her mouth stopped her from uttering more than a muffled sound.

She knew where she was. She watched plenty of those ghost shows on the television; in fact she was addicted to them. Especially the ones where they would go exploring in abandoned asylums or hospitals. They nearly always made one of the presenters climb inside the empty fridges that were kept down in the morgues for the dead bodies. She began thrashing around as much as she could as the panic took over. She had to get out of here before she suffocated. What if there was a dead body in the fridge next to hers? As she moved her head from side to side an explosion of pain made her see stars and she blacked out.

Annie hadn't slept much, short bursts in between the noise of the nurses in the wards going about their business and patients ringing bells and groaning. As the sun came up she felt relieved. As long as the consultant didn't take forever she would wait, but if they weren't here by eleven she was leaving. She was convinced the pain in her head was something to do with the dead girl she kept seeing – when Mike had hit her with the empty champagne bottle, he'd cut the *back* of her head open. Then when she'd come off the road and hit the tree it had been the *front* of her head. This pain was more to the side, above her left ear, and for all she knew she might have just passed out last night with the shock of Stu doing what he did and her ungracious tumble down the stairs. Plus it wasn't unusual for pregnant women to pass out for no reason whatsoever. A gentle knock on her door snapped her out of her daydream.

'Come in.'

Jake walked in and grinned at her, relieved to see she wasn't bandaged up or cut and bruised. 'Seriously, Annie, this has to stop. Have you got an obsession with doctors or something? It's any excuse for you to spend a night in here.'

'Bugger off. Did you only come to insult me?'

He shook his head and brought out the grease-spotted brown paper bag from behind his back. Closing the door behind him he came and sat on the end of her bed.

'No, you ungrateful wretch, I brought you food: hot, greasy sausage muffins and hash browns. You want some or you want me to leave and go and eat it on my own in the car like a saddo?'

He waved the bag in front of her nose and she felt her stomach rumble. She hadn't eaten for hours.

'Jake, I love you. I'm sorry – please stay.'

'Ha – you love the food, more like, but seeing as how I love you and you had a tumble I'll forgive you.'

He passed her a muffin.

'Here, you'd better eat that before the nurse comes in and catches us. I always feel guilty bringing food into hospital, although you would think I'd have learnt to get over it the amount of time you spend in them.'

Annie didn't speak. She was too busy eating so she nodded in agreement with him.

'Here, what about Stu then? I couldn't believe it when I heard. Will must have told you. I mean, what an idiot. Poor Ian will never get over that; he's had to go on the sick. Apparently it was a right mess; there were blood and guts everywhere.'

She felt the mouthful of muffin she was chewing stick to the back of her throat and she had to force herself to swallow it; suddenly she didn't feel so hungry. 'What do you mean? I don't have a clue what you're talking about. What happened?'

'Well, I only know half the tale but apparently Kav and Cathy were driving him home because he was too pissed to get there himself. He told Kav he was going to be sick, so he pulled over near the play park on Biggar Bank and Stu did a runner. He ended up hiding from everyone so they called all available officers to go over there and look for him. As Ian turned into the street Stu threw himself in front of the panda car. Apparently there was blood and brains everywhere. Why would he?'

Jake never got to finish his question as Annie threw back the sheet and climbed out of the bed. She ran into the small bathroom and threw up the muffin she'd just eaten. Jake knocked on the bathroom door.

'Are you OK? I didn't realise you still had morning sickness.'

Annie couldn't think straight. Oh God, poor Stu. What an idiot. What was he thinking?

'Be out in a minute.'

Her stomach lurched again as a vivid picture of the scene last night filled her mind. She could almost smell the blood; it was everywhere. Squeezing her eyes shut against the pictures, she blocked them and tried to clear her mind. *Think good thoughts, think of flowers, the apples in the orchard, the baby. Think of anything but that.*

She stood up and washed her mouth out with cold water, splashing it all over her face. She needed to see Stu, tell him she wasn't angry with him and that she realised now he wasn't himself last night. As she walked out of the bathroom Jake looked at her. She waited for an insult but none came.

'Are you OK? I don't just mean generally; I mean are you OK as in your whole, mad life? Is there something you're not telling me, because I'll find out so you might as well just spill now and save the hassle.'

She sat back down on the bed next to him; resting her head against his shoulder she began to tell him about last night, the woman she kept seeing in her house, and as she finished she told him about Tilly. She sat upright. She needed to speak to Ben . . . then she remembered she didn't have her phone; it had disappeared last night. To say she was annoyed with Will was a bit of an understatement, but she knew why he was avoiding talking to her; he wouldn't want her to worry over Stu when she already had Tilly to worry about. She borrowed Jake's phone and rang Ben, who answered. His voice was hoarse and she knew he'd been crying. Bugger – no sign of her niece then. She talked to him for five minutes then ended the call, saying she needed to ring Will.

She did ring him, but his phone kept on ringing and ringing. She knew he was incredibly busy or might be driving but it irked her that he hadn't answered. Then the door opened and in he walked. She took one look at his pale, unshaven face and felt bad for being angry with him. He walked over and wrapped his arms around her and she squeezed him back.

'I thought I'd have got here before Mr Social Media, but obviously he didn't have to come as far.'

Jake pretended to look hurt. 'I didn't come to gossip. I brought her some breakfast. Which she very ungraciously threw up, but never mind. I'll forgive her because I love her.'

Will turned to Annie. 'How many times have you been sick? Have you told the nurse?'

'Just the once and no; it was the shock of hearing about Stu – nothing else. I'm fine, I promise.'

Jake stood up, letting Will sit next to her.

'I'll be going then. Ring me when they let you out or if you need a lift home.'

He kissed her cheek and she smiled, grabbing hold of his hand.

'Thank you for my breakfast. Sorry I didn't manage to keep it down.'

He laughed. 'You're forgiven, but next time I'll bring fruit. Actually, there'd better not be a next time because I'm sick of this place.'

'Me too, Jake.'

He left them, closing the door behind him, and Will pulled her close.

'God, I missed you last night. I woke up and thought it had all been a bad dream and then it hit me that it wasn't. I feel like shit, but he got me so mad – I can't believe I hit him – and then . . . trying to kill himself . . . What got into him, coming into our house and treating you like that? I don't understand.'

'Alcohol is what got into him. Have you ever seen him drink more than a couple of pints, ever? Doesn't he always cry off and go home to Debs after a couple of hours on a night out?'

Will nodded. 'Tilly hasn't turned up either.'

'I know, I've just spoken to Ben – he sounds awful. Why does everything in my life happen at once? It's like someone has said, "Right that Annie Graham has had enough of a nice time, now let's break her heart and make her feel like shit again."'

Will couldn't answer her because their life was exactly like that. The last four months had been perfect – no worries or stress – and now they were back to square one.

'Come on, things will get better. Stu, I'm afraid, has been the master of his own disaster and it has a lot to do with Debs having an affair. His actions are his alone; you didn't tell him to do what he did to you. Kav didn't tell him to throw himself in front of a fast-moving car. When Stu wakes up he has to realise that all of this was his own doing.'

Will didn't add that Stu might not wake up. He'd been to see him in intensive care before he'd come to see Annie and had spoken to the consultant, who had told him at the moment they were taking it hour by hour. Debs had been coming out from the ward when he'd turned up, her eyes bright red and full of unshed tears. He'd given her a hug and told her once more how sorry he was. It hadn't been that long ago that he'd had affairs and changed his girlfriend as often as he'd changed his socks – until the day he'd set his eyes on Annie and something inside him had changed. He didn't know what it was that had turned him from the equivalent of a male slut into a completely besotted, one-woman man but he was glad that it had. She had changed his life completely and for the better; he had never felt so happy.

He knew that Debs would blame herself for the rest of her life and no one should have to carry that sort of guilt around with them. Things happened and sometimes for a reason.

'I'm doing everything I can about Tilly. I've requested a cell site analysis of her phone so we can get a location on her. Maybe she just needed to get away for a few days, have some time to herself and think about her life. Let's face it, Lisa is not an easy woman to live with; she's so opinionated and overpowering. I'd have run for the hills years ago. I have no idea how your Ben puts up with her.'

Annie cracked a smile. 'Me too. He must take after me.'

'What's that supposed to mean? I hope I'm not like that to live with?'

'Don't be daft – I meant the me before you. Afraid of what might be waiting on the other side, staying in a violent relationship because it was the easiest thing to do. You, Will Ashworth, are the very best thing that has ever happened to me and I still can't believe that you love me so much.'

He pulled her close.

'And you are the best thing that ever happened to me . . . except for the murderers – I'm not too keen on your ability to attract them from a hundred miles away, but everything else about you is wonderful.'

Chapter 23

Heath didn't eat his breakfast. Jo had made him bacon, tomatoes and poached eggs – his favourite – but he couldn't face it. His stomach was in knots; the police were still out in the woods and there was a girl in his fridge. He looked across at Jo who was tucking into her food without a care in the world. She stopped eating and put her cutlery down.

'Is there something wrong with your food?'

He shook his head.

'Are you feeling OK? It's not like you not to eat. Would you like some toast and jam, or I could make you some cereal?'

The plate whistled past her head, narrowly missing her ear, and she jumped as it hit the cupboard behind her and smashed into pieces. The egg splattered everywhere; mixed with the tinned tomatoes it looked like someone's brains had just exploded all over her white kitchen cupboard. Drawing into herself, ready for his fist to come flying at her next, she bowed her head and waited.

His chair scraped as he pushed himself back; he was raging inside at the injustice of it all. Just when things were starting to look promising the fucking police were on his doorstep. He should have buried the bodies much further away. Why after all this time had this happened? He wanted to finish his photo collection.

He pulled on his coat and boots and stepped outside the back door, needing some fresh air. He needed to clear his mind and seriously think about what he was going to do. There was a lone policewoman standing in the distance behind the tape that was stretched across a huge area of the forest. He wondered what would happen if he took her and added her to his collection. There were three more empty fridges in his garage. His feet began to walk over to her and his mind became blank as he fixated on her bright yellow body armour and blonde curly hair. She had her head bent, staring down at her phone; obviously she was bored of standing in the middle of nowhere, so what were the police still doing here? He carried on walking towards her. She had her back to him and he was very good at moving without making a noise. He knew these woods like the back of his hand.

As he got closer the radio clipped to her body armour began to ring and he heard a man's voice speak on the other end. She relayed how bored she was to him and asked him what time he would be there. Heath was almost behind her when he stood on a twig, which snapped in half. The noise was like a gunshot as it echoed through the trees and she screamed loudly, turning around. His hands flew up in the air.

'Jesus, I'm so sorry. Did I scare you? I just wanted to know if you needed a drink or something. I live in the house back there.'

The man's voice on the radio was frantic.

'Are you OK? What's wrong? I'm just parking my car.'

'I'm fine. Sorry, just had a bit of a fright.'

The man cut her off and she looked up at him then started to laugh. 'Sorry, I guess you could say I'm just a bit nervous out here on my own. It gets a bit spooky but thank you and I'm OK for now. I'm hoping to get relieved soon. I've been here four hours and I really need the toilet.'

Heavy footsteps came crashing through the woods towards them and they both turned to see Will with another couple of PCSOs following behind him.

Will stopped when he saw that Claire was in one piece and hadn't been injured or hurt herself in any way. She looked at him and smiled.

'Aw, did you run all the way from your car to see if I was OK? That's really sweet of you, Will.'

Heath recognised the policeman standing in front of him from the other day and felt his knuckles clench into tight, white fists.

Will couldn't catch his breath and bent down. When he could finally put a sentence together he stood upright. 'Yes, I did – you gave me a heart attack. People normally scream like that when there's something wrong.'

Claire blushed. Will looked at the man standing there and realised it was the guy from the cottage.

'Is everything OK? Can I help you? You shouldn't be out here – it's a crime scene.'

Claire spoke up. 'He was just checking if I needed anything, like a drink.'

'Sorry, I was just being polite. As long as you're OK then I'll get going. If you ever need anything just come and knock on the door. There's always someone in.'

He completely blanked Will, turned around and walked back towards his house. His heart was racing even more. What was wrong with him? He'd very nearly screwed everything up and he hadn't even realised what he'd been about to do. Was this what losing your mind felt like, taking stupid risks? Was he wanting to get caught, because he was going the right way about it if he was. He began to walk faster; Jo had better have cleaned up the mess; if that nosy bastard copper came to the house he'd have a field day.

Will waited until the man was out of earshot. 'Do you know him at all?'

'Nope, never seen him before in my life. Why?'

'There's something about him and I can't put my finger on it – well, apart from the fact that I think he beats his wife and he lives directly in front of our two graves.'

'Really? That's a shame because he seems nice. I mean he's nice to look at and his face is friendly. Are you sure he batters her?'

'Well, not one hundred per cent but I'd bet a month's wages on it. What do you mean, he looks nice? You should know that you can't judge anyone by their appearance.'

'Ah, that's easy for you to say. I can't help but like the handsome guys. I like you, don't I?'

Will laughed. 'Cheeky, you know you drive me mad sometimes.'

'Yes, but I make the best coffee, don't I? Anyway, at least he came to see if I needed anything, unlike a certain person who left me here for hours on my own and bored shitless.'

'Erm, I didn't leave you here for hours. I had to go see Annie. I've not long since come on duty. You can blame that on your sergeant. I'm not guilty of that one.'

'I suppose so. How is she doing? Is there any news on Stu? I can't believe it. Why would he do something so stupid?'

'Annie's fine, thanks. I wish I could say the same about Stu. Right, these two are going to take over from you and I'll drive you back to the village hall where you can make me one of your fabulous cups of coffee.'

She signed her name in the scene log and handed it over to Tina.

'At least you have someone to talk to, unlike me who was left here all by myself.'

'Yep, I suppose so, but it's still not exactly laugh a minute, is it?'

Claire followed Will, who had turned around and was now walking back to where he'd abandoned his car thinking she'd been getting attacked.

'So what's the deal? It's OK for me to be out here on my own, scaring myself witless, but those two get to stay together?' Claire said gesturing to Tina and Phil.

'I have a bad feeling about that man from the house. I don't trust him one little bit and I'm sorry you were left out here on your own – because he's now become my number-one suspect. But don't you breathe a word to anyone just yet; this is between me and you. How good are you on the old computer?'

'I'm shit-hot.'

'Right, well, I want everything on him. Get on Facebook, Twitter, anything else, and find out how long he's been running his photography business. Who are his friends, what is his favourite food.'

She looked at him.

'How am I supposed to know what he likes to eat? I'm not that good.'

Will laughed. 'That was a joke, Claire.'

They got in his car and she scribbled notes down in the back of her book. A wave of sadness washed over him. This was Stu's job and to give him his due he was pretty good at it.

Heath went into his garage, locking and bolting the door behind him. It was a good distance away from where the police were in the woods, so hopefully the sound wouldn't carry. He walked across to the bank of fridges and placed his ear against the door of the one he'd put her in last night. He couldn't hear anything, which was good in a way – he hoped that she'd suffocated, because it was too much hard work trying to keep her sedated and under control. He opened the door and shone a torch inside; the girl was still breathing but she was either unconscious or faking it. He poked her shoulder but she didn't flinch.

Pulling the sliding shelf out he stared down at her. She didn't look too good; her face was pale and she was cold to the touch. He wondered if he'd overdone it on the drugs or whether she had hypothermia. Loosening the gag he took a bottle of water, lifted her head up and held it to her lips. It spilt all over her but she coughed; her eyes flickered open but they were confused. She had no idea where she was.

'Are you hungry? Do you need the toilet?'

She tried to move her head but couldn't; it felt too heavy and she was so cold. Inside her mind she screamed the word 'No!' at him but nothing came out of her lips except for a small murmur.

She almost looked dead and he felt the stirring of excitement in the pit of his stomach – he would take some photos of her, now, in this state of semi-consciousness. This was interesting; he'd only ever photographed alive and dead. She looked almost as beautiful as the girls who he'd killed. Not quite, because her skin wasn't quite the right pallor, but it was pretty close – and she didn't have a gaping head wound that he'd need to cover up. He would call these pictures his sleeping beauty portraits.

Lifting the bottle of drugged water, he poured some more into the crack between her lips. Grabbing a rag from the side he gently dabbed at her mouth and chest, mopping up the droplets of water. Her eyes fluttered and once more she sank back down into a deep sleep; she was so sweet and innocent. She might just be his favourite up to now. He removed the gag from her neck and brushed her long, black hair. He wouldn't be able to wrestle with her whilst she was on the narrow drawer to put the white, cotton nightgown on her but he could undress her and drape a simple white sheet across her naked body. He preferred them with some dignity; he didn't like nudes and would balk at the forty-something-year-old women who would come to him for sexy photoshoots to give to their poor, unsuspecting husbands.

By the time he'd finished she looked like a work of art, a very fitting tribute to the times when death was looked upon as beautiful and a celebration. He snapped away, taking photo after photo and getting more excited with each one. He blocked out the incident earlier in the woods, his anger with Jo, his anger about everything . . . and concentrated on taking the best photos of his career. He couldn't wait to develop these and see how they turned out.

Chapter 24

Annie kissed Will then got out of his car and stood at the gate to watch him drive away and leave her once more. She waved at him and felt her heart sink. She was so fed up of being on her own, but at least he was working in the village today so he wasn't far away. She walked towards the house and felt a cold chill settle over her back; for a moment she was scared to lift her head and look at the upstairs window in case it was Betsy Baker staring back at her, but forcing herself to, she sighed to see there was no one there. Something was going on but she hadn't had the time to sit and try to figure it all out. Her phone rang and she answered it; her brother sounded awful.

'I thought you should know that Mum's here; she arrived earlier. I didn't know she was coming, but she said that she couldn't stay in France when her granddaughter was missing.'

'Oh, OK, that's good. Have you heard anything at all?'

'Nothing. The last update was that they were sending an officer to the bus station to see if there was any CCTV footage of her getting onto the Bowness bus. It's like she's disappeared into thin air. I don't understand it.'

There was a loud knock in the background.

'I have to go; the police are here. I'll ring you back after I've spoken to them. How are you, Annie?'

'I'm fine. Don't forget to ring me.'

The line went dead and she felt the familiar churning that began in her stomach whenever she thought about her mother. Everything she'd been through the last couple of years and the woman had not even phoned her to see if she was still alive, never mind dropped everything to leave her life in France to come and visit her. She hadn't even come to her and Will's wedding, preferring to send a quick Facebook message instead. No card or gift had ever arrived from her. Not that she wanted her to buy her anything or drop everything to come and see her – it was the principle of the matter and the fact that her love for Ben was far more obvious than her love for her. Annie would never treat her children like that, ever.

As she walked inside the cottage she felt bad. Tilly was missing; why the hell couldn't she use her sixth sense to find out where she was? What was the point of this psychic crap if she couldn't use it when she really needed to? She threw herself down onto the sofa and closed her eyes, taking deep breaths as she tried to make her mind empty of everything so it was a blank canvas. Far easier said than done, and took a fair few attempts before it was a blank canvas. Her eyes felt heavy. She hadn't slept much last night in the hospital. She kept saying Tilly's name over and over until she felt the heaviness take over as she began to fall into the place between waking and full sleep. No matter how many times it happened to her, it always felt strange.

She found herself getting off a bus near to the village car park. Her bag was heavy on her shoulder and she hoisted it up, then she looked around, not knowing exactly where she was. Pulling out a scrap of paper she looked down at the roughly drawn map with some writing at the bottom and a phone number. She walked towards the main road, where she forked left and headed away from the village centre. As she passed the shop near to the toilets she noticed her reflection and felt her heart sink; this wasn't her niece, Tilly – it was another girl. One with long, blonde hair that was scrunched up in a high ponytail and a pair of neon orange leggings that made her wince. She had a baggy, black batwing T-shirt on and a pair of white oversized sunglasses. This girl was also painfully thin; Tilly had a much fuller figure. She couldn't pull away from her, though, because she knew that deep down there was some connection between this girl and her niece. So she stayed, following the girl along a quieter stretch of road.

She heard the car before she saw it. It was noisy and she guessed it would be some kind of four-by-four. She guessed right, as a battered Land Rover came around the bend in the road and slowed down. It stopped when it reached her and the man inside it asked if she was lost. Annie felt her pulse racing and wanted to scream at the girl to run but she couldn't because this was a replay of what had once happened and there was nothing she could do to change it. She was helpless and could only watch. The man inside was young. He was wearing a baseball cap and black sunglasses so it was hard to see his face, but he had a big smile, which instantly put the girl at ease.

Annie couldn't hear their conversation but the next thing she knew he leant across and opened the door from inside the car and she climbed in, pushing her sunglasses on top of her head. She was so pretty and young that it made Annie's chest ache for her innocence; something bad was going to happen to her. Correction – something bad had already happened to her. The car drove off in a plume of black smoke and she began to cough; in fact she coughed so hard that she thought she was about to choke and her eyes flew open as she gagged on the dryness in the back of her throat. She heaved herself up from the sofa and walked into the kitchen; opening the fridge she took a cold bottle of water from it and gulped greedily. Once the coughing had subsided she picked up a pen and paper from the table and wrote down what she'd seen – there was some connection between the man and Tilly; she was sure there was. If she could find out who the girl was or why she'd got into a car with a stranger, that would help.

She closed her eyes and tried to see if she could make out the number plate; she had been so busy looking at the man she hadn't really taken much notice. Squeezing her eyes shut she forced herself to focus on the number plates but the one at the front was covered in dried mud, making it impossible to read, and then when it had driven away there was no plate on the back. Her niece was in trouble and the sooner she could figure out the connection between them the better. It was time to ring Will and tell him the truth.

'I think Tilly is in danger. You need to upgrade her missing person's case to high risk.'

'Should I ask how you know this?'

'Well, you can, but I don't think you'll want to know the answer. Please, Will, I'm being serious. I saw a young girl similar to her get into a battered old Land Rover with a man she didn't know and I think that girl might be one of the bodies that you found. I need to see pictures of the girls that you think could be them, like, *now*. I only glanced at them briefly the other day and my brain doesn't seem to want to remember much.'

'I'm at the village hall. Can you come here?'

'Yes, I'll be there soon. Will – whoever killed them is local or was local. So you need to start looking close to home, and I think that they still live around here.'

He couldn't say much because the detective inspector was hovering around him, and even though Annie was a colleague as well as his wife she had nothing to do with this case and he wouldn't want her interfering. Knowing him, he'd report them both to professional standards because that was exactly the kind of man he was.

'I thought as much, and I agree; however, I can't talk right now – but I'll speak to you soon.'

He hung up, making her realise that now wasn't a good time for him or for her to be putting him in an awkward position. She wondered what had been written on that scrap of paper below the roughly drawn map; it had been so small she hadn't been able to make it out. She thought about driving the short distance to the village, but then decided against it; if she walked it would buy her some time so that whoever had been hovering around might have left and she could speak to Will.

As she left the house she wondered how Jo was today; reaching the village hall she saw the assortment of cars and clocked the super's Land Rover. Not wanting to put Will in an awkward situation, she decided to walk the other way. It wouldn't hurt her to check in with Jo, see if she was OK and make sure her bully of a husband hadn't been getting too handy with his fists. It was much cooler today, which was a relief; the burning-hot sun had been nice on holiday, but it wasn't the same when you had to walk around in it. Finally Jo's cottage came in sight and she walked towards it. After knocking on the front door, she waited and waited. Surprised there was no reply she walked around to the side of the house where Jo's husband's studio had its own entrance. There was a car parked in the drive so someone was home. She knocked on that door even louder; there was no reply.

Too tired, and now desperate for the toilet, she knocked once more. This time she heard a door bang from inside and then footsteps echoed down the hall towards her. Relieved that she could use the toilet after all, she waited for the door to open and grinned, hoping to see Jo – but it was her husband who opened the door. His face was red and his white, sweat-stained T-shirt was untucked from his jeans. He had stubble that hadn't been there yesterday and he looked a complete mess.

'Oh, I'm really sorry to bother you. I was looking for Jo?'

'She's not in. I think she went shopping.'

'Ah, never mind. Sorry again, but can I ask you a huge favour before I walk back – would you mind if I used your toilet? Being pregnant is a nightmare. I can't go ten minutes without needing the loo.'

A scowl spread across his face, making him look much more menacing than he had the last time she'd met him, and she felt the tiny hairs on the back of her neck stand on end. Her early warning system was kicking in, but she ignored it because he faltered and then gave her a huge grin.

'Of course you can. Sorry. I was busy in the darkroom, so I never heard you knocking. Come in. I'll show you where the toilet is.'

Annie followed him inside, closing the door behind her. There was something about him that seemed so familiar but she had no idea what. He led her down a dark corridor, which opened up into a huge, light-filled studio with solid oak floors and white walls. Along one side was a mirror that almost filled one wall.

'Wow, you have an amazing studio. I didn't expect it to look like this at all.'

'Thank you. I've worked long and hard to get it just right. It's a bit of a pain being out in the middle of nowhere, but it doesn't seem to make any difference to my business. I still get plenty of clients. In fact if you want that baby bump portrait you really need to get booked in before I can't fit you in at all – I'd hate to let you down.'

'I will. I haven't seen much of my husband lately – he's been working a lot – but I'll ask him after and definitely let Jo know.'

He pointed to a door in the corner of the room and she smiled at him, crossing the floor to get to it. There were two huge framed portraits on the wall and she stopped to look at them. As she stepped closer she felt her spine tingle and a chill made her shiver. It was the girl from her vision, she was sure of it – only she looked as if she was asleep. Annie tilted her head and the shock of what she was looking at hit her so hard she felt her legs tremble as they threatened to give way. Aware that he was watching her every movement she stepped back, forcing herself to smile at him. As she did she noticed a familiar black Vivienne Westwood bag underneath a chair in the corner of the room; it was exactly like the one she'd bought Tilly for her birthday. It even had the same black and gold cat keyring attached to the gold chain. Annie frantically tried to work out how her niece would know this man or for what reason she would be here.

'They are beautiful photos. Are they recent? I like how they almost look asleep.'

'Thank you. No, they're old ones but I really liked the composition and the lighting on those two. I've come a long way since then, but I like to keep them there to remind me of the early days.'

She nodded and walked towards the toilet door, trying not to let her legs betray how she really felt. Scared to speak she opened the door and stepped inside, sliding the tiny brass bolt across, a bolt so tiny even with her swollen stomach and ankles she would be able to kick it in. She had seen enough dead bodies in her time to know that those two girls in the photographs on the wall were well and truly dead. She lifted the toilet lid up and sat down, pulling her phone from her pocket. She needed to buy herself some time and to get hold of the police, because outside the toilet door was the man she had no doubt had been the one she'd seen in her vision and who had killed then buried those two girls in the woods. He also had something to do with her niece's disappearance.

She pressed the switch to make the phone go onto silent and dialled Will's number, but there was no signal. The sickness that had been churning inside her stomach rose up her throat. Next she tried Jake, then she dialled 999 but there was no signal to connect her. Typing out a message to Will she pressed send but the little red circle telling her there was no network appeared. Standing up, she flushed the toilet and pushed the phone down into her bra; hopefully when she moved out of the toilet into a more open area the message might send automatically. She washed her hands in the tiny sink, trying to think about what she was going to do, then she realised that the only thing she could do was pretend everything was normal and she had no idea who he was or what he'd done. She needed to walk out of here because she was in no position to fight him, not without getting hurt or worse still letting the baby get hurt. She opened the door to see him standing over by the long bench, messing with one of his cameras.

'Would you like a drink before you go?'

'No, thank you, I'll only need the toilet again. Honestly, I had no idea when I found out I was pregnant that it meant spending nine months with backache and wasting more time in the toilet than on the sofa. I've taken up far too much of your time already. Thank you so much – I was busting.'

He smiled at her and she began to walk across to the door that he had led her through. It wasn't too far away; she just had to stop acting like a freak and get to it. She didn't give the pictures a second glance this time and had almost made it to the door when he spoke behind her.

'Tell me, Annie, what do you really think about my photos? You looked a little shocked after you'd studied them. What did you see in them that no one else ever has? And believe me, there have been a lot of people in this studio since I decided to put those two extra-special photographs on my wall, and no one has given them more than a fleeting glance. I'd be interested to know why they stand out for you.'

'I think they're fabulous. I was a little – and please forgive me for being so rude – but I was surprised by just how good you are. I was kind of expecting you to be average, if you know what I mean.'

He laughed. 'I should take that as some kind of backhanded compliment then, should I? Are you sure you wouldn't rather wait for Jo? I could take a couple of test shots of you while we're waiting, see what you think of them. You could even take them home to show your husband how good I am.'

'I can't – sorry. I've just remembered I have an appointment with the midwife and she'll be expecting me.'

She could feel the fine film of sweat that was forming on her brow and she knew that her voice sounded strained.

He nodded. 'If you're sure. I don't have anyone booked in this afternoon because they cancelled at the last minute, and Jo could be a while yet. It's just you and me.'

He gave her that big smile, the one his much younger self had given the girl in her vision, and her heart felt as if it was going to explode straight out of her chest. Annie knew that he knew she'd made the connection.

She turned to open the door to the outside world – to her freedom, to Will who she would get to come back with a search warrant and a team of men with very big guns . . . but she knew deep down that he wasn't going to be letting her leave any time soon. Her hand clasped the cold brass handle. She was so close to her freedom, but before she could pull it down he was behind her. He wrapped a rope around her neck and pulled it as tight as he could. Her fingers flew up to the taut rope, pulling at it, trying to free it from her neck. He walked backwards, dragging her with him, and the pressure on her neck made the room swim.

She lifted her foot and kicked her leg out behind her as hard as she could. It connected with his knee, giving her enough time to break free. With all her might she ran back towards the door, but he reached out for her arm; grabbing tight hold of it he yanked her and she felt herself begin to fall. Before she hit the floor he was there with a piece of white rag that had been soaked in some foul-smelling liquid, and he pressed it against her nose and mouth – making her gag. She opened her mouth to bite his hand, but he shoved the rag straight into it then punched her in the face. The world swam as a hundred hot pins and needles burned her eye socket and this time she couldn't stop herself from blacking out.

Chapter 25

Jo put the groceries onto the conveyor belt and stared across at the headlines screaming out from the front page of the local newspaper. She looked up at the rest of the papers to see similar headlines and she felt sick. Those poor souls had been buried behind her house in the woods for all those years and she never had the slightest inkling. Well, technically it was Heath's house; she'd moved in with him, selling her cottage to fund the build for the studio, leaving her with very little money. She did have a tin hidden at the back of the cupboard with almost two thousand pounds in – her emergency get-away stash – but she'd never had the guts to take it and use it to actually get away. Twice she'd come close, but then her nerves had got the better of her and she'd talked herself out of it. Weren't all men thugs and bullies? She had nowhere to go and not enough money to start over again.

The cashier had to ask her to pay twice, she'd been so absorbed in her daydream. Her cheeks burning, she'd apologised, taking the money from her purse and handing it over. As she wheeled the trolley across to the counter at the back of the shop to pack her bags she'd been oblivious to the queue behind her and hadn't noticed her old boyfriend, the doctor, standing behind her. As she put the last of the shopping into her bag for life she felt a warm hand brush against her shoulder and she jumped, turning around. If Heath was here she'd be in trouble for taking so long that he'd had to come looking for her. The relief must have shown on her face when she saw it was Paul and immediately he apologised.

'I'm sorry, Jo, I didn't mean to scare you. Is everything OK? You seemed so distant.'

She tried her best not to, but she couldn't help it – the tears filled her eyes, burning them, and before she knew it they began to roll down her cheeks. Mortified, she grabbed her bag and dashed out of the shop. She almost collided with a group of nine-year-olds on a school trip; muttering her apologies she realised that she sounded like a madwoman and wondered if he would have her committed to an insane asylum. Maybe that was what she needed; at least it would get her away from Heath. As she briskly walked away from the shop she tripped over the uneven kerb and fell to the ground in a muddle of tins of tomatoes, broken eggs and orange juice. Two strong arms lifted her up and began to check her over to make sure she wasn't injured.

'Are you hurting anywhere?'

She shook her head, wanting the ground to open up and swallow her and the crushed shopping that was scattered at her feet.

'Wait there. Don't you dare move.'

She flinched and he reached out to touch her arm.

'I meant don't run away again. We need to talk. But if you don't want to, then you really don't have to . . . but I'd like it if we could.'

He didn't look up at her because he was too busy salvaging what shopping he could. When he straightened up he shook his head.

'I can't believe that I've stood back and watched you for so long. I don't care about your husband or what he thinks. You've had a shock and I'm taking you back to the surgery to make sure you're OK and not hurt. We need to talk, and if there's a problem then I want to help you. I can't stand to watch you lose yourself anymore. Look what he's doing to you, Jo.'

She didn't trust herself to speak. It had been so long since she'd been able to speak freely that she was afraid once she did she wouldn't be able to stop. Paul took her by the arm, leading her away from the crowd of kids who were all arguing and shouting outside the shop, and walked her towards the surgery and his home.

Will had come out for some fresh air and witnessed the whole thing. He had been about to run to help Jo up when the doctor – who he only knew because of Annie's many appointments – beat him to it and had picked her up. For a minute he wanted to applaud them; they looked much better suited than she did with the man she was married to, and he would bet that the doctor didn't believe in beating women any more than Will did. He found himself rooting for Jo, hoping that she would open her eyes and make the move away from her husband like Annie finally had before it got too bad.

The surgery wasn't far from the shop and before long Paul had his key out, had the front door open and was ushering her inside. Instead of taking her into his consulting room, he led her through the small, deserted waiting room and into the lounge at the back of the house where he gently sat her down. He went out of the room and came back in with a small glass of amber liquid. Jo shook her head.

'Drink it – doctor's orders.'

'I don't drink. Heath doesn't like it.'

'I don't care what he doesn't like. I'm asking you as a friend to drink it, not him.'

With hands that were shaking she took the glass from him, lifting it to her lips. She pulled a face and he nodded his head; then she tilted her head and downed it, sticking her tongue out and coughing. Passing the glass back to him she shuddered. 'Urgh, that was foul.'

'All the best medicine is. You should remember that from when you were a kid.'

He laughed and felt his heart fill with joy at the smile that spread across her face; suddenly she looked more like the Jo he used to know. Sitting down next to her he took hold of her hand; he expected her to pull away from him but she didn't.

'Look, I know this is none of my business. God knows I've kept my nose out for more years than I wanted to – but I can't do it anymore. I can't bear to see you like this. I know that he hits you, bullies you and makes your life a misery. What I don't know is why you let him . . . but that's easy for me to say. You need to get out of there before he kills you – because he will. It's just a matter of time. Each time I see you the injuries are worse. He never used to hit you where it could be seen, but now he doesn't seem so fussy. He's worn you down to a shadow of your former self. Have you looked in the mirror lately? You always had a lovely figure but now you're just skin and bone. No wonder you bruise so easily.'

She didn't want to speak because she knew once she did it would all come out, but the brandy had warmed her up, soothed her a little.

'Don't you think I know that? I've thought about it more times than I care to remember over the years, I really have – but I have nowhere to go if I left. I know for a fact that he'd come looking for me and kill me. He wouldn't think twice about it. As much as I have a crap life I still love being alive, I enjoy living in this beautiful place, the warmth of the sun on my face and singing out of tune to the radio . . . I don't want to die just yet.'

'Then please let me help you. Why don't we phone the police and tell them everything? Hell, if we walk fifty yards down the road there's a village hall full of them. If you give a statement and he's arrested he won't be allowed to come near you.'

Jo laughed. 'You always were such an optimist; that's what I loved about you when we were dating. That might work for a day or two, but then do you really think he's going to let me walk away from him? He'll find a way and come after me, then he'll kill me – and you, if he finds out you talked me into it.'

'How do you know? They might just be empty threats. Most men are shameless wimps when faced with the harsh reality of prison.'

'If he thought he was going to prison for giving me a good few slaps now and again then he would want to make it worth his while. Thank you for caring, Paul, I truly appreciate it, but there's nothing I can do – it's hopeless.'

She stood up because her stupid eyes were filling with tears again and she didn't want him to think she was a complete loser.

'What if I help you? You can come and live here with me. I have three spare bedrooms so you can take your pick. I don't mean as anything other than a friend. I also have a state-of-the-art security system because of the drugs kept on the premises, so he wouldn't be able to get near you because I'd be here to stop him and the police would be here in minutes.'

'Why would you want to do that for me? Why would you want to put yourself in so much danger? I'm not worth any of the hassle or heartache that I'd bring with me, Paul.'

'Isn't it obvious why?'

She shook her head. She had no idea. She didn't know if he was married, divorced . . . hell, he could even be gay for all she knew. It had been a very long time ago that they'd been lovers and it had only been a brief relationship that hadn't lasted more than six months.

'I love you, Jo, I've always loved you – but you would never let me close enough to make it clear, and back then we were both so young. Then you got together with Heath and at first I thought it was OK, that I could cope because I was so busy being newly qualified and a junior partner in the practice. I didn't have time to be lovesick so I let you get on with it, even though deep down I was broken-hearted. I did marry eventually, years later, but she was never you and she left me three years ago for a lawyer – would you believe it? Anyway, what I'm trying to say is that I can't stand watching you shrink into yourself anymore – you were always so loud and funny. So kind and caring, not to mention passionate. I'll help you to get away from him. I promise you I won't let you down.'

She didn't know what to say. She had never in a million years expected this when she left the house an hour ago to buy some eggs.

'What about the scandal? Won't it hurt your practice?'

'This lot in the village get excited about a missing dog, so yes there might be a bit of gossip, but nothing that either of us can't handle and with the discovery of those remains I'm pretty sure we won't be in the limelight for very long. Come on, Jo, what do you say – I'd love to see the woman I fell in love with all those years ago find herself again.'

He had hold of her hand and was now kneeling in front of her. She forced herself to look into his dark brown eyes and nodded.

'I can't just up and leave right this minute. I need to go back and get some things together. He's been so preoccupied lately that he might not even notice what I'm doing. As soon as he locks himself into his studio I'll ring you to come and get me. I'm not telling him anything. I'll just pack an overnight bag.'

For the first time in over ten years she felt a spark of hope, that her life might just be about to change for the better. Paul grinned, then bent down to kiss her cheek.

'I think you've made a very wise decision. I have some holidays booked for the end of next week so we can get away. I was going to stay here and sort the garden out but we could go anywhere you like – and for now I'm more than happy to be friends. I don't expect you to jump into bed with me; I just want to help you get your life back.'

This time the tears did fall but they were tears of hope and joy – the thought of being her own person and free was almost too much to believe. She couldn't wait to tell Annie; she'd known from the moment they'd met that Annie knew a kindred soul when she met one. Jo had also known that they would become great friends, and to think that she would be able to visit her whenever she wanted without the shadow of Heath looming over her made her smile even more. She stood up and hugged Paul.

'Thank you so much. I'm just checking – you do realise that he won't let me go without a fight, don't you?'

'Yes, I do, but nothing would give me greater pleasure than to dish out everything that he deserves. Of course I would only resort to violence if I had to. I was never the fighting kind, but I do have a good left hook.'

He winked and Jo pulled away.

'I'd better get back now because I've already been far too long. I don't want him to suspect anything.'

He crossed to the desk in the corner of the room and picked up a mobile phone, handing it to her.

'I bought this after the last time I spoke with you because I was so worried. It's only a cheap, unregistered pay-as-you-go but I've topped it up and programmed my number and the police's into it. Keep it hidden from him and if you need me then ring me. I'll be here. Oh, and leave it on silent so he doesn't know about it.'

'Thank you so much – I will.'

She tucked it into her pocket – that small bundle of black plastic was the lifeline to her new life and she would never let it go, or let Heath find it. She made her way to the front door and picked up the bag with what was left of her groceries inside. Too excited at the prospect of finally being able to get away from him, she never thought to bin that bag then go back and replace the damaged contents.

Chapter 26

Jake had taken it upon himself to check the CCTV cameras at the main bus stop in Bowness to see if Annie's niece had got off the bus at any point yesterday from when she left her house until the time Ben had reported her missing. He was sitting with a bottle of Diet Coke and a huge tuna salad, because his normally kind and caring husband, Alex, had hinted that his sleek, toned six-pack was turning into a slightly flabby four-pack. Jake had spent twenty minutes this morning looking at his reflection in the mirror after his shower. He'd always been slightly vain; he couldn't help it that he'd been blessed with thick, black hair and good looks. Since Alice had come into their lives the gym had become far less appealing; instead he'd rush home from work to spend time with her and Alex, who was lucky enough to work from home so they didn't need full-time childcare. It wasn't his fault he had a huge appetite; he liked food.

He wondered how Annie was – she was always on a diet; she'd be able to lend him some of her slimming books. In fact he would drive through to see her as soon as he'd watched this last bit of film. He was up to almost seven p.m. and hadn't seen anyone that even resembled Tilly getting off the bus – with her long, black hair, she was quite easy to identify. There was no way she had come to Bowness on the bus. The phone on his desk rang and he answered it to a breathless Smithy.

'Got a location for her phone. Can you go and do an initial search? If you can't find it I'll get a task force to come in and do a fingertip search of the area.'

'Where?'

'In the area of St Mary's church. Do you know it?'

Jake inhaled. He did indeed know it – and far too well. It was where he'd had his first encounter with the supernatural and watched Annie do battle with the scariest thing he'd ever seen in his life. It was also the place they'd buried Betsy Baker's remains when they'd dug her up from Annie's front garden. Something wasn't right; for a place of worship that church sure attracted a lot of trouble. He sighed, relieved they might have a tangible clue but also wary of going to the churchyard on his own.

'Yes, I do. I'll go and have a look around the grounds now but they're some size. I'll get back to you.'

He put the phone down, snapped the plastic lid back on his salad then went and put it back in the fridge. He was starving but not that hungry for rabbit food. He wondered if Father John would be in – he always had the most amazing cakes. He might just have to give his door a knock for a catch-up, and of course a slice of homemade cake. His stomach let out a loud growl at the thought of some sugary, covered-in-buttercream delight. He didn't bother getting the van keys off the board; he would walk the short distance to the church – at least that would count as exercise.

Annie would wet herself laughing if she could see him now. He would go and see her as soon as he'd finished up with this. He hoped they found Tilly soon because the worry was giving him heartburn. He missed Annie like crazy and she would tell him the truth about how bad he looked if he asked her, because apart from Alex she was the one who spent the most time lusting after his body. He left by the side door of the police station, avoiding the busy front desk area, which was full of tourists wanting to report their lost cameras and phones. As he walked up the street, the spire of St Mary's came into view. He walked through the gates and looked around. How had her phone got here? He didn't think she'd actually been here and it was all a bit too strange. If Tilly hadn't stepped foot in Bowness then someone had put her phone here, and if someone had dumped her phone there was a reason for that. It hit him like a brick – someone had taken her and was trying to cover their tracks. He typed Smithy's collar number into his radio and waited for him to answer.

'None of this makes sense. I'm telling you now – someone has her. She hasn't run away at all. She's been abducted.'

'Have you found her phone?'

'Not yet but I've checked the train and bus CCTV – there is no sign of her coming into Bowness, and she doesn't drive or have access to a vehicle. We need to upgrade this because someone is holding her against her will and we need to find out, like, yesterday.'

'Fuck, I'll go see Kav. This needs CID, not some plod with a shitload of shoplifters and angry neighbours to sort out.'

'Tell Kav to phone me.'

Smithy ended the call.

'Good afternoon, Jake. What brings you here to visit on your own? Where's my lovely Annie?'

Jake jumped at Father John's voice.

'It's a mess, a right bloody mess. Sorry, Father.'

'Don't worry, son, I've heard much worse. What's a mess? Is Annie OK?'

'Yes, for a change she's fine, but her niece is missing and now we've traced her phone – which is showing up as being in the church grounds or somewhere nearby.'

Father John's tanned face turned white as he pulled a pink iPhone from his trouser pocket. 'Mrs Phelps found this behind her husband's grave this morning. I was about to wander down to the station to hand it in; I meant to do it this morning but I've been busy. I'm sorry, Jake, I hope I haven't messed everything up?'

He held the phone out to Jake, who pulled a small plastic evidence bag from his pocket and put the phone into it without touching the plastic casing.

'Sorry, it will have both mine and Mrs Phelps' prints on it. I just assumed it was one of the local teenager's or a tourist's. You know what they're like.'

'Don't worry, Father, that's brilliant – thank you so much.'

He pressed the home screen from outside the plastic back and was relieved to see a picture of Tilly giving her best pout appear. Good, at least it was her phone. Then he rang Will and left him a voicemail.

'Will, my friend, we have a major problem. I've found . . . well, actually, Father John has found . . . Tilly's phone in the churchyard. I've checked the train and bus cameras – there is no sign of her coming into Bowness at any point. I think someone has her, and that they dumped her phone to throw us off her track. Ring me back. I'm driving through with it. Where are you?'

'Jake, will you let me know what's happening? Are you sure Annie's in no danger?' asked Father John.

Jake smiled. 'No, for once our very pregnant Annie is safe and sound back at her house. She's not in work at the moment – and is in fact driving us all mad because she's bored. I'll let you know. Thank you for this, but I need to go now.'

'Take care, son. I hope you find Annie's niece safe and sound.'

'I will, Father, and so do I.'

Jake jogged back down to the police station. He needed a van now. Damn, it always went tits up when he went out on foot. As he got back to the station, out of breath and sweaty, he ran straight into Cathy.

'Whoa, what's the rush, big man?'

'What do you mean, big man?'

'As in tall, muscular, big hunky man. What's up with you?

Feeling a bit sensitive today, are we? Is it your time of the month?'

She started to laugh at her own joke and Jake shook his head.

'Nothing. Do you know where Will is? Father John had a phone handed to him and it belongs to Annie's niece who's missing.'

'Hawkshead village hall last time I heard, drinking coffee and trying to pretend he knows what he's doing.'

She walked away, then stopped dead and turned around. 'What's her phone doing in the churchyard? Where is she?'

'If I bloody knew that I wouldn't be panicking, would I? Bollocks. Forget it, I'll go find him myself.'

'Hang on, we need that churchyard searching properly, Jake, in case there's anything else of hers there.'

Jake nodded. 'Like what? Yep, good idea. You sort that out, boss. I never thought of that.'

He grabbed a set of van keys and ran out towards the door.

Cathy muttered under her breath, '*Like a dead body, you idiot, Jake.*' She rushed to her office, telling the two PCSOs in the refs room to leave their lunch and get to the church.

'Do not – I repeat, *not* – let anyone into St Mary's churchyard. I don't care if there's a funeral or a wedding, it's out of bounds to everyone.'

'Including the priest?'

'Yes, including the priest.'

They both looked at each other but stood up to walk the short distance up to the church.

'And take a roll of crime scene tape with you in case there's more than two ways in; block it off and guard it with your lives.'

'Yes, boss.'

Cathy barged into her office and began placing calls to get the nearest task force team and a dog handler here. Once she'd organised that she phoned Annie, who didn't answer, and left her a voicemail. Then she rang Kav and voiced her fears to him. Today had started off OK, but now it was about to go down the shit pan quicker than she could imagine – and that cheese and onion pie she'd had for her dinner was now giving her killer heartburn, and she had no indigestion tablets with her. Time to go find a rookie and send them to the shop. Today was going to be a long one.

Jake rang Annie's mobile, which went to voicemail, then he rang the house phone – which also went unanswered. He didn't think it was strange at this point because he could never get a mobile signal on a good day when he went to visit Annie. She could be asleep. Or out shopping, or driving, so he left her a garbled message to ring him. Then, turning on his blue lights so he could get through the traffic, he put his foot down. He wanted to speak to Will before he left. They couldn't afford to mess around – this was serious, and he just hoped they weren't too late.

Chapter 27

Annie gagged. She had no idea where she was – but wherever it was, it was cold and so very dark. She opened one eye; the other had swollen shut. At least she was still alive, so there was a bonus to all of this. She couldn't think straight. What had happened? She tried to move her hands but they were tied in front of her. Shifting her shoulder it hit a cold, metal surface right next to her. Rolling slightly the other way her other shoulder did the same – she was in some kind of box. Kicking her feet they clanged against more metal. A wave of sickness made her head feel light and she squeezed her eyes shut.

She had called to see Jo . . . The image of the girl from her vision and the dead girl in the photo in Heath's studio filled her mind. Oh shit, she was in big trouble. And so was Tilly, because that had been her bag stuffed under the chair. She tried to think . . . Everything was fuzzy. It was hard enough trying to figure out what she was going to do to get out of this situation without anything else popping into her head. Where was she? Did he have ready-made coffins in his garage for his victims? If he did that was some pretty fucked-up shit, and where was Jo – did she know about her husband? Annie's stomach churned. Maybe poor innocent Jo wasn't the victim she'd been portraying after all. She knew that women could be just as dangerous and lethal as any man could. Hadn't it been a woman who had almost killed Will?

She closed her eyes trying to think what she could do. A cold shiver ran down her spine. It was freezing in here – and then it hit her. She was in a fridge. One that had been built for the sole purpose of storing dead bodies. How many times had she been to the path lab and watched Matt the pathologist open a drawer and pull out the sliding tray with a body on. She kicked against the metal with her feet, fear taking over her rational thoughts. She needed to get out of here, and *now*. She carried on kicking, but nobody came.

Worn out, and crying tears of frustration, she stopped and heard the faintest bang on the wall next to her. Shuffling towards it, she pressed her head against the cool metal and listened. It happened again, slightly stronger than the last one. She tried to shout with the gag in her mouth but it was hopeless – all that came out was some mumbled offering. A similar sound came through the wall and Annie knew then that there was a good chance it was her niece. She closed her eyes and prayed that it was, because at least it meant that they were both still alive and there was safety in numbers as long as he kept them both that way long enough for her to figure out what to do.

The thought filled her mind once more: did Jo know what he was doing? Had she known all along her husband was a sick and twisted killer? The more she thought about it, Annie didn't believe that she did. There were couples who liked to kill – look at Henry and Megan – but they were thankfully few and far between. Jo had seemed genuinely embarrassed about her situation and Annie had to hang on to that, because the thought of her being a party to all of this was too much to bear and would send her over the edge.

Jo walked home, eager to get back and decide what she was taking with her to Paul's – although she didn't own very much.

After all this time, he still loved her – it was unbelievable. She no longer felt like a trapped bird in a cage because soon she was going to be free; she was actually going to be able to have a life again. One that wouldn't be shrouded in secrecy and loneliness.

As she walked into the house she almost collided with Heath. She put her head down and apologised. He smelt funny, like some kind of chemical or medicine – but she had no idea what. It must be some new solution for developing his films.

'Where the fuck have you been?'

'Sorry, I just nipped to the shop. I met Annie and we got talking.'

He looked down at the ripped carrier bag and felt a white-hot rage fill his chest. She was lying to him. Meek and mild Jo was lying to him, and he couldn't even say she was because she'd want to know how he knew that – and he couldn't exactly drop it into the conversation that he actually had Annie in his garage. Locked into a mortuary fridge and slowly freezing to death.

'What's up with the shopping? Have you been juggling with it? You're making a mess all over the carpet.'

His hand came up and slapped her so hard across the face the shock made her stumble backwards. She looked down at the bag to see it was leaking orange juice onto the floor. She braced herself as he pushed her to one side and stormed past her, but she couldn't help notice the bite mark on his hand. She wanted to ask him how he'd got that, but it would be more than her life was worth. What was he up to? He ran upstairs to the bathroom, slamming the door and turning the shower on. A loud knock on the front door broke her from her trance. Running through to the kitchen she put the carrier bag into the sink then went back to answer the door. The lovely policeman from the other day was standing there with a huge man in full uniform. He looked worried and she wondered what he wanted.

'Hello, Jo, sorry to bother you but have you seen Annie today?'

Ice water filled her veins and she prayed that Heath wasn't listening from behind the bathroom door or she'd be getting more than a slap because he'd know that she'd blatantly lied to him. She stepped outside and pulled the door shut behind her, shaking her head and lowering her voice. 'I'm sorry, I haven't. Do you mean the pregnant Annie?'

'Yes. I'm really worried about her. This is Jake, her best friend, and neither of us can get in contact with her. I dropped her off at home a couple of hours ago but no one has seen her since then.'

Will realised that Jo hadn't made the connection as her face clouded over with confusion. 'I'm sorry, I should have explained better. I'm Annie's husband.'

'You are? Oh gosh, I feel so stupid. I had no idea. I'm really sorry, but I haven't seen her at all today.'

'It's OK – thank you. If you hear from her, please will you tell her to get in touch with me?'

'Of course I will. I hope she's OK and you find her soon.'

Will smiled and ran back to the police van. Jo stepped back inside the house, praying that Heath was still in the shower and hadn't heard any of the conversation. For once her prayers were answered and the shower was still running. It stopped and she heard him moving around upstairs. Her mind was a jumble of thoughts. Just who had bitten her husband's hand and where on earth was Annie? She walked through to the kitchen; going over to the tattered carrier bag in the sink, she took the leaking carton of orange juice from it. She turned on the tap to rinse her hands and screamed at the thick, red liquid that dripped from the faucet in big splotches, all over the white carrier bag. It gurgled as it trickled from the tap and then all of a sudden it exploded everywhere. Blood splattered from the tap, coating the sink, cupboards and herself. She grabbed a towel and tried to turn the tap off but it was stuck.

Heath came running in and pushed her out of the way, reaching over and turning off the tap. He slowly turned to look at her and she couldn't take her eyes off the bright red splotches of what looked like blood that covered his white T-shirt. She lifted a finger and pointed to him; he looked down at himself but could only see wet patches where the cold water had soaked him.

'What the fuck is the matter with you, Jo? Have you gone mad, screaming at nothing? Are you trying to get the police here? Because if you are, you're doing a bloody good job.'

She shook her head, trying to clear her mind. As she looked down into the sink all she could see was clear water mixed in with the leaking orange juice. She stepped closer and looked around; the only splashes all over the worktops and Heath's T-shirt were clear water.

'I'm sorry, I don't know what's wrong with me. I haven't really felt right since I hit my head a few days ago.'

He shoved her and tutted, running back upstairs to change into a dry top.

All she could think about was Annie. The village wasn't big enough to lose someone in. An awful thought began to fill the edge of her mind and she tried her best to block it out, but it wouldn't let her.

Those two bodies out in the woods were lost for over twenty years, though, weren't they, Jo? Right outside the back of your house . . . and now your new friend is missing and someone has bitten Heath's hand. Why would someone want to bite him?

He came thundering down the stairs in clean clothes, with a black plastic bin bag in his hands. He grabbed the car keys from the bowl on the sideboard and looked at her.

'I need to go and get some stuff from Barrow. Make sure you clean the carpet before that juice stains, and the mess in here before everything gets water-stained.'

'I will – sorry.'

He turned and walked out of the front door, letting it slam behind him. The churning in her stomach was making her feel sick, but she waited until she heard the engine start and then she ran and flicked the latch on the door so he couldn't get back inside with his door key. She didn't want to but she had no choice; she needed to go into his workshop and see what was going on. The evening paper was pushed through the letterbox and she jumped back, screaming at the door. She realised what a fool she sounded and shouted 'sorry' through the heavy wooden door; the paperboy had his earphones in and was humming away to himself, completely oblivious – thank God. She was turning into a nervous wreck.

She picked the paper up and felt the room swim. There were pictures on the front page of the two girls who'd gone missing twenty years ago – one of them was the girl she'd seen in the mirror a few days ago. The dead girl with her head caved in on one side . . . and why would a dead girl be in her house? She knew the answer but was far too afraid to speak it out loud. And why did he need those fridges? She wasn't as stupid as he thought she was; she knew they were morgue fridges.

If he'd gone to Barrow she had a good ninety minutes before he'd be back. Running to the kitchen and the studio door, she tried the handle – but it was locked, just as she'd known it would be. He was acting so strange he wouldn't risk her going inside and snooping around. The only way she could get into the studio was from the outside door; he kept a spare key in the bedside table in a small box. She knew because she'd seen him put it in there years ago, but had never until now had any reason to want to go in there without his permission.

Forcing her legs to move she ran upstairs and opened the drawer, half expecting it to have been moved – but the box was still there, underneath a black diary. She grabbed the box and dropped it onto the floor; it was so cold it had burnt the tips of her fingers. Picking it up once more she lifted the lid and took the small brass key out. She didn't bother to shut the drawer because she didn't plan on being here when he came back.

She ran downstairs, terrified of doing this and going against his wishes, but she had to go and see what was inside those fridges. For too long she'd buried her head in the sand, ignoring everything he did because she was scared of him. Well, she was still scared of him but not enough that she wouldn't go and check it out. Her friend could be in there, needing her help, and if there was one thing Jo was it was loyal.

She put the key in the lock and turned it. As she stepped inside the light-filled room she couldn't see anything that looked out of place. She crossed to the two huge portraits on the wall; she'd only ever briefly glanced at them before but this time she walked over and studied them. Her heart began to race. It was the girls from the paper. They looked different – they were sleeping, but it was definitely them. As she turned around she noticed a black handbag under the chair in the corner and tried to rack her brains to remember if Annie had a bag like it. Bending down she opened it and saw an iPod, make-up, perfume, chewing gum and a purse. Picking up the purse she opened it to see if there was any ID inside. There was a small plastic driving licence and she lifted it up – the name said Matilda Graham. Where had she heard that name before?

The fear of being caught in here by Heath was nothing compared to the ice-cold shard of fear that was now lodged in her spine. There were far too many coincidences . . . the radio – she'd heard that name on the radio. A missing person's appeal. It had been playing in the shop, but she hadn't taken much notice. With legs that were trembling, she walked across to the garage and opened the door.

Heath hadn't gone to Barrow like he told her. Instead he'd gone to the recycling centre in Bowness to get rid of his clothes that he'd been wearing for two days and which were covered in God knows how much DNA from the girl in the fridge and that nosy bitch Annie. He'd put them in one of the square bins for some kids' charity. It made him smile to think of the poor sod who would open his bin bag of stinking clothes. They would just bin them, with no idea where they'd come from. He didn't know what he was going to do with the two women in his fridges. The police were going to be all over looking for Annie – she was a local policewoman, for God's sake!

He didn't really want to kill a pregnant woman either – if only she hadn't decided to become best friends with his pathetic excuse of a wife, then none of this would have happened. It was her own fault – and Jo's. If she hadn't been so desperate for someone to talk to they wouldn't be in this predicament. It was everyone's fault except his own. Some solution would come to him. He had his baseball cap pulled down low over his head and sunglasses on, because the village was crawling with police. He needed to go home and stay inside – 'out of sight, out of mind' was his dad's favourite saying. He got back into the car and began the short drive back to his house.

Will jumped out of the van and ran to the cottage. 'Annie, Annie, are you home?' The house was silent and he knew that she wasn't, but still he went inside and checked every single room just in case she'd blacked out again. He checked the noticeboard in the kitchen just to be sure she didn't have any hospital appointments – but there was nothing on the calendar for today and no cards pinned anywhere next to it. He ran his fingers through his sandy blond hair. Where the hell was she? It didn't make sense. He'd left Jake with his phone in the van, ringing around everyone on his contact list. Her car was outside so she hadn't gone far; she was in the village somewhere and he was probably being a complete wanker and getting all stressed out over nothing . . . but with everything that had happened the last two years he wasn't prepared to take that risk. He knew the phone signal was crap here but he just couldn't think of where she might have gone. He went out to the van and Jake shook his head.

'I spoke to Ben's wife – God, that woman can talk. She never shut up but she did say that she hadn't heard from Annie at all today and Ben was on his way up here to go and look for Tilly.'

'Jesus Christ, what a fucking mess. Not only can we not find my wife, I can't find her niece either. It doesn't add up, does it? Where the hell are they? It's not as if we live in the middle of London, is it? This is a fairly quiet Lakeland village.'

'You losing your touch, Mr Golden Boy Detective? It seems like you can't keep an eye on any of the women you love.'

Will stared at him in disbelief and Jake realised how terrible what he'd just said sounded.

'Oh Will, I'm so sorry. I didn't mean that. It was a tasteless joke. I have no idea what I was thinking – it just came out.'

Will rolled his eyes. 'Take me back to the village hall. I want to organise some groups of people to start searching the village for Annie.'

'Anything you say, boss. I've already phoned the esteemed Cathy and Kav, who are going to leave the safety of their cosy offices and help look for her. I think you should get Annie a GPS microchip inserted in the back of her neck; that way we could track her and we'd never lose her again, just like those chips vets inject into dogs.'

'Shut the fuck up, Jake. I can't take much more of your bullshit. Although to be fair it's not a bad idea. I just want to find her and make sure she's OK. My heart feels like it's about to burst from my chest. How does she do this to me?'

'And to me, and to everyone she knows . . . it's only since she met you, to be honest. I mean we'd get into scraps down Cornwallis Street with the drunks on a Friday and Saturday night, but nothing more than a cut eye or bruised fist. Not like the full-scale "I'm about to be murdered by a serial killer" crap that's happened the last couple of years. I mean, come on, we didn't even have a serial killer in this part of the country, ever. Now they're popping up left, right and centre.'

Will felt a cold chill settle over his back. Something was seriously wrong and he knew it. He just didn't know what.

Chapter 28

It was dark inside the garage. Jo felt along the wall for the light switch before she dared to step inside. She was terrified of what she might find in here, but knew there was no choice – she had to see. The watery light illuminated the room and she stepped inside. She shivered; the air was much cooler in here. The bank of four steel fridges stared at her. What would anyone in their right mind want with them, unless they were starting an undertaking business? Forcing herself across to them she opened the bottom one – it was empty and so was the one next to it. Her fingers crossed now, she hoped to God the others were and she'd just let her imagination run wild; that way she could go inside and pack her stuff, get the hell out of here and never look back.

Grasping the metal latch of the next one she tugged it open and gasped to see someone inside. Pulling the steel stretcher out it took her a few seconds to register that the semi-conscious woman lying in front of her was Annie. Her face was swollen on one side and she was gagged. Jo lifted her head and untied the gag.

'Oh my God, Annie, I'm so sorry. Are you OK? Please talk to me. We need to get you out of here because I don't know how long he'll be and if he comes back and catches us he'll kill us both.'

Annie opened her eyes, relieved to see Jo standing there; the look of concern etched across her face wiped away any fears that she might be working alongside her husband. As the dirty rag was taken from her mouth she coughed and sucked in big gulps of fresh air.

'Thanks – there's someone in the next drawer and I think it might be my niece. We need to get her out and phone the police.'

Jo helped Annie off the stretcher and she leant against the wall, feeling dizzy and still queasy from whatever drug he'd given her. Annie watched as Jo opened the next fridge and dragged the stretcher out. Relief filled her entire body to see the shock of long, black hair that belonged to her niece, Tilly.

She wasn't responsive like Annie had been and Jo panicked, listening to her chest. 'She's breathing but she's unconscious.'

Annie stumbled across to see what she could do. 'We need to get out of here, Jo, because he could come back at any time and catch us.'

Jo took the small phone from her pocket and dialled 999.

'Ask for urgent assistance, officer down, and give your address, then hang up.'

Jo did that, then she dialled Paul's number – it went to voicemail. 'I'm in big trouble, Paul. He's been killing women. I've phoned the police, but he might come back. Can you go and get the police from the village hall to come to my house?'

She didn't listen to see if he answered because she heard the hammering on the front door and dropped the phone in shock. 'He's here.'

Annie looked around for something to protect them with.

'No, get back inside the fridge and I'll pretend I don't know anything – it will be safer for you.'

Jo pushed the stretcher with Tilly on back inside the fridge and shut the door; before Annie could find a weapon or even think about climbing back into the fridge a loud clapping noise echoed around the garage.

'Brav-fucking-o! I never thought I'd see the day that you

actually grew a pair of balls, Jo. Now tell me – what the fuck are you doing in my workshop when you know fine well it's out of bounds?'

His voice had risen to an angry scream as he strode towards her, grabbing a handful of her hair.

'What have I told you, again and again?'

He dragged her away from the fridges and Annie. Jo clawed at his hands, drawing blood and scratching him as hard as she could.

She screamed, 'It's all over Heath – the police are on their way.'

He smiled at her. 'It might be all over for me but it's also all over for you.'

He grabbed her head and slammed it into the brick wall; an explosion of black and silver stars filled her mind. Then she kicked out at him in anger; this time she wasn't going down without a fight.

Annie pushed herself away from the fridges she was leaning on to go and help Jo, but her legs were too wobbly and she fell to her knees. Her phone slipped from her bra and she picked it up, speed-dialling Will. 'I'm at Jo's house, come quick – Heath's going to kill her and he killed those girls.'

Heath heard her speaking and threw Jo to the floor, turning to look at Annie. He was in front of her in seconds and snatched her phone from her hand, threw it to the ground and stamped on it. She watched horrified as it cracked and splintered into pieces. Turning back to her he wrapped his hands around her throat and began squeezing, cutting off her airway. Annie tried to kick and stamp on him, scratching at his hands, but he was much stronger than her and she could feel herself losing consciousness. All of a sudden his hands let go as shock registered on his face and she fell to the floor, scrabbling to get away from him. Annie could see Jo standing behind him, holding on to an axe that was now dripping with bright red blood from where she'd buried it into his back. Annie's voice was hoarse but she croaked, 'Hit him again, Jo – now.'

But the shock of what she'd just done had all but rendered Jo incapable of moving. Heath swung around to face his wife and grabbed the axe from her hands. The door flew open and Annie was relieved to see Jake, Will and several uniformed officers standing there with Tasers drawn – they had already been on their way back to search the house and workshop.

It was Jake who stepped forward and red-dotted Heath. As Jake shouted his warning to him not to move, Heath swung the axe towards Jo. The Taser hit him, making him fall to his knees, but not before the axe hit Jo's neck – sending a spray of arterial blood across the room. Someone fired a second Taser and this time Heath collapsed on the floor. Annie screamed as Jo fell towards her. She held out her hand, catching the woman who had just saved her life and praying that she could save hers. Will ran across the room, ripping off his shirt and rolling it into a tight ball. He bent down, pressing it with as much force as he could against the gaping wound in Jo's neck whilst screaming for someone to get an ambulance.

Paul, who had got Jo's message and driven straight to her house, ran from his car carrying his black doctor's bag faster than he'd ever run in his life. He raced towards the back of the house where he could see police vans and officers standing around. Telling them he was a doctor they stepped to one side to let him through. In seconds he assessed the scene and went to where Will was cradling Jo in his arms, trying to stop the bleeding. He knelt down and looked at Jo, who was losing far too much blood, and he felt the panic rise in his chest. He didn't want to lose her now.

'I'm here now, Jo. I'm going to take care of you. I promise you'll be just fine, but I need you to stay awake. Keep looking at me, OK? Try not to go to sleep.'

He turned to Will.

'ETA for the ambulance?'

'Any time.'

Jake came running back in with some bath towels and rolled them up, passing one to Paul who pushed it against Jo's neck with all the pressure he could. After what seemed like forever the sirens finally came closer and Paul breathed a sigh of relief when two paramedics came running in.

Will helped Annie up from the floor and hugged her, pulling her close.

'Did he hurt you?'

'Not much but I have no idea what he's done to Tilly.'

She pulled open the fridge door and slid the stretcher out. The teenage girl looked lifeless. Annie tried her best not to but she couldn't stifle the sob that escaped from her lips.

Will shouted to Jake. 'We need another ambulance, now.'

'It should be on its way. I requested two.'

Heath lay on the floor stunned and bleeding from the wound in his back, but he was alive and no one gave a flying fuck. Two coppers were standing over him with their Tasers drawn as Will pulled the cuffs from his pocket.

'It's over, you sick bastard. One of you two read him his rights. I can't bear to look at the piece of shit.'

'I'm bleeding – I need an ambulance. She hit me with that axe in the back.'

Will turned around – about to kick him so hard in the nuts he'd never be able to use them ever again – when Annie dragged him away. Jake had taken his jacket off and wrapped it around Tilly; he'd also untied the gag from her mouth. Pressing two fingers against her neck, he smiled. 'She's got a pulse! But it's weak. We need to get her to the hospital – the sooner the better.'

The look he gave Will conveyed exactly how urgent it was for them to get her to the hospital. They looked up to see Kav parking the big police van outside. He wound down the window.

'The other ambulance has been diverted to a motorcycle accident on the A590.'

'Are you having a laugh, boss? We need it like *now*.'

Kav shook his head. Jake scooped Tilly into his arms, running towards the van with her. 'Hospital, now.'

Will opened the door and helped Jake to get the girl into the van. They laid her down across the back seats and covered her with an assortment of police jackets that had been left in there – trying to bring her body temperature up. Next, Will pushed Annie up into the front of the van next to Kav.

'Buckle up.'

She fumbled with her belt but finally snapped it in. The sliding doors slammed shut as Will jumped in the back to help Jake keep Tilly as safe as possible whilst they blue-lighted her to the hospital. The sirens screeched into life as both the van and the ambulance prepared to set off, the ambulance following the police van.

Annie couldn't speak – all she could see was that axe hitting Jo's neck and the spray of blood. There had been so much blood. Will's white shirt had been covered in it; so was the short-sleeved white T-shirt he'd had on underneath. Kav reached across and squeezed her shoulder, then put his hand back on the steering wheel as he made it through the narrow, twisty lanes at record speed, clearing the roads for the following ambulance. The journey was bumpy, fast and uncomfortable, but before long they were screeching to a halt outside the front of the accident and emergency department. Thankfully the paramedics had pre-warned the hospital and there was a team of doctors and nurses waiting to greet them with trolleys and wheelchairs. Jo was rushed through first with Paul by her side, still holding the rolled-up, blood-soaked towel against her neck. Kav opened the doors and Tilly was carried out onto the waiting trolley and then rushed through.

Will opened the door to help Annie out; she was pale with the shock and the rough journey here, had angry purple and black bruising around the swelling by her eye and was covered in specks of blood – but she had never looked so wonderful to him, because she was alive. She got out and clasped hold of Will. Jake jumped out and shook his head; he didn't know what to say. A nurse offered her a wheelchair but she shook her head and walked through the double doors into the waiting casualty department where the waiting room was full of people staring at them. The shirtless man covered in blood, the pregnant woman with a black eye and the huge policeman next to them. The nurse led them straight past the waiting room and into the all-too-familiar cubicles.

A doctor stepped out of the resuscitation room covered in Jo's blood and Annie blanched; poor Jo had finally stood up to her bastard of a husband to save both her and Tilly's lives – but at what cost? Paul stepped out and walked towards Annie, who he knew from her antenatal visits. He was covered in more blood than Will. Annie gently took hold of his hand. 'How is she?'

He nodded, tried to speak but couldn't, and had to cough to clear his throat. 'She's lost a lot of blood, too much blood really to survive, but she's hanging in there – just. They're about to rush her to theatre.'

The doors opened and the trolley appeared – surrounded by a team of doctors and nurses, Jo looked so tiny lying there completely lifeless. Will squeezed Annie's hand, knowing fine well that she was blaming herself for all of this when the only person to blame was Heath Tyson. Another trolley was rolled in; this one had a policeman either side and Will was glad to see they had handcuffed him to the metal guard rails on each side. They were taking no chances; he was an extremely dangerous man. Annie turned away. Will pulled the curtain across so she wouldn't have to look at him.

'Please find out how Tilly is, and can you phone Ben and tell him?'

Kav stepped through the curtains. 'Already taken care of. I've sent Cathy to go and collect them.'

'Cathy as in our Inspector Cathy, who has even less tact than I do?'

'Yes, Jake, and, believe it or not, the woman is not as bad as you might think – she wouldn't be inspector if she was, would she?'

'Well, you would say that, wouldn't you, because you and her are shagging. On your head be it, Sarge.'

Annie giggled and Kav decided not to bollock Jake because seeing Annie smile amongst all this chaos was worth a little cheek from Jake.

'Shut up, Jake – don't be so rude. And thank you, Kav. I really appreciate it.'

Will stepped through the curtains to go and find the doctor looking after Annie's niece; what a headache this was going to be. The crime scene back at the house was a complete mess and would take days to process; he decided he would take all the help he could get and if any of the powers that be said he couldn't work this case anymore because of the family connections he wouldn't be so precious for once.

He was so tired of it all. He'd thought that coming back to work had been the right thing to do, but maybe it hadn't. He'd never felt exhaustion like this, ever – if he was honest with himself he was feeling overwhelmed by it all. They had the killer; now it was only a matter of time before those bodies were officially identified. If they couldn't link the bodies to him at least they had him for the abduction of Tilly, Annie and attempted murder of his wife, Jo. Will just hoped that she pulled through surgery and the charge of attempted murder wouldn't have to be upgraded to murder.

They all heard Lisa's voice the minute she walked into the department, and even Jake cringed. Will had already told Annie that Tilly was responding well to the treatment for hypothermia and although she wasn't likely to wake up any time soon – because of the amount of sedatives in her system – by tomorrow she should. Annie had buried her head in her arms, relieved for her niece, but she was still worried about Jo. They were both alive because of her, and Annie would never be able to repay the debt; she owed her everything.

Paul was taken to the small but comfortable relatives' room in the intensive care unit, where they'd sat him down and told him it was quieter and he could wait until Jo came out of surgery because she would be brought straight to the intensive care unit. They didn't say how long it would be, though, before she would be stable enough for him to see her again and he knew that it could be a long time yet. The last few hours kept replaying in his mind and he wondered if this was all his fault? If he hadn't taken her back to his house and then begged her to leave Heath, would she be fighting for her life in surgery right now? He knew the answer to that question, without a doubt, was that – regardless of his intervention – it would have come to this sooner or later.

A nurse brought him some hospital scrubs to change into; his own clothes were heavily bloodstained and the woman from CSI, who introduced herself as Debs, had come to find him and ask for them as evidence. He'd changed in the small toilet, scrubbed his hands and face with the antibacterial gel and then put his clothes into the brown paper sack that she'd given him. His face was grey and the woman in the black polo shirt and combat trousers had taken the sack from him, sitting down opposite him.

'Thank you. I hear you were quite the hero and probably saved her life.'

'I just did what anyone would have done. It was the detective who probably made the difference by putting pressure on the wound within seconds. Or at least I'm praying to God that between the pair of us we made the difference.'

Debs sighed. 'I'm sure it will have. The staff are really good here. She is one very brave woman. I don't know too much about it because I've just been called in, but I know she saved the life of one of my colleagues and her niece.'

Paul looked at her. 'She was incredibly brave. I would never have thought that she'd have it in her, but it's amazing what you can do when faced with a desperate situation.'

'Oh, you can say that again – my husband is in there.' She

nodded her head in the direction of the double doors, which were shut but led into the ward.

'I'm sorry to hear that. How is he?'

'The truth is, he's a complete mess. He threw himself in front of a police car travelling at speed because he was drunk and thought it was the right thing to do.'

Paul sucked in his breath. 'Oh my goodness, that's awful. You must be devastated. What have they said his prognosis is?'

'That when he wakes up he'll either be fine – maybe have some slight memory loss and a limp. Or he'll wake up a vegetable. If he wakes up. They can't make up their minds at the moment how bad he is.'

'That's terrible. I hope he wakes up soon and proves them all wrong.'

'Me too. We were having a bit of a rough patch and had split up. The thing is, he wouldn't be in here if he hadn't found out I'd been having an affair, so it's my fault that he so got drunk and decided to.'

Paul leant over and patted her knee. 'It's all terribly sad, there's no denying that, but you didn't push him in front of that car, did you?'

She shook her head.

'No, I thought not, and this is going to sound cruel – but it was his decision, not yours, so you can't blame yourself for what's happened. Life doesn't always work out how we imagined. People fall in and out of love for all sorts of reasons. I'm a big believer that things happen because they're supposed to.'

She smiled at him. 'Thank you so much; you're very kind and that's very good advice. I hope you listen to your own advice because I get the distinct impression that you're sitting here blaming yourself for what's happened to your friend.'

He laughed. 'You're very astute. Yes, I feel terrible and I do think that it's all my fault.'

'Well, it's not. From what I've heard your friend made the

decision to intervene all by herself. You should be very proud of her and, when you get the chance, make the most of every moment that you can. I have a feeling that you two were destined to be together.'

Paul's eyes filled with tears, making his vision blurry. The woman stood up and, grabbing the bag, she turned to leave.

'I'd better get back to work. I've taken up enough of your time. Take care.'

And she was gone. He let the tears fall because he couldn't hold them in any longer. He cried hot, salty tears of guilt, regret and disgust that he had let it come this far.

Chapter 29

When Will finally led Annie out of the hospital, she was tired and wanted nothing more than to go home to bed and sleep forever, cocooned under the duvet next to Will – but she knew that wouldn't be an option just yet. Will had so much work to do and she felt terrible for him; he'd been so quiet and not himself. She wanted to help, but he wouldn't talk to her. Every time she asked him what was wrong he shook his head and smiled, but something was wrong and she hated that he thought he couldn't talk to her about it. The last thing she wanted was for either of them to start keeping secrets from one another.

Alex was waiting outside, parked in one of the on-call doctor parking spaces, with his engine running. Alice was fast asleep in the car seat in the back and Annie climbed in next to her, whispering, 'Hey, beautiful baby girl . . . I missed you.'

Will slid in next to her. She laid her head on his shoulder.

'I'm getting too old for this and I'm starving. Please could we go to the drive-through, Alex? I need a big juicy Quarter Pounder with Cheese.'

Alex nodded. Jake came running out to the car. He unzipped his body armour, opened the boot and threw it in along with everything else.

'Sorry, you're going to have to drive me back to Windermere station after we've dropped these two off. I need to drop my kit off and get my car. Do you mind?'

'Not at all but we have to make a detour first. Annie's starving.'

'Makes a change . . . of course not. Where we going?'

'McDonald's,' chimed all three of them.

Jake groaned. 'Fuck it, I've been on a diet for most of the day and I'm bloody starving – not to mention stressed out, and I get so hungry when I'm stressed. No wonder you don't stick to them, Annie – it's torture. I need lots of greasy food and a huge chocolate milkshake.'

Annie mustered up enough energy to lean forward and poke him in the side.

'Cheeky. I can't stick to them because I'm always working with you and you never stop eating.'

Jake laughed. 'It's a shame the vet's isn't open; we could have made a little detour and called there on the way. Will and me have come up with a great plan for you. We're going to get you microchipped like they do with dogs, so we can keep an eye on you.'

Will held his hands up. 'I never said that – he did.'

'I don't care – in fact, it might be a good idea. I only went to see Jo to pass half an hour, so I could then go and speak to you in private. I had no idea that Heath was the man responsible for everything and that he was going to try and finish us all off. I'm still in shock about what happened – I just can't believe it.'

'Let's not talk about him. It boils my blood thinking about him and what he's done to those girls, Jo, Tilly and you. Tomorrow we're all going to have to relive every minute of today when we give statements so let's just try to forget about it for now and get some rest.'

'I'm really worried about Jo; she lost a lot of blood. Do you think she'll be OK? I wonder if she's out of surgery yet.'

Will's phone rang. 'Hello.'

'Will, it's Paul, Dr Miller. Jo's out of surgery. Can you tell Annie that she's OK? They've managed to stop the bleeding and repair the damage. She's gone into intensive care, but it's just a precaution.'

Will stuck his thumb up at Annie, who breathed out a sigh of relief.

'That's fantastic news, Paul; I'm so glad. We'll come and see her tomorrow. If you get to speak to her tell her I said thank you, from the bottom of my heart.'

'I know, it's a miracle – thanks to you. I think you saved her life, Will, and of course I'll tell her when she wakes up. She's a pretty amazing woman.'

He ended the call and Will chuckled.

'Go, Jo! She's a right little fighter underneath that timid exterior. It looks as if she has the good doctor to look out for her as well, which is a nice end to this horror story.'

Annie smiled. She couldn't wait to see her and thank her in person.

One week later

Annie had bought the biggest box of chocolates she could find in the shop; once Jo was home she would send her flowers as well, but they weren't allowed in the hospital. She had spent the entire week doing nothing much – Will had forbidden her to leave the house unless she was with someone, which was fine by her. The whole experience had left her exhausted. Tilly had been released three days ago into the arms of a tearful Lisa and Ben. When Will had questioned her about how she had come into contact with Heath Tyson, she had told them about her dreams of becoming a model. Will could have kicked himself; he had seen the stack of *Vogue* magazines in her bedroom and hadn't made the connection.

Before Lisa could begin to berate her for being so stupid, Annie had grabbed hold of her niece and held her tight, telling her that she would indeed make the most amazing model, but she was to go about it the proper way with a reputable photographer, whom she and Will would vet before Tilly even set foot through their door.

'Thank you, Annie. I thought you would all laugh at me.'

Annie had kissed her and looked across at Tilly's parents. 'Isn't that right, guys? If she wants to be a model then we'll help her all the way, won't we?'

Ben had grabbed tight hold of Lisa's arm and nodded. 'Of course we will. Anything you want to do, we're here to help you, aren't we, love?'

All eyes had fallen on Lisa, who everyone expected to rip Tilly's dream to shreds in a thirty-second rant, but she'd whispered, 'Of course we will; we'll help you all the way.'

Annie drove around the car park, looking for a space near to the hospital main entrance. Her back had been aching so much since she woke up this morning, it was hurting her to walk far. After driving around three times a car reversed out and she pulled into the last space outside the accident and emergency department. As she got out of the car and leant in the back to get the chocolates, which had fallen to the floor, a sharp pain spread from the middle of her back into her side, making her inhale sharply. It lasted a minute then subsided; she rubbed her belly, not sure what it was. *Don't even think about it, kid. I'm not ready and neither are you. So I'm just ignoring you.*

She made her way into the hospital and walked along the long corridor until she reached the lifts. Jo had been transferred to a general ward to recover. As she got to the ward the pain came again, making her pause to catch her breath. Surely not – she was only seven months pregnant; it was far too early and she'd still not finished the damn cot, which had more parts to it than an entire fitted kitchen. She walked into the small private room that she'd spent time in not that long ago and smiled to see Jo and Dr Miller sitting there. Annie rushed across and hugged her tight, careful of the bandage around her neck.

'Thank you so much, Jo. I don't know what to say. You saved our lives.'

Jo smiled back at her, holding on to her just as tightly. She croaked, 'You also saved mine, Annie, in more ways than one. I hope we can still be friends. I can't stop thinking about eating a slice of that cake from the village coffee shop.'

'Friends? You will never be rid of me. Have you thought about where you're going to stop when they release you? We have plenty of spare rooms at our house. You'd be more than welcome.'

Jo looked across at Paul and smiled. 'Thank you, but I have my very own doctor to take care of me now. Paul and I go back a very long time, but I was stupid and chose the wrong man. He has a room all ready and waiting for me. I can't go back to my house; well, actually, it was always Heath's house. I don't want to go back there and, besides, I think the police won't be finished with it for a long time yet. Will came to see me yesterday and told me what was happening with the investigation – it's so horrific. I can't even begin to imagine how he could do those wicked things to those girls. Leaving them all alone and burying them when he knew their families would be out looking for them . . . It's just so horrific. Oh, by the way, that was incredibly sneaky; you never once stopped me when I was telling you how dreamy and gorgeous Will was that day we went for coffee.'

Annie felt her cheeks burning. 'Sorry about that, but I wasn't thinking straight – and it seemed funny hearing someone else tell me how dreamy he was. I mean, I've always thought that he was but it just didn't seem right saying that it was my husband you were talking about. I didn't want you to think I was some crazy, possessive woman.'

She winked at Jo who laughed. Paul joined in.

'Hang on a minute, what about me? Am I not dreamy?'

Jo sat forward and grabbed hold of his hand. 'You've always

been dreamy, but I kept my head buried in the sand and hadn't looked at you for so long that I'd forgotten.'

He stood up and kissed her tenderly on the head. 'Perfect answer and I can live with that. Right, I'm off; I have to go and do some work. My patients' haemorrhoids and sprained wrists won't mend themselves. You take care, Annie. It's great to see you.'

'Bye, Dr Miller.'

'You can call me Paul, you know. I think we've gone past all the formalities now, don't you?'

'Yes, I suppose we have, but it just seems so cheeky, especially if I want you to sort my haemorrhoids out.'

She grimaced at him and they all laughed.

'I have a feeling we'll be seeing quite a lot of each other, Annie, so please do. I was never big on the doctor title and if you need a prescription let me know.'

He left and Annie sat down in his chair, letting out a sigh. 'You know, he's quite dreamy as well. Look at us. I never got the chance to tell you about my ex-husband, Mike, did I? He was a bit like Heath and very handy with his fists. In fact he almost killed me one night and when I woke up in the hospital I decided then that I was never going back.'

'Oh, Annie, I had no idea. I'm sorry to hear that. I can't believe that someone as strong as you had an abusive husband.'

'I don't talk about it really; I still get ashamed – but look at us, two women who had to fight for our lives against abusive husbands to finally find happiness with a couple of dreamboats.'

'Well, why not? Don't we all deserve a happy ever after?'

'Yes, we certainly do and if I had a glass of champagne I'd drink to that.'

'Me too. What will happen to Heath now? I mean, will he ever be let out of prison? I really hope not because I think with him out of my life I might just be able to finally start living again.'

'He'll go to court for a full trial, because Will said that he pleaded not guilty when he was interviewed. It will take months for them to gather the evidence and for it to get to court – which means even more agony for those girls' families. Hopefully Will's team will find more than enough evidence to prove to the world what a complete liar he is.

'Why would he plead not guilty? I can't believe it. I mean he had those photos of those girls enlarged and hung up on his studio wall for everyone to see. I can't understand why I never noticed before or why none of his clients thought they were strange.'

'Probably because they just thought they were supposed to be some kind of dramatic statement, a tribute to his art and skill.'

'It's so creepy to know that he had pictures of dead girls on the wall; that's not normal behaviour, is it? Wouldn't he be better off pleading guilty?'

'It would certainly save the families having to go through the horrors of a court case but most killers enjoy the attention. They are quite often living for the thrill of daring to do what no one else would. He'll get to relive it all over again through the courts and the newspaper coverage.'

After ten minutes the door opened and Paul came back into the room.

'My stupid car won't start and the tow truck won't be here for another four hours; apparently they're having a record-breaking number of call-outs and being a single male with no screaming kids or elderly parents I'm not a priority.'

'I'm going now, so I can drop you off. But how will you get back for your car?'

'I'll bring my motorbike. I can leave that here for now because I rarely use it and besides they might not be able to get the car started so it might need to go to the garage. At least then I won't be stranded.'

Annie hauled herself up and hugged Jo once more, holding her tight.

'I'll see you soon, Jo. Thank you again. I don't think I'll ever stop thanking you. Now make the most of this being waited on by the nurses, because you'll be home before you know it.'

'Where I'll take over and wait on her hand and foot. I always knew my medical training would come in handy one day. Not to mention my fabulous baking skills. I'll have you fattened up and feeling better in no time at all.'

Paul kissed Jo one more time then left with Annie.

Chapter 30

Heath Tyson's house on the edge of the woods stood out now it was surrounded with blue and white crime scene tape. Like some morbid fairground attraction, it had been named 'The House of Horrors' by the local paper; the nationals had picked up the story and when Will had called into the village shop the black and white photograph that had been taken by a local photographer – the one he really didn't like – had screamed at him from the front cover of every single newspaper.

Inside and outside the house had been photographed, videoed and searched from top to bottom several times over; it had been Will who had found the hidden safe yesterday that none of them could gain entry to, despite several of them trying. It had taken them until today to find someone to come and open it. The locksmith had spent the best part of forty minutes cursing under his breath and wiping sweat from his brow but he'd finally done it. Will had watched the entire time, holding his breath and keeping his fingers crossed behind his back because up to now they hadn't found anything concrete that proved Heath had killed those two girls. They had the death photos of them on the studio wall and that was it; he hadn't actually killed Tilly or Annie, thank God, although he very nearly had – but not in a cold-blooded way.

He had left them in the fridge, drugged up and hypothermic, but not dead.

Most killers would have just got on with it and it was puzzling him why Heath hadn't killed Annie whilst he had the chance either – not that he'd wanted him to, God forbid, but it was niggling away inside him. He'd only hit Jo with the axe in retaliation for her hitting him first and if he got a good lawyer they would claim it had been nothing but self-defence. They needed some kind of concrete proof that would result in the right conviction against him. Will wanted him locking up and the key throwing away so he'd never be able to look at or photograph any more women.

The bright flash from the crime scene investigator's camera broke his daydream as the contents of the safe were photographed in situ. His white paper suit was uncomfortable and his rubber gloves were irritating him; it was warm outside and he could feel the beads of sweat forming on the back of his neck. He still felt tired, even though he'd slept all night. When he'd asked the chief super if someone else could take over from him because this case was too personal, his answer had been that they were short-staffed and he was already up to date with the case. Much to his dismay, the man had told him that it didn't make sense to take him off it – and he'd actually had the cheek to say that no one in his family had died, so Will could carry on. That was probably the closest he had ever come to punching a senior officer; the man was so insensitive – thank God no one had died, but it had been a close call for Tilly, Annie and poor Jo, who had come off the worst of them all.

Will leant down and looked inside at the contents, hoping to find a murder weapon, but all that was inside was an antique, brown-leather photo album with the words *Memento Mori* in gold script on the front. Where had he heard that phrase before? He couldn't remember. After taking it out he began flicking through the pages. It was very old and most of the photographs were black and white with the subjects wearing Victorian clothing.

Most of the pictures were of babies and children, but there were a few snaps of adults as well. He shivered – they truly made him feel uncomfortable as he stared at them. They were awful; not the sorts of photos you'd want to put on the mantelpiece for everyone to stare at.

He realised why the words were familiar. A while ago he'd seen similar pictures on the internet; they were called *Memento Mori* – mourning photographs of the dead. As he flicked through them, intrigued by the quality and the effort that had gone into them, he shivered. They would stick in his mind for ever.

As he got three-quarters of the way through it there were some much more modern photos – an elderly woman in her nightgown who had quite clearly died at home in bed, her yellowed, sunken skin and slack jaw making her look a lot different to how her family would want to remember her. He turned the page and this time it was the same woman but her false teeth were in her mouth, her eyes were shut and she had a slight smile across her lips, making her look much better. Her thinning, wispy grey hair had even been brushed and she looked as good as a corpse could look. Will frowned. Why would he have these pictures? Why would he even want these? The woman was still under the same duvet cover as in the previous picture so she hadn't been moved to a funeral home where you would expect that sort of work to be carried out. There was a black leather doctor's bag on the chair next to her.

He flicked the page to see an elderly man who was dead in his armchair, his eyes frozen open, staring into another world, a look of horror on his face that would certainly upset his family or whoever it was that found him. He turned the page; this time the same man had his eyes and mouth closed, again in a half-smile.

Will didn't understand what he was looking at. How on earth could Heath have gained access to these people who were recently deceased to take their photographs, without family members complaining or telling him to fuck off? It didn't make any sense whatsoever. He flicked the page – another woman, this one middle-aged but with a plastic bag over her head. How had he got access to these most private, final moments? None of these had been taken in his studio. Unless he'd killed them as well, but how would he manage that without arousing suspicion from their families? They needed to find out who these people were. It was as if he was trying to recreate the vintage Victorian photographs from earlier in the album.

Next there were the girls from the stills that had been hanging on the studio wall. There were a lot more of these photos; he must have enlarged his favourite shots of them because he had taken so many. He lifted the album closer to his face; these photos had definitely been taken in this studio, but there was someone else there when it happened. He stared at the blurred image in the background to the far right of just one of the photos. It wasn't Heath because it didn't match the position he would have had to have been in to get the shot.

Turning the pages, he flicked backwards and forwards until he realised what he was seeing. On the next page there was no one except the dead girl in this picture, but there was something on the floor that he did recognise. A black, leather doctor's bag like the one from the earlier photo of the elderly woman; a bag that looked exactly like the one Paul Miller had been carrying the day they found Annie. When it had all gone horribly wrong, Will had been shirtless because he'd taken it off and had been pressing it against Jo's neck to try and stem the bleeding. He had been so relieved to see the doctor come running in he couldn't help but notice that he had his black bag with him. It had puzzled him then because how had he known that they would need medical help? But in the chaos that had ensued he'd forgotten all about it.

A cold feeling spread down Will's spine as it all came crashing together and he could see the full picture of what had happened. He stood up and began giving out orders to the officers who were standing around.

'We need to find Dr Paul Miller – like *now*. I think he's the killer – Tyson was just his puppet and his official photographer. Where is he? Someone go get me a search warrant. We need to search his surgery and house. We need to find him now. I want armed task force officers to the hospital right now because Jo Tyson could be in grave danger.'

He took out his phone and dialled Annie; it went straight to voicemail.

Annie chattered with Paul about anything and everything on the drive back to the village, but he seemed quite distant. She put it down to the week they'd all had; they were all still in shock about it, not to mention tired. It was so sweet how Jo had found her knight in shining armour, just like she had found Will. Halfway along the road to Hawkshead he asked her to turn off onto a narrow lane.

'Would you mind? It's a bit rundown and bumpy, but I keep my motorbike in my dad's barn. I don't have any room for it at my house. Parking is bad enough at the best of times and I'd hate it to get damaged. It's my pride and joy.'

'No, of course not, although I have no idea where we're going so you'll have to direct me.'

He smiled at her. He'd known all along that he couldn't have her in his life – she was far too big a risk. If Jo was to be a part of his life then that meant her new-found best friend would want to be, and it wouldn't work. No, it wouldn't work at all because she was a copper, her husband was a copper and every fucking person she knew worked for the police – and he hated the police. It would only be a matter of time before she realised that he wasn't the nice man they all thought he was. Oh, he wasn't a wife beater like his loser of a brother, Heath. No, he had some morals inside his twisted head – but he did like the power of being able to dictate whether someone should live or die. He knew without a doubt she would see straight through him. At some point he would let his guard slip – it was inevitable because he wasn't invincible; he was only a man at the end of the day.

He directed her to the rundown house that had once belonged to his and Heath's father, but which was now empty and had been for the last fifteen years. Well, it was empty if you didn't count their father's corpse that was buried out in the barn. He'd had a grand old time killing him whilst Heath had waited in the house with his camera, desperate to take photos of him once he was dead, but not of the killing. Heath was a thug and a bully but not a killer – no, he'd left that part of it to Paul, which was a good job. He didn't mind it. His medical training had taught him early on that life was a fragile thing. Sometimes you lived and sometimes you didn't; there was nothing more to it.

He tried to keep his voice calm. He didn't want Annie to suspect the frenzy he was silently working himself into. It was a shame Heath wasn't around to photograph this one; he'd never done a pregnant woman before. Although, to be honest, Heath would probably have chickened out with his twisted set of morals. But after he'd killed her he could have photographed her and her dead baby; they certainly would make stunning pictures.

'You have to take a sharp right turn, which will lead you to the drive up to the farmhouse; it's only a few more minutes and then you can get on your way. I'm sure you have lots to be doing, but I really appreciate the lift. It's so kind of you and it means I can get back to see Jo much quicker.'

Annie opened her mouth to speak but a small gasp came out as the pain came again, this time far more severe than the last one. He looked across at her. 'Is everything OK?'

She nodded her head. 'Yes, at least I think so. I've had a couple of twinges since I arrived at the hospital.'

'How far on are you again?'

'Seven months.'

'You'll be fine. I wouldn't worry too much – they'll be Braxton Hicks contractions and they're quite common at your stage of pregnancy. It's just your womb having a practice run. When you've dropped me off, go home and run yourself a warm bath, take a couple of paracetamol and try to get some rest. You've had a hell of a week and your body needs a break – doctor's orders.'

Annie laughed. 'Yes, doctor, I will. That sounds like a great idea.'

She pulled into the overgrown drive and wondered why it was such a mess; his dad must be a bit of a recluse if he lived like this. She stared into the rear-view mirror and felt the hairs on the back of her neck stand on end. The girl with the long blonde hair was staring back at her; Annie watched as a trickle of bright red blood dripped from the gaping wound at the side of her head down her cheek. Her blue-tinged lips were moving but Annie couldn't hear her or read her lips because she was trying to keep calm and not run the car off the narrow, overgrown drive and into a tree. Her heart was pounding; she didn't understand why the girl was there. Annie had made the connection, once she'd seen the photos on Heath's studio wall, that the girl who had visited her was the same one who was lying dead in the picture, and who had been buried in the unmarked grave that Will had been called to. They had found her killer; surely she should be able to move into the light now? She shouldn't still be stuck here, following Annie around.

Annie shivered. The temperature had dropped in the car and she saw tiny particles of ice forming in the condensation on the bottom of the windscreen. The farmhouse came into view and she was shocked to see just how decayed the building was; no one could possibly live inside of it because the roof had all but collapsed and there was ivy growing out of every window and doorframe. Annie looked in the mirror, hoping the girl had gone – but she was still there, staring at her, trying to tell her something that she couldn't hear, so she began to talk about the first thing that entered her mind.

'What a shame such a beautiful building has been left to go to ruin. It would make a beautiful family home. Maybe one day you and Jo could renovate it and move here.'

'I know. My father died almost fifteen years ago. It was in a right old state before then and I've been too busy with the practice to do anything about it. My brother could have made an effort, but he never did. He doesn't come here now. Not since my father's death.'

'Oh, that's a real shame. I didn't realise you had a brother, although I don't know why I would, to be honest. It's not any of my business. I guess I just imagined you as an only child.'

He wondered what the best thing to do was – to kill her now in the car, or to get her out of the car. Yes, that would be best. He didn't want her blood and his DNA all over the car – it would make it far too easy for the coppers who would eventually find it. He directed her to a large, half-collapsed barn around the side of the house.

'My bike is just in here. Thank you so much for the lift, Annie. Would you mind just hanging on for five minutes in case I can't get the bike started? Otherwise I'll be stranded here.'

She wondered why he would even leave an expensive motorbike in a decrepit barn that belonged to a ruined farm in the middle of nowhere. Rural theft was rife; she would be amazed if the bike was even in there. It had probably been stolen long ago.

'No, of course not. I don't mind at all.'

She gasped as the pain came again, taking her breath away.

'Why don't you get out of the car and have a walk around? It might be cramp? Stretching your legs will help ease the discomfort and pain.'

She opened the car door and hauled herself out. Why would she have any reason not to listen to him? He was a doctor and knew what he was doing, or at least she hoped he did because she didn't fancy giving birth here in the middle of a ramshackle barn with no Will to hold her hand and wipe the sweat from her brow. He walked across to the huge barn door and pushed it open, stepping into the blackness inside. Annie tried to straighten up;

this one was taking its time to go. When the pain eased off she took out her phone to ring Will and tell him where she was, just in case she needed him. She dialled and heard the beeps that told her there was no signal. *Bloody story of my life.*

The best thing she could do was get in the car and get home, ring him from the house phone. She waited to hear the sound of a motorbike engine revving but there was none; in fact there were no sounds coming from the barn at all. She walked towards the slightly open door and the darkness that waited beyond.

Will was pacing up and down outside on the drive. He couldn't breathe inside the cottage; it was too stuffy. His mobile rang; he answered it to a breathless Jake.

'You're not going to believe this. I'm at the hospital and Jo is fine. Paul was here but he left with Annie. He told her his car had broken down and he needed a lift.'

Will had to undo his top button and loosen his tie; he couldn't breathe and he felt his head swimming as his face went white. He'd been here before, only it had been a dark night and him who had been kidnapped. *Not again, please God not again.* And then he collapsed to the floor.

'Will, answer me. Will?'

'Jake, it's Claire. He's collapsed – oh my God, what did you say to him? He just went white and fell to the floor.'

'Fucking hell, Claire, who's there with you? Is he breathing? Is he fucking alive?'

'Stop shouting at me! Yes, he's breathing but he's a funny colour – he might have had a heart attack.'

'Slap him a few times on the face. I need him awake now; he hasn't got time to fanny around.'

Tina came over with a plastic bottle of water and knelt down; lifting his head she tried to pour some water into his mouth and missed, pouring it down his front instead. He opened his eyes and looked at them in confusion.

'What happened?'

They both shrugged.

'You tell us.'

He pushed himself up and Jake's last words to him rushed into his mind. Annie was with Paul, Dr Miller, the man who had murdered those girls and God knows how many of his patients. Claire passed the phone back to him.

'Will, are you with me? Because right now we have a huge problem. He has Annie and she has no idea that he's the killer and she's in danger.'

'I know – I think they might be brothers, him and Heath. I'm just waiting for confirmation. I can't do this, Jake. I can't take it. I don't know what to do – my head is a complete mess. I can't think straight.'

'Look, Will, we got it wrong, but how were we to know there were two of them? He told Jo he needed a lift to his father's to collect his motorbike. She said she doesn't know the exact address, but has given me a location on a map. Task force are on it but you're the nearest officer because Jo said it's somewhere near to Hawkshead village. There are officers blue-lighting it to the area, but it might not be good enough. I'm sorry, mate, but I can't sugar-coat it. He's going to kill her, and yes you can handle it because that's the love of your life and your unborn baby we're talking about – so snap out of it and stop feeling sorry for yourself.'

He nodded. Both Tina and Claire pulled him to his feet. He took the half-empty bottle of water from Tina and drank it.

'Get me an address for his dad, Jake – now!'

'Comms are trying to find it on the computer as we speak; they're doing intel and address checks. Who's there to help you? Are there any officers with you?'

'No, I sent them for lunch. There's just the CSI, Tina and Claire.'

'Well, they'll have to do . . . Hang on, I've got an address. Get one of them to drive you to High Fell Barn. It's two miles before you get to the village; there's a sharp turn on the right, which will lead you to a lane. Tell them they can wait at the road to flag down task force, or all three of you will be in a whole world of shit with the chief.'

Tina looked at Will. 'Fuck that – we can help. We never heard any of the last part of that conversation, did we, Claire?'

Will smiled at them. They were all going to be screwed if anything went wrong, but he was grateful that they weren't going to leave him on his own. All three of them ran out to the front street; there was Will's BMW or the shit heap that was the PCSO van. Will headed for his car but Claire grabbed his arm. 'That van's a pile of shite, but it has blue lights and sirens so we can drive faster through the lanes without having a head-on collision than we could in your car.'

Tina rolled her eyes. 'Yes, we can – if the fucker doesn't break down on us, that is. Can you drive, Will, or do you want me to?'

'Can you drive fast, Tina?'

'Does shit stick to a blanket?'

Despite the graveness of the situation he smiled and climbed into the van next to her.

'I haven't got a clue how to turn those sirens on, though; they only showed us how to drive the heap of junk.'

Will leant across and pressed the buttons on the handset for the lights and sirens. Tina started the engine and screeched off, making both Will and Claire fumble for their seat belts just in case she had to do an emergency stop.

Chapter 31

As Annie was about to step into the barn she felt a cold hand on her shoulder. She turned around but there was no one there. The voice that whispered in her ear was firm. 'He's coming for you.' She had long ago learnt to trust the messages from the other side and suddenly she sensed just how much danger she was in. She didn't know how or why, but something had changed; the nice doctor who had been so kind was waiting inside that barn for her to step inside so he could kill her. With no hesitation she turned and began to half run back to the car, as fast as her swollen stomach would let her. She almost made it when the most horrific, breathtaking pain made her double over and gasp. It froze her to the ground. She could hear his footsteps as he came out of the barn, but she couldn't move. Glancing behind her she saw the huge axe that he had in his hands – it made the one that Heath Tyson had used on Jo look like a penknife.

Clutching her side she forced herself to move and managed to get the car door open; throwing herself inside she pressed the lock down, which made the central locking kick in. She couldn't reach her keys, though; they must be in her pocket. Feeling wildly for them she patted her pockets frantically, but they weren't there and he was getting closer. Looking down into the footwell in case she'd dropped them she swore because they weren't there either. A loud thwack on the car bonnet made her scream – he'd buried the axe into the shiny black metal that Will had spent all Sunday afternoon so lovingly polishing, and was standing in front of her dangling her car keys with a huge grin on his face.

'Did you lose something? It doesn't look like you'll be going anywhere soon. Why don't you come out and talk to me face to face? Then we can discuss who deserves to be Jo's best friend the most. I'm sure you will have a compelling argument, but I've known her for over twenty years, which sort of gives me the advantage, don't you think?'

She shook her head, not taking her eyes off him. Her phone was on the passenger seat and she grabbed it, dialling 999. *Please ring, please ring, please ring.* The operator answered and Annie screamed her location to her as he pulled the axe out of the bonnet of the car and ran around to smash his way into her side of the car with it. The toughened glass cracked into a million splinters but held for the next three blows. When it finally gave in, showering her with minute shards, she lifted her hands to her head to protect her face. His hands reached in, lifting the lock up. Annie tried to move across to the passenger side so she could make her escape but her stomach was too big to let her move fast enough and then the door was pulled open and he was dragging her from the car by her hair.

She screamed and screamed, hoping the noise would put him off, but he was past caring now and he kept on dragging her. Once she was out of the car he threw her to the ground. She shut her eyes, not wanting to see what was coming next. As his shadow fell over her, she wrapped her arms around her baby and felt the hot, salty tears fall from her eyes. *This wasn't fucking fair at all. She'd done nothing to him. She'd never have guessed he was the one who was the killer.*

A loud screech filled the air as sirens wailed onto the lane she had driven down not long ago. He turned to see what it was, giving her just enough time to get to her feet and start to run like never before. Her chest burning and legs aching she ran towards the drive and the oncoming police van. He realised that she'd got the better of him and began chasing her. She could feel the axe as it sliced through the air behind her, narrowly missing her. She almost made it when another pain stopped her in her tracks, forcing her to her knees at the side of the gravel drive, right in front of the oncoming van. Paul stepped behind her, past caring now – he knew it was all over so he might as well finish what he'd started.

He raised the axe and Will screamed, 'No,' about to throw himself from the van. Tina swerved, just missing Annie but managing to turn the van to the side. She ploughed straight into the man who had been about to bury the huge axe into Annie's head. He flew up into the air then bounced back down and hit the bonnet again, cracking the windscreen, then fell to the ground. She stopped the van.

'Oh, shit, I hope that bastard's dead.'

Will got out of the van and ran around the front to check that Paul couldn't get up and hurt Annie or any of them. He snapped handcuffs across Paul's arms, who let out a scream as they all heard his already fractured wrist bone crack with the force Will used. The man was bloodied and dazed and his leg was bent at a funny angle – but he was alive, which was much more than he deserved. A trio of sirens screamed in the background behind him as task force arrived, followed by a van being driven by Jake with Kav and Cathy sitting next to him, then an ambulance. Will ran to Annie, who was curled up in a ball, and knelt down in front of her.

'Did he hurt you?'

She looked up at him, her tear-stained face shiny and red from the exertion. 'No, but he was going to kill me. Why would he want to do that? I never did anything to him. I didn't even know.'

Will held her, pulling her as close as he could. 'I know; I'm so sorry. I should have realised it was him sooner. Tyson was just his puppet.'

Cathy shook her head. 'None of us realised. This isn't anybody's fault so don't you lot get all soppy on me. But what I'd like to know is who the fuck ran him over?'

Tina stepped forward. 'I did, ma'am.'

Cathy looked at her then broke into a smile. 'Top effort, Tina. I'm amazed you could get that van to go past thirty, but thank God you did.'

'So am I, but I think that it's had it now – because it won't even start.'

'Don't worry – it was a heap of shit anyway. I will personally see to it that you lot get a decent one. However, and I mean it, this is the one and only time you are allowed to run members of the public over. Do I make myself clear?'

Kav laughed and clapped his hands. 'I'm impressed, very proud of my girls in blue.'

He winked at them and they grinned back.

Annie winced and doubled over as another pain came, taking her breath away.

'What's the matter? I thought he didn't hurt you. Are you OK?'

She couldn't speak because the pain was that intense.

Cathy bent down and took one look at her. 'Oh bugger me, she's in labour. She's having a contraction – we need to get her to the hospital. How long have you been having them?'

She looked over at the ambulance where the paramedics were in the process of loading Paul inside, who was now handcuffed to a very big task force officer dressed in black with a gun by his side.

Annie gasped. 'Since this morning.'

'Come on, you strapping lads are going to have to carry her into the back of the van and we'll drive her there.'

Annie shook her head and gritted her teeth as Jake and Kav bent down and lifted her as gently as they could, walking her to the back of the police van. They managed to get her up and she laid herself down on the seat. Will climbed in next to her, taking hold of her hand. Finally able to speak again, she looked at Will.

'I swear to God I'm not having this baby in the back of this bloody van with you lot watching.'

Jake and Kav turned away and got into the front; Cathy climbed into the back with Annie and Will.

'No, don't you bloody dare. I'm already a van down because of Tina's road-raging. I can't have another one out of action because you've splattered your waters and placenta everywhere. Hang on until we get to the hospital – and besides, it would be cruelty to children to have those two ugly buggers present at the birth.'

She nodded her head in Kav's direction, who muttered, 'Charming.'

Will kissed Annie's forehead; as Kav turned the van around, Cathy leant across Kav's shoulder and shouted out of the window to Tina and Claire, 'Sorry, but can you two guess what I need you to do for the next couple of hours until we sort this disaster out?'

Tina and Claire looked at each other and shouted back in unison: 'Scene guard.'

Cathy stuck her thumb up at them.

'Now then, Kav, drive as fast and as safely as you can to the hospital, before our Annie here does what she's so good at – causing high drama – and gives birth in the back of my van.'

By the time they reached the hospital the contractions were coming fast and furious. Annie didn't let go of Will's hand, even though he couldn't feel his fingers. It was all too sudden; neither of them was ready for this. When Kav finally stopped outside the maternity unit Jake jumped out and ran to get a wheelchair. Between them they managed to get her into it with only minimal swearing. As the midwife rushed Annie and Will through to the labour suite, they watched the double doors shut behind them, leaving Jake, Kav and Cathy in the waiting area – which was thankfully empty.

Jake looked at them. 'Now what? Do we wait or go back to

the station? How long does it take to have a baby? Days, hours?'

'I would say not very long; she was close to giving birth, but the poor kid was hanging on and I can't blame her. I wouldn't want to spread my legs for you lot to have a good gawp at in the back of a police van either.'

Jake sat down in a bright yellow chair that looked the same colour as his stab vest. 'What a week. I'm knackered and I've never been so bloody stressed out in my life.'

Kav nodded. 'I have to agree with you. I'm definitely too old for this. I'm glad I've only got two more months before I retire.'

'What about you, Cathy?'

'Me, I bloody love it, I do. I love the grey hairs that you and Ms Graham are giving me on a daily basis. My life has never been so exciting.'

Kav and Jake laughed. Forty minutes later the doors opened and a midwife eyed all three of them up.

'This is against hospital rules, but I said you could come in for a couple of minutes.'

She held the doors open for them to follow her through. 'Don't forget to use the hand gel. I have no idea what you lot have been up to but I've been assured it was all in the name of public safety.'

She led them to a room and stopped outside to knock on the door; they could hear the high-pitched sound of a baby crying and the midwife opened the door. A sweat-soaked Annie lay on the bed in a hospital gown holding a tiny screaming bundle of baby. Will, who looked more shell-shocked than any of them, was standing next to her looking down at the wriggling baby in her arms. She grinned at them.

'I thought you three should be the first to meet Alfie. He's a bit early but he's got ten fingers and toes. Not to mention a set of lungs on him Jake would be proud of.'

Jake crossed the room and bent down to kiss her head.

'Congratulations, he's amazing. I can't believe it. You did this – I mean, you and Will made him, without any help. Who knows

– he might grow up and marry my little Alice. Wouldn't that be amazing? Well, it would be as long as he doesn't turn out to be gay, that is . . . not that it would matter if he did.'

Cathy and Kav both stared at Jake, who started to laugh. 'You know what I mean.'

Annie smiled. 'I think that Alfie is the luckiest boy alive to have such amazing godparents to take care of him. That is, if you want to be – of course you don't have to.'

'With your track record, my love, that kid will probably need us at some point – unless you become a recluse and start knitting.'

Annie poked Jake in the ribs. 'Cheeky, this is it – a whole new chapter of my life, one that's filled with nothing but love and laughter.'

Kav put his arm around Cathy and nodded his head. 'Thank God for that. I don't think my heart can take much more.'

All three of them kissed Annie in turn, shook Will's hand and made silent promises to watch over Alfie. The midwife came back into the room and ushered them out. When they were alone, just the three of them, Will finally found his voice.

'I love you more than I've ever loved anyone in my entire life, Annie Graham. Thank you so much – I can't believe we have such a gorgeous son. But now we need to talk seriously about you taking up flower arranging or opening a cake shop – because this all has to stop. I want to grow old and watch my son grow up; I want to watch him playing rugby and cheer him on with you by my side. No more of this chasing killers or getting mixed up with anything remotely violent.'

'For once I think I agree with you. I won't put him at risk – I love him and you far too much.'

She looked down at the baby in her arms and felt a bond of love so strong and warm inside her heart that she knew nothing would break it.

'Anyway, did I ever tell you I always wanted to be a florist when I was a kid?'

Epilogue

'So, Heath – I don't quite understand how this all worked. I mean, I managed to figure out there were two of you – but this, it was pretty clever stuff. Not like anything I've ever seen before, so who was the mastermind behind it all?'

Heath Tyson's bruised, pale face stared back at Will, defiantly daring him to try and work it all out for himself.

'No comment.'

'Was it true that you and your brother once fell out over Jo? How did that work out for you, Heath? How did you end up kissing and making up so you could then go out and murder teenage girls in cold blood?'

'No comment.'

'So is it true that you were just your brother's puppet? I think that obviously you were, and did exactly as you were told. You are nothing more than a weak, pathetic man who likes to hit women. Isn't that right?'

'No fucking comment.'

Will looked at Heath's solicitor and shrugged. She was normally straitlaced and very professional, but she looked as if she was way out of her depth.

'Let's go back to your relationship with your wife. You must have been so angry when you realised Jo had got the better of you. That she had figured you all out?'

Heath had begun to drum his fingers on the plastic table in front of him; his feet were also tapping and Will knew that he was getting under his skin. The solicitor reached out her hand, placing it on his arm as she silently warned him to keep calm.

'It doesn't really matter anyway; this is all just a formality because we already have a full and frank confession from your brother, Paul. I bet you didn't realise that he would take all the credit for it; he couldn't wait to tell us how this was all his idea and how he'd planned it all. According to his confession it only worked because of him. He said that you were too weak and pathetic to carry it out.'

Heath launched himself from his chair across the table at Will, who managed to jump back. As he did the chair overturned and he slammed his hand against the red panic button on the wall. The door burst open as several uniformed officers came running in. Will managed to push the solicitor out of the way while they restrained Heath, who was almost foaming at the mouth he was so angry. His beetroot-red face curled up in anger as spittle flew from his lips; he growled at Will. There was a loud, satisfying thud as Heath's head hit the table. It took three big, burly officers to control Heath and he was carried back to his cell in handcuffs and leg restraints wrapped around his ankles as he fought with them all. Will stood there watching; they would give him some time to calm down and then start all over again. One of the detention officers came in with two steaming mugs of tea for the solicitor and Will.

'Thought you might need a brew.'

He took it from her and grinned. The solicitor took the other one.

'You thought right.'

'Were you deliberately goading my client, Will?'

'Not at all; it's all very true. He's just not very good at accepting the truth.'

'Hmm, well, off the record I completely agree with you, but for the record let's just get it over with. I need a cigarette. If he decides to play ball I'll be out the back trying to calm my nerves down.'

Will put the table straight and picked up the chairs, resetting them. With a bit of luck he had wound Heath up just enough for them to get a full confession from him. There was no need to tell him that technically they hadn't got a word from Paul; he was much brighter than Heath. After twenty minutes there was hammering on the door of the cell that Heath had been thrown into. Will smiled at the solicitor. 'Someone's ready to talk. You and me might get to enjoy our evening, after all.'

'I hope so. I'm going out for a meal at eight.'

The detention officer stuck her head back in. 'He's promised to behave himself; said he needs to tell you what happened.'

'Bring him back then.'

Will sat in his seat, watching as Heath was led back into the small room. This time his handcuffs were kept on. He dropped onto the hard plastic seat.

'I want to tell you everything, what happened. Whatever he's said about it, he's lying. None of it was his idea; it was all mine.'

Will stretched out his arms and crossed his fingers together.

'Tell me how it was then. How did it all begin?'

'We were pretty close as kids, but when we were teenagers for some reason we grew to hate each other. We fought all the time and drove our mum mad. But Paul always thought he was better than me, than our parents. He thought he was better than everyone, but he wasn't. I knew that he wasn't; he was clever, though. He used to sail through his exams without much revising and I would have to spend hours poring over my textbooks and still get crap grades. He got a scholarship to a posh boarding school at St Anne's and he left without so much as turning around to say goodbye.'

'Did you have different dads? Why did you have different surnames?'

'No, we had the same dad; as soon as he was eighteen, he changed his name by deed poll. Said he didn't want to be a Tyson; he wanted a whole new identity. He did really well at college and university; then he went off to be a doctor, but as soon as he'd qualified he came back. At first he wouldn't have anything to do with any of us, but he'd started to come down the pub for the quizzes. That was where he met Jo; they went out with each other for a while. He was so smug and up himself, it really pissed me off. So I did what any self-respecting man would do – I got my revenge and stole his girlfriend from him. He didn't like that; in fact he beat me up in the car park of the pub one night, but he crapped himself in case I went to the police. I wouldn't have come to you lot, but after that he started being nice again.

'We didn't see a lot of each other, but then he came round to my house one night and we got drunk. We started to reminisce about our childhood and the day our granddad died. I told him about the photograph album I'd found hidden away at the back of his wardrobe that I'd taken. Well, the rest you know, don't you?'

'We know some of it, not all of it. Can you tell me why you killed those girls, Heath, and buried them in the woods where no one would find them?'

'I never killed them; I just liked to photograph them. It was all Paul. They came to me to have photos taken. The first time it happened was when Sharon Sale had come to have a portfolio done. Paul was in my workshop whilst I was in the studio taking the photos. I almost chickened out but I wanted to take the photographs of them whilst they were dead. I went to change my camera and before I knew it Paul had gone into the studio and killed her. The shock when I came back in and saw that she was dead was terrible, but . . .'

Will sat forward, leaning his arms on the table. 'But what?'

'But the excitement of having a dead girl to photograph took over and I didn't care after that. He wasn't interested in her when she was a corpse; he enjoyed having the power to take someone's life and it didn't matter to him whether they were young or old. He doesn't have an artistic bone in his body, but I could see the endless possibilities of having a model to pose for me who would never complain or want to take a break.'

Will saw the look of horror on the solicitor's face and wondered if she'd ever met anyone quite so sick as the man she was supposed to be defending.

'So Paul Miller killed Sharon Sale?'

'Yes, and Wendy Cook, but I kept their bodies as models and when they started to decompose I had to dispose of them. The only place I could think of to bury the girls was out in the woods; it's so quiet out there. Well, most of the time it is.'

'What about the other photographs in your book? Did Paul kill those elderly patients?'

'Not really. They were at death's door – he just gave them a helping hand.'

'And you were there, ready to take the photographs in the background?'

Heath nodded. 'Yes, but it wasn't the same as the girls in my studio. I didn't really like taking those photographs – I just did it because the opportunity was there.'

'What about Matilda Graham? Why did you decide to drug her?'

Heath grew fidgety, and his leg began to twitch slightly under the table.

'She wanted a photoshoot. I didn't plan it, but it was too good an opportunity to miss. Only I panicked after I'd drugged her, when I realised you lot were all over the woods with sniffer dogs. So I put her in the fridge.'

'Were you going to kill her?'

The tapping under the table became louder.

'Yes – I mean no. I didn't know what to do with her. It was too late once I'd drugged her to just let her go. I was hoping she'd die on her own and if she hadn't then I was going to ask Paul to do it.'

'To do what?'

'To kill her.'

Will had put his hands under the table, his knuckles were clenched so hard. He wanted to punch the man in front of him so much, he was having to sit on his hands. He didn't want to ask about Annie, but he had to know what would have happened if Jo hadn't realised and saved them both.

'What about the other woman?'

'Who? The pregnant one who'd decided to become my wife's new best friend?'

'Yes.'

'Well, she figured it out. If she hadn't stuck her nose in she wouldn't have got into that situation, would she?'

'I don't know, would she?'

'No. I didn't particularly want to hurt a pregnant woman, but she didn't leave me much choice. She was the only person in twenty years to look at those photographs on my studio wall and realise that the two girls were dead. She didn't leave me much choice, did she?'

In his mind, Will saw himself launching across the table to batter the shit out of the handcuffed man in front of him, but he had to snap out of it. His fingers hovered over the tape recorder – 'interview suspended at 16:46' – then he stopped it and stood up. He needed to speak to the DI; he couldn't do this anymore – it was too much. Too personal. He'd got the most important information out of him. He was going home to his family and he wasn't coming back for a few days. Someone else could sort this mess out.

Will left the station exhausted. He'd spent all afternoon interviewing Heath Tyson and his brain was a mess now. All he wanted was to go home to Annie and their baby. He pulled into the drive of their house and rolled his shoulders. Annie would be desperate to know what had happened, how it had happened and what the connection had been between the two men that had bound them to commit murder together. He slammed the car door shut and waved at the camera on the outside of the house in case Annie was watching him from the monitors. He opened the door with his key and heard Alfie crying. Kicking off his shoes then loosening his tie he hung his suit jacket over the end of the banister and followed the sound of crying into the living room. Annie was pacing up and down, rubbing Alfie's back.

'Thank God you're home; I'm starving and I need a wee. He's been really unsettled the last hour and wouldn't let me put him down. The more I thought about wanting a wee, the more desperate I got.'

She passed the tiny bundle wrapped in a blue blanket over to Will and watched in mock horror as their son stopped crying.

'No way, I'm not having that. He can't be a daddy's boy already?'

Tutting, she walked off to the cloakroom, not showing Will the huge grin on her face. It was the most amazing sight to see him standing there holding their baby, and it filled her heart with warmth. After she came back out she went into the kitchen where she took a bottle of her favourite rosé wine from the fridge and two glasses from the cupboard. Filling a glass full for Will and half for her, she carried them through into the living room where not only was Alfie now fast asleep and lying in his Moses basket but Will had lit the log burner and a fire was beginning to take hold. She handed him a glass and he took it, placing it on top of the mantelpiece; then taking the other one from her he did the same. Pulling her towards him he held her, then kissed her on the lips with so much passion she almost forgot that she'd only given birth a few weeks ago. He let her go and tugged her down onto the sofa where she curled up, lying against him.

'What was that for?'

'Because I've missed you both and I bloody love you so much. Anyway, since when did I need a reason to kiss you?'

She laughed. 'You never need a reason to kiss me. So are you going to tell me how it went or would you rather not talk about it just yet?'

Will didn't want to talk about it, ever – but it wasn't fair on Annie. She'd been involved and she had every right to know . . . but it just felt wrong speaking about Heath Tyson and Paul Miller in front of their four-week-old baby. At least Alfie was fast asleep. Will didn't want to taint his tiny ears but he knew he was being daft. All Alfie would hear was their voices; he thankfully wouldn't have a clue what they were talking about, and he hoped it would always stay that way.

'No, I don't mind. I mean, I'd rather not talk about it – but you need to know.'

Annie stood up and picked up the wine glasses; passing Will his, she sipped from hers. Hoping to quell the churning inside her stomach, she wanted to know everything, every last sordid detail because it had been driving her mad. Wondering how they'd managed for all this time to kill and photograph dead people without being caught. Will drank half of his glass without stopping and she winced; he'd had a bad day. After a few minutes he began to relive this afternoon.

When he'd finished she turned around and kissed his cheek. 'Thank you. I had to know even though I didn't want to. But no more. I don't want to talk about it or think about it – at least not until the court case. I want us to concentrate on Alfie and having a normal, relaxed life. I'll go and get you something to eat. You must be starving.'

Annie made her way into the kitchen. She heard Alfie crying and the sound of Will pulling himself off the sofa. At least Alfie would keep them busy and they could try and put everything to the back of their minds. As she plated up the beef casserole she'd had on the go all day in the slow cooker, she put it on a tray with a fork and carried it through. Will was fast asleep on the sofa and snuggled in his arms was their tiny baby, who had also gone back to sleep. Annie knew that this was it. Her life had changed and she would do her very best to keep it this way.

Acknowledgements

This year has been an incredibly tough one for not just my family but so many others. I'm very touched and inspired by the amazing work of the wonderful, beautiful, inspirational ladies of the Lookin GOOD and Feelin GREAT charity group. These amazing ladies are all fighting or have fought cancer. In fact, they are not just fighting it but indeed kicking its arse and still managing to raise money for charity and give each other the support that anyone suffering from this dreadful illness so desperately needs. If there's one thing this year has taught me it's that you never know how strong you can be until you're faced with no other alternative.

I'd also like to thank my lovely editor, Victoria, for putting up with me this year – it hasn't been easy – and the rest of the team at Carina UK.

Once again huge thanks to my friends Sam, Tracy, Tina, Caroline, Gail, Phil and Iain, for your support and making me laugh at times when we really should be tearing our hair out. Sam, I haven't forgot about the mouse incident and it will appear somewhere along the line.

Thank you to the very funny Heath Tyson who wanted a bad man named after him. I just wanted to say that the real Heath Tyson is nothing at all like his evil counterpart.

I'm forever indebted to my lovely blogging friends, The Write Romantics. You all keep me sane and understand how tough it is once you've made your dream come true. Thank you so much Jo Bartlett, Julie Heslington, Jackie Ladbury, Lynne Davidson, Helen Rolfe, Alex Weston, Deirdre Palmer, Sharon Booth & Rachael Thomas.

Last but not least I'd like to say to my family that I love you all very much. It's been a hard year but the Phifers have proved how tough and strong we are. Without you none of this would be possible and I'm so proud of you all.

Love Helen xx

**Ready for the next thrilling instalment in the
Annie Graham series?**

THE FACE BEHIND THE MASK

Annie Ashworth is on maternity leave from her police job, enjoying spending time with baby Alfie. Perhaps her days at home are a little boring, but after all of the horrific crimes she's witnessed, that's fine with her.

But when she starts having strange dreams – dreams that turn out to be linked to a local murder – she can't stop herself from digging. There's an eerie connection to a serial killer from the 1950s, and Annie fears that the same dark forces are back.

And maybe it's just new-mum tiredness playing tricks on her, but she's been noticing a cold presence lingering around Alfie late at night. Could her baby be the target of whatever evil is haunting them? And will she have what it takes to protect him?

Out in paperback and audiobook August 2025.

Out now in ebook.

Dear Reader,

We hope you enjoyed reading this book. If you did, we'd be so appreciative if you left a review. It really helps us and the author to bring more books like this to you.

Here at HQ Digital we are dedicated to publishing fiction that will keep you turning the pages into the early hours. Don't want to miss a thing? To find out more about our books, promotions, discover exclusive content and enter competitions you can keep in touch in the following ways:

JOIN OUR COMMUNITY:

Sign up to our new email newsletter: http://smarturl.it/SignUpHQ

Read our new blog www.hqstories.co.uk

X https://twitter.com/HQStories
f www.facebook.com/HQStories

BUDDING WRITER?

We're also looking for authors to join the HQ Digital family!
Find out more here:

https://www.hqstories.co.uk/want-to-write-for-us/

Thanks for reading, from the HQ Digital team